The Reporter, a Ferret and a Hurricane

Steve Martaindale

Copyright © 2012 Steve Martaindale

All rights reserved.

ISBN-10:
1481111612

ISBN-13:
978-1481111614

DEDICATION

To the person who has insisted my dreams are worthy of pursuit, that no time is misspent when it is applied to doing what you love and that we are surrounded by goodness, my Leah.

CONTENTS

Two Stories

ACKNOWLEDGMENTS

It took me longer than many journalists to decided I wanted to write a book. By that time, more than a hundred different people had come and gone as co-workers in several different small newspapers. I had also lived and worked in a number of incredibly different towns and interacted with a broad range of people. All of these elements influence, to varying degrees, the fictitious town and characters which make up "The Reporter" stories. One thing a reporter learns: "Everyone has a story."

1 THE REPORTER AND THE FERRET

Had there been life behind the open eyes, the once-clear blue orbs could not have avoided following the darting black and gray creature. It would be in the lap of the dead woman and then running behind a chair. At one point, the ferret picked up a shiny object beside the kitchen counter and secreted it in the fleet fur ball's favorite hiding place.

THURSDAY – 8:22 A.M.

"JP! Where's JP? C'm'ere a sec."

The command came from the slightly rotund city editor, who always seemed too busy to speak without using contractions, incomplete sentences and abbreviated words. Not that JP Weiscarver noticed; after almost five years together, he and Stanley Hopper usually thought on the same wavelength.

"What do you have, boss?" JP asked while slipping his 6-foot, once-athletic frame onto the pea green sofa against the wall of the office.

"Know Irma Hodge?"

"We don't exactly run in the same circles, but I know who she is."

"Was."

"Was?"

"Was. Found dead this mornin' at home." Hopper hardly looked up from the oak desk that had served city editors going back to World War II, each of whom had written his or her name on the pull-out writing shelf. There was plenty on the desk to keep his attention, pile after pile of papers and clippings and press releases and photos.

"Put together a nice little piece," he continued while shuffling through a particularly important-looking stack of papers, "who she was, what she did, how much Oldport will miss her, the usual." There was a slight pause, as if he had found what he wanted. "And Weiscarver." Hopper looked up and a slight pause gave weight to his declaration. "Hit the deadline."

"Sure thing, boss. Suspicious death?" Hopper was concentrating on diving into his third pile, sure this one would produce the corporate form his editor wanted turned in yesterday.

"Not your concern, Weiscarver. Jennifer will take care of the cops angle; that's her beat now. You deal with sweetness."

"Gotcha. One sugar overload coming up before 5 o'clock," JP said as he exited the city editor's glassed wall office, tossing a smile at the typist who also functioned as Hopper's assistant.

"Four!" Hopper bellowed, the glass quivering as if it were frightened. "Deadline's 4 o'clock, Weiscarver, and you good and well know it."

Yanking his boss' chain was one of JP's many pleasures, especially when Hopper handed him a rookie assignment such as this. But he knew better than to complain. That's the price he had to occasionally pay for having a general assignment beat on a small daily newspaper.

During his first four years with the Oldport Odds and Ends newspaper, JP had done it all. Just like current rookie Jennifer O'Hanlon, he started by covering cops, fire departments and a few trials. Eventually he moved to the school beat, the city beat and finally helped Hopper convince Margaret Edmonds, the editor, that the Odds and Ends had grown enough to warrant a full-time general assignment reporter. Actually, Edmonds was the easier sell because she was still a newswoman, even if she was never on the front lines any longer. JP knew she had the tougher job, that of convincing the publisher that he should release a little more of his profit margin to enhance the news product with an additional reporter.

Once that was achieved, though, JP usually picked up choice assignments, such as a celebrity visiting town or maybe digging into possible government corruption. In fact, Hopper depended on JP to keep himself busy most of the time and relished the fact that his GA reporter did not need much babysitting. But having no clear beat made JP the easy person to hand a late story that didn't really fit anybody else's regular assignment, like the death of a well-to-do woman who had lived in one of the city's nicer homes.

"Hey, Patricia, what's shaking?"

Lifestyles editor Pat Baird always knew JP wanted something when he called her Patricia.

"Forget it, JP, my dear, Lifestyles is not doing your Hodge piece for you. It's Thursday and we're up to our elbows with this weekend's section."

"Wouldn't dream of it, Pat, but how is it you seem to know my assignments before I do? If I didn't credit you with having better taste, I might think there was something going on between you and Hopper."

JP often teased that Pat Baird had been doing lifestyles since before he was born. Truth is, he was off by only a few months, but Pat saw no reason to draw too much attention to the fact. Not yet, anyway. She pretty much adopted JP when he moved to Oldport, helping him find a place to live and instructing him in the finer points of getting along in a busy newsroom.

"Thank you for giving me the benefit of doubt," and she punished JP with her mother's-mad-at-you look as she added: "I might be in Lifestyles but I'm still a reporter and I notice what goes on around me. Now, what do you want?"

"Information. I know good and well you probably have a thick folder of goodies on the late Irma Hodge and I thought it might give me something to start with."

"My, but aren't you a clever reporter," Baird teased, "thinking of that all by yourself." She waited just a second to see if JP would take the bait, but he was eagerly waiting for her answer. A Lifestyles folder on Irma Hodge would save him an awful lot of boring digging in the newspaper morgue, the filing system of old stories.

"You will not believe how lucky you are," Pat continued. "Lydia just finished a story on Miss Hodge earlier this week as part of a series we will be doing about leaders of the Palmetto Club. Have you heard of it?"

"Only because I read your pages. My impression is that it is a group of older women with money and either a desire to help the community or at least a guilty enough conscience to make them feel compelled to do so."

"I'll let you slip by with that definition, but you might want to keep it between us. In fact, you might drop the 'older' part even with me. Regardless, Lydia's story is useless now, though I'll probably have her rewrite something of a tribute, especially since Irma Hodge was to be honored as the Palmetto Club's Woman of the Year."

"That sounds great," JP said, ready to get started on the story so he could put it behind him and move on to something more interesting. "Do you and Lydia mind if I use it?"

"Of course not, my dear boy, but I have a request. You know how badly Lydia wants to get out of Lifestyles and onto the news side and you should know how much she idolizes you."

She waited for JP to acknowledge that he knew what she was talking about. Actually, Lydia Murray embarrassed JP a bit with her adoration. She was trying to break into journalism the hard way. With only a year of junior college behind her, she won a job in Lifestyles as a typist and soon was able to do occasional rewrites, bottom-feeder type of stuff for someone who really wanted to be a reporter. It wasn't the preferred route to a news job, but a poor financial situation put Lydia in the position of needing fulltime employment and she correctly assumed that typing society releases would get her to that goal more quickly than flipping burgers. She was not bashful about making her objective known. Though she knew she was not yet ready for a reporting job, that didn't keep her from reminding Stanley Hopper that she was preparing for just such a role. Nor did it keep her from continually seeking out JP's advice on her stories.

JP silently nodded that he knew what she meant.

"If you find her information at all useful, please put a 'Lydia Murray contributed to this article' footnote on your story. It would give her quite a boost to have a part in one of your stories."

"I cannot say that I understand this idolization you speak of, but I will happily give credit where it is due. Now, where will I find this file?"

"I have already put the folder on your desk," Pat promptly replied, unable to quite contain her smile.

"Wow! You do know how to scare a guy. I owe you one." The last comment bounced off the partition to the empty sports department because JP was already headed toward his cubbyhole.

"Forty-one," Baird yelled, something she was not normally known to do. "You now owe me 41, but who's counting?"

Miss Irma Hodge, according to Pat's file, did not get around in the town's social circles nearly as well as her name did. In fact, JP determined mainly from reading between the lines of carefully clipped and filed articles from the past, she was a minor recluse. Of course, what got her name around town and into the Odds and Ends Lifestyles section was her money. It was her money because it had been her father's money, earned from a profitable shipping supply company, and she had been his only survivor. Her father, Cletus P. Hodge, already widowed, left the entire business to Irma when he died 35 years ago. Within three months of Cletus' death, Irma had sold Yardarm Shipping Supply Company for a tidy gain.

Evidently, nobody faulted Irma for selling the company, which dominated the Oldport docks, especially since she had no background in the family business, or any business for that matter. In fact, it seemed that Daddy Hodge had kept his little girl pretty much sheltered since her mother had died when Irma was only nine years old.

Lydia's article summed up all that information in such a way that it did not sound like Irma Hodge's pending Palmetto Club Woman of the Year award was solely because she was so supportive financially, but the young writer certainly could not generate other, false, reasons to justify the honor.

Apparently, Irma Hodge had never married, but JP did a double take while reading Cletus' yellowed obituary, which listed survivors as his daughter, Irma, and grandson, Michael.

"Hey, Pat," JP called out, "what's this about Irma Hodge's son?"

Not wanting to yell across the newsroom a second time in one morning, Pat Baird did not answer until she sat in the uncomfortable, brown chair JP kept at his desk for guests. He did not like visitors getting too cozy while they were taking up his time. If he did want to entice someone to stay and talk, he would invite them into one of the conference rooms with the deeply cushioned chairs and would offer coffee or, maybe, even dig into his pocket to buy a soft drink from the office machine.

"You must be slipping, my boy," Pat said as she adjusted her ample body into the chair. "I expected that question five minutes ago." Pat was fond of JP and couldn't help but think of him as she would a son, but her favorite way to make a point was through needling his ego a bit. Fortunately for them both, JP understood. When he graduated college, he would never have thought that he could learn as much from a "society" editor as he had from Pat Baird. She continued talking after giving up on making herself comfortable.

"It was quite the juicy story some 40 years back – I was just a kid, mind you – when Irma Hodge came up pregnant at about 25 years of age. It never was actually announced who the father was and she certainly never married, but the popular thought was that it was a 17-year-old dockhand who worked for the old man. He became the prime suspect when, about the time Irma began showing, he came into a rather decent amount of money and made a big to-do of leaving town to, as he put it, make a name for himself, which sounds particularly funny when nobody seems to remember his name. I bet you Michael himself doesn't know his father's name. I wouldn't be too surprised if Irma didn't. She certainly never talked of him; Michael was just her 'little gift from heaven.'"

"OK, then," JP began as he rubbed his chin, something he often did while thinking but would promptly stop once he became aware of it, "whatever became of Michael?"

"That's another story. Apparently, Michael was not all that heavenly for Irma, after all. Think about it. She had hardly known her mother and had little more than innate instincts to guide her in raising a child. Additionally, even at that age, she was very much caught up in leading the good life. Well, Cletus, seeing the possibility of having an heir to continue the family name, would not even consider allowing Irma to put Michael up for adoption, but he did agree to an 'arrangement' where a family would take care of the boy. Presumably, Michael would benefit from having two 'parents' and a sibling or two."

"So they just packed him up and sent him out?" JP asked, drawn once again into one of Pat's stories.

"Don't get ahead of me, son. No, first of all, Bob and Midge Moore moved into the Hodge Mansion, as most people called it back then, just one big and happy family. But when Cletus died and I guess Michael was 6 or 7, Irma chased them out. Nothing that dramatic, you understand; she just made arrangements for the Moores, their own son and Michael to move to Queensland in the next county. Actually, I guess that took place after she sold the company and she had plenty of money. She sent a check every month, but Michael never really got to know his mother, if you know what I mean."

"So, did they ever make amends?" JP was taking notes on a yellow legal pad while Pat talked.

"Irma did not abandon him or anything. They kept in touch and all, she continued to support him, and I heard a rumor about six or seven years ago that she helped bankroll a restaurant venture for him. That almost severed any relationship because the restaurant was a big-time money drain and she eventually turned off Michael's supply line and the business soon folded. That's the last I heard about him."

"Hey, O'Hanlon," JP said as he directed his attention over Pat's head toward the cops reporter, "are you listening to this story?"

"Can't help it," Jennifer said. "Mrs. Baird always spins an interesting tale."

"Tell me what you think, cops lady: who makes the better suspect as Irma Hodge's murderer – her son Michael, his unnamed father, or the sweet couple who took Michael to raise?"

THURSDAY – 10:01 A.M.

JP Weiscarver had never heard of Oldport prior to five years ago. After graduating college up north, he had taken the reporter's job at a very small daily newspaper less than an hour's drive east of school and an hour west of home. Being the only reporter for a small-town afternoon paper meant he did everything from city council meetings to high school wrestling matches. And if there was a fire at 2 a.m., he carried a camera to take photos to run with his story.

With two years of such experience, JP felt he had the seasoning and the clips – samples of his work – to be considered for a larger paper. He found a classified advertisement in Editor & Publisher, a trade magazine, for an entry-level cops reporter in Oldport, a Southern coastal town of almost 50,000 people. The Oldport Odds and Ends, even though its name sounded like that of a tiny weekly publication, covered a nine-county region of mostly small towns and had a circulation of 35,000. It wasn't as easy as JP thought it would be to get the job. Hopper made it clear there were plenty of young reporters anxious for the position, but something clicked between the two and JP got his chance. Hopper even pitched in three hundred dollars to help on moving expenses, something that certainly did not happen often.

JP fell into the new routine with ease. He still responded to fires and shootings when he was awakened in the middle of the night by the portable police scanner that he carried with him 24 hours a day. He became like a mother to the scanner. As long as the cops were chit-chatting and running license checks and answering family disturbance calls, the reporter slept soundly. But, when tension crept into the law officers' voices or if there was the sound of a siren, JP responded as if the radio had cried his name.

In addition to relying on the scanner, he soon had a pretty good network of police and fire officers who had his phone number and who would try to call when something major was happening. They appreciated the fact that he would work the same awful hours they did and that he did a thorough and fair job in his reporting. He actually found the nights to be much easier than his old job since the Odds and Ends was a morning paper, which meant that the night editor finished the final pages by midnight and the press was rolling by 1 a.m. So a story that broke overnight didn't have to be finished until the 4 p.m. deadline the next day, which gave JP the chance to go back to bed and get a decent amount of sleep.

After his move to general assignment reporter, JP seldom got out in the middle of the night unless he was filling in for the cops reporter. But he still left the scanner running at home, like many former cops beat writers who never got over the urge to know what is going on. In fact, it came as a bit of a surprise just two or three years ago when he realized that he no longer listened to music in the car and always kept his television turned down enough at home that it did not interfere with hearing the scanner. Almost 29 years old now and not married, he wondered if he could find a woman who wouldn't mind listening to police chatter all night.

JP decided to start working on his story by visiting City Hall, partly to keep in touch with city officials because he had not seen some of them for a while. Not that he really minded.

He didn't quite detest dealing with city officials, but many of the people there were not that interesting and seldom were helpful. Regardless, he made it a point to keep in touch; after all, one never knows who or what may provide a strong story tip. When he lived up north, the town's mayor was the one who tipped him off on the upcoming arrest of a popular librarian who was actually selling kiddy porn over the Internet. Had JP not managed to be in the area when the arrest was made, he would not have gotten such a great photo of the librarian flashing an obscene gesture at the camera, nor would he have heard the detective quip, "Book him."

After parking next to City Hall, JP reconsidered and first headed across the street to the police station. It wouldn't hurt to see if he could come up with something about the death of Irma Hodge.

"Hey, Sarge, what's shaking in the world of thick coffee and thicker doughnuts?" JP all but shouted as he entered the phone booth of an office that was the second home of Oldport Police Department's PIO – public information officer – Sergeant Tad Bellew.

"Weiscarver, you waste of perfectly good ink and paper, you've got some nerve showing your face around here," Bellew fired back. "What's it been, three or four years since you've been by to visit?"

"Try two or three months, Tad, but then again, you cops aren't expected to get facts straight, are you?"

"What can I say, JP? All I know is what I read in the papers."

With the obligatory good-natured slashing of each other's person and/or profession out of the way, the two clasped hands and Bellew offered JP a cup of his famous coffee, a talent he attributed to his Jamaican mother.

The reporter noticed that his host was already wearing his long-sleeve uniform. It was late September and nowhere near cold, and likely would not be cold until January, but the cop had always kept to his own schedule: long sleeves after Labor Day and until Easter.

Bellew was working the streets as a patrol officer when JP first moved to Oldport and the two hit it off from the beginning. The cop, with a dozen years of experience at the time, appreciated the young reporter's willingness to put in the work to get a story right and his ability to do so without making a pompous jerk of himself, something he had found to be fairly common among both beginning reporters and rookie cops.

JP, on the other hand, found a police officer who knew his job and who was willing to be straightforward with him. The cop knew JP would ask the questions he needed to ask. The reporter knew Bellew would give an honest answer, even if it were "I don't know" or "I'm not going to answer that right now." In contrast to the legendary battles between reporters and policemen, these two were able to both do their jobs and respect themselves and each other at the same time.

After complaining that the coffee was too strong, something he usually did after drinking his second cup, Weiscarver got around to the point of his visit: "Tad, I'm working on a story about the Hodge death and I was wondering if y'all had found anything suspicious about it." Southern dialect was creeping its way into JP's life, but it always seemed to come out more quickly around his police contacts.

"That's funny," Bellew replied without missing a beat, "but Jennifer O'Hanlon said the same thing just a few minutes ago. And it has been her beat for some time now." He paused to give JP a chance to explain his interest, but an interruption came over the telephone's intercom from the dispatcher that the shift captain wanted to see the sergeant.

"Walk with me, JP, and let me see if this meeting will take long," Bellew said as he immediately got out of his chair, taking the radio from the charger and sliding it into his belt with the practiced ease of someone picking up a key ring. The PIO always wanted to know what was happening in the field and hated to hear about something first in the form of a question from a reporter. Getting back on track since JP did not pick up the bait, Bellew continued to press him.

"In fact, Miss O'Hanlon mentioned that you were assigned a fluff piece about what an asset our community lost in the death of Mrs. Hodge, excuse me, Miss Hodge. True?"

"All too true, Sarge," Weiscarver said before grinning and shaking his head. "And I've been doing just that, but something seemed kind of out of place in what I was hearing, so I decided to get it straight from the source. So, what's the scoop?"

Arriving at the captain's door, Bellew held up a flat hand to put the question on hold and stuck his head inside the door. "This gonna take long, Captain?" JP could not hear the reply, but the PIO's behavior gave it away. "All I know, JP, is that we've got an older, well-known lady who died in her home of what so far seems to be natural causes. That's not final, yet, but I ain't heard nothing to make me think differently. Now, I need to get in here for a bit. Anything else?"

"No, Tad, but you give me a call when you get something new, OK?"

"You know I will, bud. By the way, what I just told you is exactly what I told Miss O'Hanlon and don't you lead her into thinking otherwise. I'm still training her, you know."

THURSDAY – 10:19 A.M.

Thinking it might be a good idea to do at least some work on his assignment and leave Jennifer to her assignment, JP headed across the street from the three-year-old police station to the 80-year-old city hall to get a quote from the mayor about how "impossible it will be for the city of Oldport to replace someone as generous and kind as Irma Hodge." As JP took his leave, Mayor Jeanne Goodrum asked the reporter if he had been by Hodge's home. "I understand she left quite a menagerie orphaned, thought that might make an interesting angle to your story."

JP thanked her for the idea but with only a dollop of sincerity. It wasn't like the third-term mayor to go out of her way to help a reporter, least of all JP Weiscarver, so he knew that she would be reminding him of the favor if the tip did indeed pan out. He quickly shook off any concern, however, for she never had been able to get JP to play along with her little political games.

Both county and city animal control trucks were in the paved, circular drive of the old Hodge homestead on Alligator Way when Weiscarver nosed his 10-year-old yellow pickup to the curb across the street and a house past the scene. The practice was another holdover from his cops days, when he learned to not park too close to a crime scene. First of all, it upset the people you needed to get information from. Secondly, it put you in the position of being blocked in by official vehicles. Learning that lesson took only one instance of sitting two hours after covering a fire, waiting for firefighters to roll up hoses that surrounded his car.

As he walked the shrub-lined driveway to the two-story stone house, JP surveyed the scene, framed by trees just beginning to think about changing the color of their leafs.

"There must be an ark's load of animals, judging from the turnout," he said softly to himself, a process in taking mental notes. "Two city trucks and one from the county. Place does look nice, though. I bet she dropped a pretty penny each month just keeping the grounds in order. I can't imagine one person living in a house so huge."

"Hey!" he cried out as a gray-and-black fur ball zipped between his feet, causing JP to exhibit a bit of fancy footwork while his brain assimilated the brief visual information and decided the … whatever it was … was not a threat. Quickly, the town's leading reporter gathered his wits. "What the blue blazes?" he yelled the second time the streak of fur startled him. This time, though, he got a look at dark eyes peering at him from within a black mask. Surrounding the mask was a beautiful gray coat that turned black again at the feet and the end of the tail.

"Hold that ferret, would you, buddy?" yelled a winded young man in a gray uniform. JP couldn't help but wonder just how the man expected him to hold something that darted around the way the animal did. Ferret, he thought to himself … of course, he knew that. He had never seen one quite so close before, or moving that quickly.

"Whoa," said the man in the uniform, which stated its occupant's name was "Juan" and that he was an employee of the Oldport County Animal Control Department. He had cornered the ferret and it acted as if it fully intended to end the chase there.

"Easy does it, fellow. You're eager to play, aren't you? You miss your owner already, don't you?" Then, at the same time Juan gathered the ferret into his big hands, he looked up apologetically at JP. "I'm sorry, mister, that was thoughtless; you're probably a family member."

Suddenly realizing he had become a sculpture on the beautifully manicured lawn while watching the playful encounter between Juan and the runaway ferret, JP gathered himself and handed a simple, black-and-white business card to the animal control officer.

"No, sir, I'm JP Weiscarver with the Odds and Ends," he began. "But if I were a relative of the deceased, I would be impressed with how lovingly you're handling her pet." A little bit of grease was always a good investment on a prospective source of information.

"Thanks, Mr. Weiscarver, we try. But, to tell you the truth, if a relative or somebody doesn't step up and claim some of these animals … well, let's just say they won't likely be with us very long."

"Miss Hodge had that many pets?" JP asked, flipping open his always handy notepad and clicking the pen he removed from his shirt pocket. "Call me JP, please. What's your name?" It was something he did as second nature and the years of practice were reflected in how smoothly he eased into an impromptu interview.

"My name's Juan Mendoza. Yeah, she has ... uh, had ... quite a bunch. Last I heard, we're looking at six dogs, maybe twenty cats – but it's hard to tell 'cause they come and go – fourteen birds and hundreds of fish."

"Fish? I never thought of you 'rescuing' fish."

"They're animals, too. We'll place them if we can."

"How many ferrets?"

"Just this one, it seems. Cute, huh?"

"Yeah, I've never handled one before. May I?" Juan answered by handing over the three-pound mammal. "What's his name," JP asked as he awkwardly accepted the creature.

"Who knows? Whatever you want to call him, I guess." Juan gave a big smile. "Yep, you two were meant to go together, all right."

"Hold it, hold it, hold it," JP stammered, "I'm here to write a story, not become part of one."

"That's a shame 'cause I doubt we'll have room for him at the shelter," and Juan smiled again, attempting to set the hook. He, too, was practiced at easing people into his way of thinking.

THURSDAY – 3:17 P.M.

"As much as the residents of Oldport will miss Irma Hodge, the death of the 66-year-old heiress will also have a dramatic impact on the lives of hundreds of pets that were orphaned Thursday." It was Stanley Hopper reading the lead to JP's sidebar from the editor's computer terminal. He liked to read stories aloud, to hear what they "sound like," he said.

"What's wrong with that," he thought aloud. "Oh, they will 'miss' Irma Hodge, huh? You tryin' to be cute, Weiscarver? They will miss Miss Hodge? Let's say 'the residents of Oldport may grieve for Irma Hodge.'"

"Sorry, boss," JP confessed. "Yet another reason you get the big bucks."

Hopper did not appear to hear, already into the next paragraph, still reading aloud but with the volume reduced to the usual whisper as he continued through the piece, occasionally inserting a comma or making some other change from his keyboard. The only big change was the deletion of what he deemed a superfluous paragraph.

"Well, Weiscarver, I'm not sure what to say; I'm stunned," the city editor finally said as he scrolled back to the top of the story in preparation for forwarding it to the copy desk.

"Gosh, boss, it might be a good piece, but it's not exactly contest material, you know."

"Oh, the story is merely adequate. I'm stunned 'cause it's only 3:25 and you've actually beat the deadline. Seriously, JP, I know this isn't the type of story you like to cover, but you're givin' the readers a nice look at an important person most of them never got to know. And it helps me justify your GA beat every time Mrs. Edmonds has to defend her budget to the publisher."

"Sure thing, boss, and I even enjoyed it. You know, just watching the animal control folks, the care they showed all those animals, well, it was pretty interesting. I'm sure you'll be reading a story about them soon."

"So," Hopper asked, looking up from his desk in that manner he has when he feels like he's about to corner someone, "how many pets did ya take home?"

"Hey, boss, you know I don't get personally involved with my stories."

"Yeah, right – the girl who needed leg braces, the family livin' without electricity, the idiot practicin' dentistry without a license …"

"OK, OK," JP said as he threw up his hands in surrender. "But I haven't taken any home … yet."

"Ha! I knew it …"

"I tell you what I'm thinking about boss. I didn't mention it in the story, maybe because subconsciously I didn't want to advertise it, but, uh, well, do you know anything about ferrets?"

"Isn't that the same thing as a weasel?" Hopper asked.

"I don't know, probably…"

"Heavens, no, they're not the same!" The exclamation from outside the door of the city editor's office surprised both men inside. Seldom did Hopper's assistant, the barely five-foot-tall Andrea Munoz, enter a conversation uninvited, especially when it was going on inside her boss' office, although the door was usually open. As a matter of fact, she seemed to have surprised herself. "Oh, I'm sorry for butting in like that," she said and turned back toward her computer.

"No, please," JP said, turning away from Hopper. "I want to know about them. Do you have a ferret?"

Thus empowered, Andrea entered the office.

"No, but I've studied up on them a bit. I've wanted one for years, but, well, you know how I am, not one to jump out and do anything radical. So, I got a cat instead. Anyway, the ferret is related to the weasel, but it's also related to the skunk and the mink and even the otter. I guess the biggest difference is, well, have you ever heard of a weasel as a pet?"

"What else?"

"Well, ferrets are very playful and actually love humans. You need to set aside time to interact with them, just to be a good daddy. They're neat and supposedly make great house pets. They are real curious and will explore anything. Well, Stanley, I've heard you say something before about a reporter ferreting out a story. That's where it comes from."

JP was rubbing his chin but caught himself, stopped and addressed his informant. "Andrea, what do you think? Should I adopt this ferret? And, if I do, will you volunteer to keep him if I have to leave town for a few days?"

As she pondered the question, JP realized he did not know much about her. Andrea was not the type to hang out with the reporters after hours and kept to herself most of the time. He figured her to be in her mid-40s, remembered her saying she was divorced and he was pretty sure she had no children.

"Yes, you should," she finally answered. "And, sure, I'll help when you need me. Maybe that will make me decide to get my own ferret sometime."

"That does it. I'm going to the animal shelter and," but he was cut short by a brunette whirlwind blowing into the office.

"Hey, boss … oh, sorry."

It certainly wasn't the first time for Jennifer O'Hanlon to interrupt a conversation, even that of her city editor. Only four months into her first reporting job, she was always moving at a fast pace. She walked fast and talked fast. Barely 100 pounds, one wondered if it was possible for her to gain weight, given how she was constantly in high gear.

"It's the Hodge story," Jennifer continued before Hopper even had a chance to invite her to do so. "Everything might not have been quite as natural about her death as they first thought."

"Ha!" JP almost yelled. "I told you; didn't I tell you? Don't mess with this reporter's nose." He cast a smile at Andrea. "I've got a ferret's nose for a news story."

"Before you accept that nose of the year award," Jennifer said, staring into JP's brown eyes to get his attention and delivering the rest of the line much slower than usual, "please note that I said 'might'."

JP Weiscarver loved it when Jennifer got sassy about her beat, mainly because he still had the habit of thinking about it as "his" beat and he wanted somebody with just a touch of a well-placed attitude in charge of it. Jennifer was a good six inches shorter than JP, but seemed to add height and weight when she was defending her turf. And she enjoyed turning up the heat on the senior reporter because she knew he severely judged every cops beat reporter who had followed him. There were two others before O'Hanlon, including current city reporter Archie Hanning. The other guy found the hours and pay not to his liking and took a public relations job with a small company a ways inland.

"Hey, while we're speaking of you, I understand you were treading on my beat today," Jennifer said, her joking attitude revealed through a slight smirk.

"What's wrong with me visiting a few of my old contacts?" JP said, looking around the office for support. "What do I mean 'old' contacts? I'm the GA reporter now; all my 'old' contacts are still my contacts. Besides, I got a good lead there … kind of."

O'Hanlon broke out laughing.

"Sergeant Bellew told me that would get you," she said. "Oh, and he made me promise to apologize for him; he didn't know any of this until an hour or so ago."

Hopper finally re-entered the conversation with, "Know what? If you two are through playin', why don'cha fill us in? Maybe, just maybe, we can get some of this out to our readers by mornin'." Andrea quietly slipped back to her desk on that note.

"Oh, sorry, boss," Jennifer said, unaware she had recently picked up the habit from JP of calling her editor "boss." It sounded strange coming from her because she almost religiously referred to anyone but her immediate peers by an appropriate courtesy title and their last name.

"Actually, there's not much that's solid and not really anything that we can print except that the cause of death has not been determined. I had to work Sergeant Bellew over a little bit," and she glanced to make sure Weiscarver had picked up on that, "but he finally went on record saying that they are looking at the 'possibility of foul play.' Off the record, they seem to feel that it is a probability, but I still don't know why that's so."

"Got the coroner's report yet?" Hopper asked, now fully into editing mode.

"Only the preliminary and, from what I understand, it didn't confirm an awful lot, just raised a bunch of questions. We've got the details of how she was found and all … but I tell you, Sergeant Bellew convinced me that this will eventually be classified a homicide. Obviously, we can't say that but I would like to play up things like the amount of time police spent on the scene, the number of detectives called in, that sort of thing, to prepare at least our more astute readers with the thought that Miss Hodge was murdered."

JP took a break from stroking his chin. "I can toss you a couple of quotes from neighbors who said they had seen her recently and she seemed to be in good health."

"Get on it," Hopper commanded. "You've got twenty minutes 'til deadline, but I'll give you a little longer to make sure it's done right. Andrea," he called out, "check with the librarian and get the best recent photo of Hodge. And one more thing, O'Hanlon: are you sure Bellew will call you this evening if anything breaks?"

"Of course, Mr. Hopper. He knows I have no private life."

"Well, I should hope you don't. Now get to work on that story."

As JP passed the promised quotes to Jennifer, Lydia Murray quietly slipped into his chair. Her take-no-prisoners attitude about working her way into the news side of the paper was not reflected in her demeanor, especially when she was around JP. She did not look like a person who would take charge of an interview. The fact that she was slightly overweight may have caused her to look a little frumpy, but JP assumed she had neither the background nor the current wherewithal to do those little things that make a young woman look dressed up. Not that he actually knew what those little things were, but he knew some women could apply cosmetics in such a way that their entire appearance was enhanced.

JP felt a little bad for not thinking to thank the girl for her help, even though it really had no great affect on his story, so he spoke up as soon as he caught sight of her.

"Hey, there, Lydia, good job on the Hodge story. Too bad it won't be able to run, but I sure do appreciate having the information. Stanley promised he would make sure your name is tagged onto my article."

"Cool, that will be my first credit of any kind outside Lifestyles. Watch out, 'cause I'm working my way in. I thought you might be interested in the interview I had today with another of the Palmetto Club honorees. Mrs. Edith Hasterley went on and on about Miss Hodge's death."

That stopped JP's efforts to try and slip away from the eager writer. The animal shelter would be open until 5 o'clock.

"You don't say. Tell me about Mrs. Hesterley."

"Her husband, John Hesterley, made their money by getting in on the convenience store craze early on. He was maybe the first in the area to give up on being a small grocery store and to aim instead at the mobile crowd. He definitely did have the city's first gasoline pumps that accepted credit cards and then the first that accepted cash. His stores also feature quality pastries and a variety of coffees every morning."

"Oh, you're talking about the Kwik N&Out stores; I love those places whenever I'm after a fast meal."

"You know what I mean then. For me, it's the fix-your-own chili cheese dog with all the toppings. Well, obviously he's been just as innovative since the early days and it has paid him well."

"And Mrs. Hesterley?"

"Apparently, she's in charge of outgo. I don't mean that in just a negative sense, though she certainly does take good care of herself, too. For the interview today, she had an honest-to-goodness fox stole on. Here? Especially this time of year? She also let it slip, surely on purpose, that she lets her mood determine which car she drives. I'm not sure if it's different types of cars, different colors or both."

While JP enjoyed picturing Lydia's new rich friend, he found himself anxious to get moving.

"What were her thoughts on Miss Hodge's death?"

"All right, you're going to love this. She has it on good authority that Irma Hodge was snatched from her home, that her body was transported to a UFO and that she was too old to survive the shock of the tests these aliens performed on her."

JP just sat there.

"And you know how she knows this?" Lydia asked.

"I'm a little afraid to ask, but my guess would be that your dear Edith Hesterley had previously scouted out the alien spacecraft."

Lydia let slip a delightful giggle, something JP had not heard from her before.

"You've got it," she said. "But, wait, there's more. Where do you think John Hesterley got all his great inspirations for his trend-setting business ideas? Edith says he's never admitted it to her, but she knows for a fact that he has been guided by the aliens. In fact, she thinks that he might be a spaceman himself and that is why they have never been able to have children."

"Hang onto those notes, Lydia. They could be useful when you decide to write your memoirs from your reporting days."

That vote of confidence sent another giggle through the reporter-to-be.

THURSDAY – 4:33 P.M.

For all his self-assurance an hour earlier, JP hesitated as he got out of his truck in the parking lot of the county animal shelter, which was less than a mile outside Oldport on Queensland Road, the two-lane county road that had connected Queensland and Oldport since 1898. He wondered if it was called Oldport Road near Queensland.

"Hey, JP!" and Weiscarver instantly recognized the voice of Juan. "I knew you would come for that ferret. You did, didn't you? And I've got good news for you. I found the answer to your question."

JP's head was spinning a bit because he had been vacillating on whether or not to go through with the adoption and here Juan had apparently already made the decision for him. However, getting questions answered always appealed to him. "What question was that, Juan?"

"His name. Remember, you asked his name and I said you could call him whatever you want. Remember?"

"Yeah, that was when you let me hold him," JP said, recalling the moment, and then he was certain for the first time that he should adopt the ferret. "So, how did you find out?"

"Once we got things sorted out inside, we found a pet carrier that was being used as a home. There were a couple of others that she must have used to carry the dogs and cats to the vet or whatever, but just this one was used for bedding. You saw how active the ferret was earlier. Well, you need to know there's a tradeoff for that. Ferrets can sleep 18-20 hours a day and, since they are burrowing animals, prefer a dark, quiet place with pillows or blankets they can bury themselves in. But I'll give you plenty of literature on that.

"Anyway, we found this carrier in the hall closet, which also had a swinging pet door – the perfect place for a ferret. I peeked inside and found gray and black hairs and then the ferret ran inside. His name was painted above the door of the carrier."

"This all sounds like good news, like he won't miss me too much while I'm at work. So, what's his name?"

"First," Juan said, flashing that same mischievous smile, "what were you going to name him? I know you had something in mind, people always do when they first meet their pet."

"OK, I was thinking about 'Murrow,' after …"

"Edward R. Murrow, the famous World War II news correspondent," Juan said. "Great choice."

"Hey, I'm impressed you know that."

"Why's that, JP? Because I'm a 'dogcatcher' or because I'm Latino?"

"Whoa!" and JP threw up his hands in self-defense. "I just don't expect non-journalists to take note of ancient news personalities, I guess. And, OK, maybe somewhat because you work in animal control, to be perfectly honest."

Juan laughed. "It's understandable, but I'm sure you know better than to let appearances fool you. I work in animal control because I want to. I love it. But, to make sure I always had something to fall back on, I first got my master's degree in European literature. I figure I can usually get a teaching job and," he paused for effect, "they're always looking for reporters." The grin was back.

"I stand rightly reprimanded, Juan. But you still haven't told me the ferret's name."

By now, they were inside the shelter away from the humid, coastal heat and JP had not even noticed they were moving. This guy could probably make a killing in sales, he thought.

"Better you see the carrier, yourself," Juan said. "Besides, you don't have to stick with it and Murrow is such a perfect name, given a ferret's tendency to stick his nose into everything," and he opened the door to a small, darkened room. "I left him in this examination room so he could rest up. We gave him a pretty exciting day."

As Juan turned the blue carrier's door toward JP, the reporter saw two eyes peeking from the cave. The ferret stuck his head out and JP instinctively reached for him. That was when he saw the name, hand painted in bright red: "Bubba."

A rich, deep belly laugh rose from the ferret's prospective owner, one like he had not experienced in days, maybe not since the last time he and his girlfriend, Sherry Miller, were able to spend an entire evening without one of them having some sort of business call. She was a registered nurse who worked in the emergency room at Oldport County Hospital and would sometimes get called in when the understaffed hospital was facing a problem. For the first time, JP wondered what Sherry would think of Bubba and felt instinctively that they would become fast friends.

"I've got to admit, that wasn't quite the reaction I was expecting," Juan said.

"Oh, no, it's the perfect name, Juan. OK, the truth is, I'm not exactly the type of person who fits in with the hoity-toity world that Miss Hodge was associated with. Seeing 'Bubba' so lovingly painted onto that cage makes me think that maybe she didn't exactly want to be a part of it either. I mean, wouldn't you think she would more likely call him 'Silver' or 'Black Coral' or, I don't know, 'Jules Prescott the Third'?"

It appeared that Juan finally didn't know what to say, and he returned to the overriding topic, "So, whether it's going to be Bubba, Murrow or JP III, do you … hey, JP III! Is that what JP Weiscarver stands for, Jules Prescott?"

"Uh, no, it's just JP," he stuttered, "but, yes, to your unasked question, I would like to take Bubba home with me. Maybe he can help me ferret out what happened to Miss Hodge." And he couldn't wait to introduce Bubba to his girlfriend.

THURSDAY – 5:33 P.M.

Sherry Miller was headed for the door when her replacement, Joe Baker, reminded her to clock out.

"You seem out of it, Sherry," said Joe, who had been her training partner when she first joined Oldport County Hospital. "Tough day?"

"Not at all," she said, placing her purse on the counter before heading to the workroom to punch the clock. "Typical Thursday. Guess I'm just a bit wacky today, that's all."

In spite of being a nurse, Joe was still male and immediately accepted the answer as being female code for an "it's that time of the month" dismissal of concern.

Sherry was en route to the door again, again without saying bye to anyone, when Joe called her name from behind the horseshoe-shaped counter and held up the telephone receiver, the mouthpiece covered by his grip. "Sounds like lover boy," he said and flashed a grin, hopeful that would lift her spirits. The news put a smile on her face, but she still gave the phone a business-like answer: "Emergency Room; Miller."

"Hey, ER Miller, isn't it about time you headed home?" JP asked. Big granny knots seemed to slip out of her shoulders at the sound of his voice. Joe couldn't help but notice her relax and was glad she wasn't having boyfriend problems. Joe was also quite the romantic.

"Well, if it wasn't for some nosy reporter, I would be on my way home now. Fact is, next time I start for the door will be my third, and I hope my last, effort at leaving."

"In spite of your wise-cracking attitude, I'm glad I caught you. Instead of going home, come by my place. I've got something I'm dying to share with you. Speaking of dying," and JP inwardly reprimanded himself over the coarse segue, "did you hear about Irma Hodge? Well, what I've got to tell you about is related, but wait, I don't want to give away anything."

There was a moment of silence.

"You there?" JP asked.

"Yeah, I'm here, just thinking. Not tonight, JP, you know I like to get out of my uniform and shower right away. And I'm a bit beat, you know. I don't think so…" She knew she was mumbling now but seemed unable to help herself. None of that mattered to her boyfriend, though.

"Then you need me to take you out to dinner. Go home, shower, change, and I'll pick you up about 6:30, my treat."

Sherry decided she did not have a good enough reason to stay at home and she gave in. "Make it more like 6:45 and I should be ready," she said. "Where are we going? Maybe the White Cap?" She was smiling again.

"You name it, but first we have to come back by my place for the surprise."

As he hung up the phone, JP actually considered changing clothes for the evening. The thought quickly passed and he decided instead to create a home for Bubba.

THURSDAY – 6:53 P.M.

The White Cap had become what they referred to as "our restaurant." The food was good but not fancy. Built over the surf atop 20-foot pilings, the view of the Gulf of Mexico was unsurpassed even though it may have been paralleled several times over by other shoreside eateries in Oldport. The ambience fit the couple well with waitpersons who took care of them without hovering. And the price range was just within their reach as long as they did not visit too often. The White Cap was also closer to Sherry's apartment than it was to the small house JP rented, so Sherry suggested eating first, but JP would have nothing to do with it.

On the drive to Weiscarver Manor, as he delighted in calling it, Sherry tried to remember the last time JP was so excited about a secret. There were often things with his work that he would not talk about, stories he was working on and unconfirmed information he wouldn't repeat, but none of that made him act like a six-year-old boy, as he had the week prior to her birthday. And as he did now.

"John Paul, if you don't tell me what you've got up your sleeve, I'm not going inside," she teased. Sherry called him John Paul when she wanted to get under his skin because she insisted, against JP's sworn testimony, that J and P each stood for something.

JP said nothing, only casting his evil-eye glare while making a turn onto Dolphin Street two blocks before turning onto Oleander Drive and stopping at his house on the corner. Saying nothing was his usual response to her calling him John Paul, but sometimes he countered by calling her Ringo. To his chagrin, he had to explain the Beatles reference to his 24-year-old girlfriend the first time he used it. She decided she liked Ringo better than George.

Continuing their game, the couple finally reached the door and JP made Sherry close her eyes before entering. She stood inside the door with her eyes closed while her boyfriend fetched the surprise. She was ultimately ordered to open her eyes and found herself face-to-face with what first looked like a huge rat but one that was instantly chittering away.

"Sherry, meet Bubba, my new roommate."

"This is your deep, dark secret? You beast … you, not the animal … you made me think it was something horrendous, saying it had to do with that horrid woman." The "horrid woman" reference obviously surprised JP.

"Maybe I should have interviewed you for my story on Miss Hodge; it seems you know something about her nobody else does because not another soul used anything like 'horrid' or 'horrendous' to describe her. What's up? Did you know her? What was so terrible about her?"

"Hold it, mister hot-shot reporter. No, I didn't know her, but I don't appreciate your surprise and I don't want to talk about it any more."

At that, Sherry turned and headed to the car, leaving Weiscarver holding a wriggling gray and black roommate that seemed to reflect the reporter's quizzical countenance. "What do you think, Bubba?" he said. "Should I pursue this topic and try to find out what's gotten into her lately?" The animal stuck its nose into the crook of the arm of its new owner. "You're right, it's probably best left alone and forgotten. I guess I've been dragging out too much of my work in front of her. After all, she's got plenty of pressure with her job. But I'm afraid it's not going to be a very enjoyable meal."

FRIDAY – 6:19 A.M.

It was a good thing JP planned to get up early because Bubba was ready for a little attention even before sunrise. Sherry's disposition improved at the restaurant the previous evening, but JP still took her home early and was ready for bed himself by the time the evening news came on. The death of "prominent local heiress Irma Hodge" led the newscast, but it was reported as simply natural causes.

"Good," he said to his new roommate. "We can always trust TV to take the path of least resistance." He considered calling Jennifer O'Hanlon to ask how her story developed but decided to hit the sack instead.

After greeting Bubba and the new morning, JP hurried out to pick up the paper and had it out of the plastic bag before he reached the steps.

"Irma Hodge's Killer Sought" screamed a banner headline. "What?" screamed a surprised reporter who hates surprises.

Barefoot and wearing sweat pants and a T-shirt, JP stood in front of his door reading by the porch light.

"When police first discovered the body of 66-year-old shipping heiress Irma Hodge in her home Thursday morning, neighbors assumed the popular but slightly reclusive woman died of natural causes.

"Concern will now be added to sorrow in the Gulfcrest Subdivision as neighbors learn that Miss Hodge is now believed to be a homicide victim.

"'After getting blood analysis reports, the coroner tells us Miss Hodge was poisoned,' said Oldport police Sgt. Tad Bellew Thursday night. 'At this point, we have not been able to ascertain how the poison was administered, but we've been assured that this particular substance would not have been encountered accidentally by the deceased.'

"Bellew would not identify the substance, saying that could impede the investigation."

The remainder of the article read pretty much like JP had expected. He knew that meant that the new information from Bellew must have come late Thursday and Jennifer just had time to rework the article's first few paragraphs.

"You know, Bubba," JP said once he eased back into his sparsely furnished living room, "it's not easy letting someone else handle a big story, especially when you realize she doesn't need your help." The ferret, which had been skittering around the room as his new owner re-entered the house, stopped and cocked his head in a perplexed fashion.

"What am I saying, fella? This was your owner who was murdered. Shoot, for all I know, you were there when it happened. Tell me, did you see who killed your momma?"

In response to the question, the ferret began pawing at the floor like an arena bull preparing to charge. JP responded by dropping the paper and falling to all fours, duplicating Bubba's actions. The ferret then jumped at JP's hand and promptly retreated to paw some more. This was repeated three more times before Bubba attacked the hand and wrestled it down. The hot-shot reporter, the description which burned him as it came from his girlfriend, rolled with the attack, gathering up the fur ball into his arms as his shoulder hit the floor. Fully into the battle now, Bubba scrambled free and started pawing the ground again, leaving JP laughing as heartily as he had in months.

"Bubba, my friend, you're going to be good for me." And the ferret playfully nipped at his hand.

FRIDAY – 7:40 A.M.

"Say, good buddy, what do you think of our cops reporter?" Weiscarver called out to Archie Hanning as he entered the newsroom. Hanning wasn't like JP about the cops beat. To him, it was just something he had to do until he could get on a beat with better hours and greater predictability. But he was on it enough to recognize that Jennifer O'Hanlon had done a good job on this morning's lead story. He also recognized the mixture of pride and longing in Weiscarver's voice; Hanning heard the same tone when he dug out the story that a paramedic was selling hypodermic needles on the side.

"Yep, JP, I believe our little girl's all grown up," Hanning teased. "But this story's far from over. It didn't sound like the cops had an awful lot to go on."

"Maybe," Weiscarver said as he stroked his chin, "but we both know that they don't tell everything, especially prior to making an arrest. Even then, there are things we won't hear about until the trial."

Pat Baird had quietly slipped into the chair next to Archie's desk, cradling a cup of coffee. "On top of that, boys, Jennifer didn't get the call until about 11 last night. I understand they held the press about fifteen minutes in order to get the updated story in."

"Is that what the high-level conference is about?" Weiscarver asked, nodding toward Stanley Hopper's fishbowl office. Inside with Hopper were the editor, Margaret Edmonds, and publisher Martin Freer, who because of a bad hip had taken his usual position in Stanley's comfortable chair.

"I don't know, dear. They've been at it since I got here this morning." Weiscarver gave her a "really?" look. Though Stanley was usually in his office by 8 o'clock, Pat was always the first person in the newsroom. Back when the Odds and Ends was an afternoon paper, she would start the first batch of coffee. Ever since the paper began publishing a morning edition, the circulation department had the coffee running at high speed before the day shifts arrived.

Before Weiscarver could comment on that, his city editor saw him and motioned for him to join the meeting. "Well, boys and girls," JP said without hardly moving his lips, "I guess we find out now."

As he approached the office, where the door was uncharacteristically shut, he lifted a questioning eyebrow toward Andrea Munoz, who gave a slight downward pat with an open hand, signaling that everything was OK. As secure as he felt in his job, JP couldn't help but worry when his three immediate superiors called him into a meeting. Actually, his greatest fear the past year has been that Freer would get even tighter on the purse strings and eliminate the general assignment reporter position. Freer was your stereotypical publisher, too often looking at the bottom line and not at the service the paper was providing the community. There was currently an opening for someone to cover county government and by the time JP shut the door of Hopper's office, he was convinced that would be his job about five minutes from now.

"Weiscarver," Hopper said, "come in; we were just talkin' about you."

"That's more than a little discomforting," JP murmured. He had no intention of making it easy for them to hang him. Hopper chuckled a bit at the comment but neither the editor nor the publisher seemed to even notice, which had the effect of pushing even more anxiety onto JP, and he shifted his weight to adjust for it.

"Sit," and Hopper indicated a spot next to him on the sofa. Edmonds was seated in the chair before the city editor's desk. "Been discussin' the Hodge story. Looks like it's gonna go somewhere and I think you need to be involved with it."

Within the span of a couple of seconds, JP morphed from casual "you can't ruffle me" repose deep in the sofa to an alert position at the edge of the seat. But it was with a calm, of-course-you-need-me voice that he said, "Oh, what's happened?"

Freer shifted in his seat, too, and fielded the question.

"I received a rather interesting call this morning, about three o'clock, in fact," the publisher said. "My head was still pretty cloudy, but it was clear what she said: 'Irma Hodge was murdered.' Of course, I had no idea what she was talking about and pretty much indicated that to her. Then she said, ' Somebody wanted Irma Hodge dead,' and hung up."

"Hmm," was all that Weiscarver produced while his right thumb and index finger gave his chin a massage, but then he started processing out loud. The newspaper honchos listened, wondering if this fresh analysis might produce an angle they had overlooked.

"That reinforces what the police are telling us, but what new information does it provide? The fact that she called you and not someone in the newsroom indicates she doesn't know how news is handled here, but a society lady would of course go straight to the top. Did she sound familiar at all?"

"No, I did not recognize the voice, but I wasn't thinking all that clearly. Now that you mention it, though, her voice had a bit of a sophisticated sound, like a 'society lady,' as you say."

"Did she sound stressed or distraught?"

"Maybe I'm reading too much into it," the publisher said, now leaning with his elbows on Stanley's desk, "but I would say she was stressed and that she was trying hard not to let it show."

"The bottom line," said Margaret Edmonds as she entered the conversation for the first time, "is still the same for us. Either Miss Hodge was murdered as we suggested in this morning's edition or she wasn't. We're not here to play cops and robbers; we're here to report when and how the police nail a suspect or, if it ends up that she did indeed die of natural causes, we must tell our readers what went wrong with the investigation. What Martin's early morning caller gives us are questions to ask."

"And that's where you come in, Weiscarver," added Hopper.

"What about Jennifer?" he countered. He was so caught up in things, JP had briefly forgotten this wasn't still his beat.

"You're to work with her," Hopper said. "The two of you obviously have a good relationship, but I'm putting you in a tough position. This is her beat and her story, but my gut tells me it's gonna run pretty deep. You're to help her, teach her, steer her in the right directions, and don't let her get bamboozled or disheartened. Got it?"

"Loud and clear, boss. One more thing, Mr. Freer, did you call the cops?"

"Well, it was only after talking with Stanley and Margaret that I began thinking it might be worthwhile. Do you think I should?"

"Definitely. You never know when some little piece of information can work with something else to make sense. As for me and O'Hanlon, we'll go catch us a bad guy." He hurried out of the office before Edmonds could restate the newspaper's role in the investigation.

FRIDAY – 8:07 A.M.

JP held back the urge to phone Jennifer right away. After finishing her story, she would have stayed until the press was rolling to see the paper, just like he would have done. Pat said that was about 1:15. And JP knew from experience that the young cops reporter would have entirely too much adrenaline playing high-speed tag in her veins to allow her to go to sleep anytime soon. But even as he began organizing his thoughts, a zephyr named O'Hanlon breezed into the newsroom.

"Jen, couldn't you sleep?"

"What do you mean, silly? I was out of here by 12:30 and home and asleep by 1. I was awake by 7, like always."

JP looked at Archie Hanning and both shook their heads.

"Well, I'm glad you made it in on time," JP said as he grabbed Jennifer's sweater at the elbow and half-pulled her toward his desk and away from the grins of Archie and Pat. "We have orders straight from the top," and he nodded toward the big fish still inside the city editor's bowl, "to solve the murder of Irma Hodge."

"Hey, hey, Mr. General Assignment Reporter," Jennifer countered as she slid away from JP's desk and toward her own. "What's with the 'we' stuff? Why are you trying to horn in on my story? Don't you have corruption to expose somewhere or maybe a feature story on a dog pound?"

JP was temporarily taken aback until he figured out that Jennifer was simply getting better at yanking his chain. But the underlying question was valid and he sensed that she was serious about defending her domain. Lowering his voice, he moved to the only-slightly-more-comfortable chair next to Jennifer's desk, allowing the discussion to take place in her territory.

"All joshing aside, Jennifer, you've proven your mettle to me. I'm proud to turn the cop beat over to you." He was stroking his chin and Jennifer had come to recognize that as something JP did when he was serious. "Stanley has asked me to assist you just because it is a big story and because you're still new to the business and new to the town. But notice that I said 'assist' and please understand that I mean it. I will slip up and start running things if you let me; slap me down if I get too pushy and possessive. Deal?"

O'Hanlon was genuinely touched by the offer and most especially by its grace. The moment was brief but it was the point where she felt she had made it as a reporter. She had already learned how competitive a newsroom could be sometimes. Jennifer O'Hanlon extended her right hand and silently sealed the deal.

"Now," she said as she took command, "what do we have?" JP filled her in on the phone call to the publisher and Jennifer immediately phoned the police PIO's office and was told by Bellew that no other developments were available. He asked Jennifer to make sure Freer called a detective, a task she deftly passed to Weiscarver.

"One other thing," Bellew said, "but this is off the record for now." He paused until Jennifer confirmed that he was now talking to her confidentially. It was an understanding they were familiar with and which both held as sacred. He knew what he was about to tell her would not be published in connection with his name unless he made it official later. She knew that it would be solid information but that which would have to be confirmed through another source or which might simply be valuable in leading to more important information. Once satisfied, the sergeant continued in a slightly softer tone.

"One, this drug they found in Miss Hodge's system is effective in stopping the heart within seconds. Two …"

"Hey, just a second," O'Hanlon interrupted, "last night you labeled it as a poison, now you're saying drug; has something changed?"

"Let me put it this way: used properly – or improperly, I guess – just about any drug can also be a poison. Two, Miss Hodge was an insulin-dependent diabetic who gave herself injections every day. That means this drug could have been administered in its most lethal fashion and we might not be able to tell because it would be just one of many needle punctures."

"OK, I understand, but doesn't that also make it possible that she could have done it herself accidentally?"

"That's possible, Jennifer, but just having this drug would mean that someone intended her harm by giving it to her or, at best, was incredibly and woefully – and probably criminally – negligent. And to answer your next question, I don't want to identify the drug because that information may still be crucial to our investigation."

"Can I quote you on that?"

Bellew paused a moment. "No, not yet. It might sound silly, but let us pursue it a bit more. If we don't come up with something, we might want to release that in order to help flush someone out. I'll mention it to the detective in charge of the case to remind him that we're still holding that card."

"Back on the record now, Sergeant Bellew … how many cups of coffee to get you going this morning?"

"Sorry, Miss O'Hanlon, but specifics to operational procedures will not be discussed."

FRIDAY – 8:26 A.M.

Jennifer had barely relayed the new information to JP when his phone rang.

"Newsroom, Weiscarver," came out in a rather clipped fashion and he hoped the caller would take the signal and keep the interruption brief.

"E.R., Miller," he heard from a notably more cheerful girlfriend.

"Well, Nurse Miller, you sound like an entirely different person. Did you get a good night's sleep or is this simply the result of the White Cap's wonderful shrimp scampi?"

"It must have been the shrimp because I didn't sleep worth a flip," Sherry said. "I'm sorry, JP. Maybe it was work, maybe it was personal problems, probably it was an accumulation of everything, but I had no cause to be sour company for such a sweet treat last night."

"It's done; I'm just glad you're OK. But, listen Sherry, I need to get back to work. This Hodge homicide – did you hear that they're now saying she was killed? – anyway, it's heating up and I've been called in to help out with it."

"I heard," she said, but she then cut off further conversation with, "Gotta run; the ambulance is pulling in with a patient." As JP said goodbye to what was probably already a dead line, he was pleased to get away quickly. However, he followed with a tinge of guilt because he had been glad that someone needed treatment in the emergency room.

"Well, Romeo," Jennifer brought him back into the newsroom, "are we ready to get to work on this puppy?"

JP tugged on his chin for a second and started talking: "Where to begin … How long had Miss Hodge been a diabetic? Did she always give herself the insulin injections? Who regularly visited in her home? Did she have any home health care? What neighbors and friends kept close contact with her? What kind of relationship did she really have with her son, uh, Michael? With the Moores, who raised him? Could Michael's father have re-entered the picture? A biggie: Who is in her will? Who would benefit financially from her death?"

Jennifer was busily jotting down notes. "Even though Miss Hodge was no longer very active socially," she said, "one doesn't become as popular and well-known as she was without stepping on a few toes, whether on purpose or not."

"Good point," Weiscarver added, even though he didn't think any of Irma's contemporaries would try to settle any dispute through murder.

"Irma," he muttered under his breath. Maybe 24 hours since he started working on the story of her death and he was already on a first-name basis with her.

It was an oddity he had noticed through the years. You can take someone such as a recently deceased lady of position – someone you would both naturally and intentionally grant the honor of a courtesy title like "Miss Hodge," whether you were speaking to a family member, a source or even the cops – and become familiar enough with her through your research that the folks in the newsroom start calling her by her given name. He turned his attention from his own notepad to Jennifer O'Hanlon.

"I think we should split up – if it's all right with you, boss lady – at least until one of us finds something to concentrate on."

Jennifer stood, stroked her chin a couple of times, which JP chose to ignore, and agreed.

"I think I'll start with her friends and neighbors," Jennifer said with authority. "Maybe Mrs. Baird can steer me in the right direction and I'll either use the city criss-cross directory to phone her neighbors or I'll just go

knocking on doors. How do you plan to begin?"
"Family," JP said. "That's always my first suspect."

FRIDAY – 9:52 A.M.

JP Weiscarver learned long ago how to make himself comfortable in almost any situation. He could grab a quick nap while waiting for the City Council to end an hours-long executive session, which was legally held outside the sight and hearing of the public and the press. He could make pleasant small talk with the ladies of the Wednesday afternoon sewing circle or expound on the current sports topic with the guys playing dominoes in the mall. He could chitchat with the president of Oldport Community College or with its nighttime cleaning crew. But he still had to gather his wits a bit before entering a funeral home.

Jason Freeman had become a pretty good friend, so JP knew he should have no concern about entering Williams Bros. Funeral Home, but he couldn't help but cringe as he felt the hairs stand on his arm when he opened the heavy door, which swung aside easily on its oversized hinges, always well-oiled to make sure they did not squeak – no small task in a coastal town.

Jason was only about four years JP's senior and the two of them sometimes played basketball together, but he was also the owner and operator of the funeral home. The last Williams brother died some 50 years ago and the business had changed hands at least four times, but the name stuck because almost everyone who lived in Oldport County very long had some family member who had been buried by Williams Bros.

JP was relieved when he peeked into Jason's small office, which adjoined a larger meeting room, or family room as the owner called it, and saw his friend seated at a neat mahogany desk filling out forms. Even a guy's guy would recognize that Jason was a good-looking man. His slight Seminole heritage was fully expressed in his dark hair and skin. He was always impeccably dressed, especially at work, and was well-educated and well-spoken. His bachelor basketball buddies were glad he was married and off the market, and that he was not a great athlete. JP knew he wouldn't surprise Jason, who undoubtedly saw the reporter enter via the closed-circuit camera, but he was always careful about popping off with any wisecrack until he knew the office was void of customers or visitors.

He was about to tap lightly on the open door when Jason wheeled around in his chair and chunked a paper wad toward him. That was his signal and JP instantly relaxed.

"Hey, you better be careful tossing around body parts like that," he warned the funeral director. "You never know when you might need one."

Another thing JP had learned from his friend was that many people in his line of work had learned to protect themselves from the uglier parts of their jobs by developing the same dark humor often found in cops, firefighters, paramedics and reporters. After a couple of minutes of banter and small talk, JP turned to business.

"The police said you picked up the body of Irma Hodge yesterday. Did you get it back after autopsy or is someone else handling services?"

"Initially, we did get her back after the medical examiners finished because no family member had come forward and we were next on the rotation," Jason said. "However, we were contacted by a member of the family first thing this morning and asked to turn the body over to Queensland Funeral Home, which picked her up about an hour ago."

All of JP's reporter alarms sounded. So, family has now entered the scene.

"Tell me," he said as he pulled his long, narrow notebook from his back pocket, "what family member called for the body?"

Jason shook his head. "Sorry, JP, but I wouldn't be comfortable telling you that; a lot of what we do is on a confidential basis and, well, I just wouldn't feel right in volunteering that information to you."

"OK, let me do the volunteering then. Was it her son, Michael Hodge?"

Jason opened his mouth as if to speak but just smiled.

"Was it someone other than Michael Hodge?"

His smile displayed a little more of his perfect teeth. There was a moment of silence.

"Jason, I thank you for your help."

"I didn't do anything, Mr. Weiscarver."

"All right, then, would you tell me how to find Queensland Funeral Home?"

FRIDAY – 10:19 A.M.

On his way out of town, JP decided to swing by the house and check up on Bubba, reminding himself that the ferret has been forced into considerable change the past 24 hours.

It was quiet when he entered his home and JP unconsciously worried about Bubba, but he shook it off upon remembering Juan Mendoza's lesson on the habits of ferrets and the fact that they sleep most of the day. He did, however, go straight to the hall closet that had been converted into Bubba's bedroom.

There was still no noise as he eased open the door, to which he had fastened a wooden block at the top so it couldn't shut and Bubba would always have access. The reporter turned the pet carrier so he could see inside and finally spied the ferret, whose slightly raised head stared back at the person disturbing his all-important slumber.

JP began apologizing, but Bubba started out anyway, revealing a familiar red and white object.

"Hey," JP severed his apology. "What's my favorite baseball cap doing in there with you?"

By now, Bubba was out of his home. "What else do you have in there?" JP asked while pulling out the pillows that formed the ferret's bed. Sliding a green and brown cushion out of the carrier resulted in a variety of sounds.

"That doesn't sound like chicken feathers, Bubba," he said to the small animal that almost seemed surprised itself. JP found that the pillow had a separated seam and the ferret must have been using it as a hiding place. Indeed, the first thing he pulled out was an earring that he remembered Sherry placing on an end table while talking on her telephone a few days ago. Next came a keyless key ring of his, a couple of coins, a cheap ink pen and last of all was a drug vial.

The small glass container made JP freeze. That was not his, so it must have come from the Hodge home, otherwise known recently as the crime scene. On the label was printed "Suxamethonium."

FRIDAY – 10:38 A.M.

"It's going to have my fingerprints on it, but only a couple," JP said as he placed the vial – now enclosed in a fold-top sandwich bag – onto the desk of Sergeant Tad Bellew, who immediately picked up his telephone receiver.

"Wait, Sarge. I expect to go over everything with one of the detectives, but I want to know something first." Bellew replaced the receiver. "Is this the substance they found in Miss Hodge's system?"

Bellew just looked at him, obviously weighing his answer.

"Look, Tad, we're off the record, OK? You know you can trust me, but none of your detectives know me that well."

"OK, Weiscarver, not only are we off the record but I must insist that you not spread this finding with anyone until we release the information." Bellew paused briefly as JP nodded in agreement.

"Suxamethonium is a muscle relaxant, an anesthetic often used during surgery, and is very potent. In fact, it's related to the curare used in poison darts by some South American native hunters. While Sux is obviously useful in surgery, an overdose can effectively paralyze the victim, leaving him, or her, unable to breathe and suffocation would follow in a matter of minutes."

"Wow, I'm impressed, Sarge. You're a walking encyclopedia."

"Listen, Weis-acre, you're not the only one capable of doing a little research. And, yes, it is what they found in Miss Hodge. Now let me see if I can get you in to visit with Detectives Good Cop and Bad Cop."

FRIDAY – 10:59 A.M.

The interview with Detectives Bill Smithson and Jackie Robbs was painless enough, JP thought as he drove back to the office, mainly to gather his wits and start anew.

While the reporter promised Smithson and Robbs that he would not reveal the drug used in Miss Hodge's death, he left no doubt in their minds that he would continue working the story. And while he was sure they believed him, they did ask to come to his house after lunch to inspect the pet carrier themselves, and he knew they would be confirming his story with Juan Mendoza at the county animal shelter.

JP was heading to his desk on automatic pilot, his thoughts in the clouds, when he almost bumped into Jennifer O'Hanlon while rounding the corner into the newsroom.

"Pardon me for bringing you back to earth, Mr. Weiscarver, but I certainly hope you did better than me," Jennifer said in her typically cheery voice, one that belied her frustration of the morning. "All I've come up with is half a score of little old ladies with just as many different stories about how wonderful Miss Hodge was and how tragic is her untimely death."

By then, JP was leading Jennifer into a small conference room so they could speak privately.

"I also checked with obits," she continued. "All they have is a pending, no funeral arrangements or other information yet."

"Actually, I've done very well," JP said while shutting the door, "except that it's a bit confusing and nothing we can print … yet."

He outlined the information that Michael Hodge apparently made arrangements to have the body picked up, but Jennifer refused to accept that as anything too noteworthy.

"After all, she was his mother."

"Biologically, perhaps, but it has been painfully obvious that there was no relationship there, that she was really nothing more than a bankroll for him."

"Granted, JP, but he was still the only family she had. If he didn't take care of her, the county would, and who would cause that to happen to their own mother, even a distant mother?" Jennifer said while circling the table to take a seat. "And let me give you another possible scenario. Miss Hodge knew there was nobody else to bury her and, even though she wasn't exactly old yet, she surely had considered what would happen and might have made arrangements with him. Shoot, if she was nothing but a wad of money to her son, as you suggest, she might have left something in her will for him contingent on her receiving a proper burial."

JP sat for a minute, his eyes again reaching toward the heavens.

"You're absolutely right, Miss O'Hanlon," he finally said as he rubbed his face. "Any son would see that his mother got a decent burial. But you're even more right to bring up the will. I would love to know what is in there."

"Sure, but that will be some time coming. For now, what should be our next move?" she asked.

"I was headed to Queensland to see what I could dig up, but that was interrupted by the most interesting part of my morning. This is a first for me … and we absolutely cannot use any aspect of it yet … but I did turn up the agent of death."

FRIDAY – 12:41 P.M.

JP had just finished heating and eating a turkey pot pie, something he knew his body was beginning to get too old to get away with, when the detectives arrived at his home. He showed them the ferret's bedding and then introduced them to Bubba, whom Robbs petted and chatted to as if he might provide them additional information.

"You're not going to give him the rubber hose treatment, are you?" JP popped off. The stony silence confirmed his suspicion that Detectives Smithson and Robbs did not possess particularly generous senses of humor. He wondered if that was true of most detectives but decided, after considering the numerous cops he had known, that these two were the exception rather than the rule.

"Have you thought of anything else since we last talked?" Robbs asked as he placed Bubba in a chair, which he instantly vacated since they now had him in a playful mood.

"No, I mean, there's so little in the first place. I went to the house, met Bubba, picked him up at the shelter, found the bottle. End of story."

And that was the end of the interview. JP knew that detectives had to follow up on a lot of dry leads, but he had never really thought about things being quite this boring.

"Bubba, old pal, I've got to get back to work. Before you distracted me, I believe I was en route to Queensland."

The seat of Queens County was about a 45-minute drive inland, giving JP plenty of time to work on the possible angles of the story. However, much to his frustration, he knew too little to extrapolate anything worthwhile. With what he had, just about everybody could be considered a suspect. He still felt like family was the best place to start, though, but the drive did not help him develop any ideas about how he was going to pursue that possibility once he made contact with Michael Hodge.

FRIDAY – 1:40 P.M.

Jason Freeman's directions led JP to Queensland Funeral Home with only one missed turn. The mortuary, like Williams Bros. Funeral Home, sat just a couple of blocks off the town square. Unlike the Oldport building though, this one was relatively new. The reporter drove past it the first time and returned going the opposite direction so he could park across the street.

After killing the engine, JP sat there, running through his mind how he might approach the situation once he entered and was met by the funeral home staff. That old uneasiness crept back … no, it rather stormed back, amplified by the fact he did not know what to expect inside and, even worse, by the doubts he had concerning what he was about to do. "This must be the worst part of my job," he mumbled to himself.

He was still running prospective scenarios through his mind when he saw the tall, walnut doors open. First through the door was a middle-aged man who had "funeral home director" written all over him, the thought of which made JP laugh when he thought how little that image applied to Jason, at least when the two of them were horsing around.

Mr. Funeral Home Director held the door open for another man of middle age but who was dressed less formally in khaki slacks and a polo shirt. At his elbow was a woman in a black dress with a veil that obscured her face. "You don't see that much, any more," JP thought, just before it occurred to him the man might be Michael Hodge.

With that realization, the reporter paid closer attention to the couple, especially the man. Maybe "middle-aged" was a bit harsh, he thought. Michael would be 43 years old, best he had been able to figure out. This man looked closer to 50, but he could be younger. He did not seem to be consumed by grief, which would stand to reason, but the veil on the woman with him was a bit mystifying. JP guessed the woman to be younger for no reason other than the fact he liked watching her walk.

As they reached the bottom of the funeral home steps, the couple paused for an old man who was slowly tottering by with the use of a four-footed cane. Michael, as JP was now calling him, spoke to the man and seemed to introduce the woman to him. The old man gave Michael a prolonged handshake and they parted.

JP waited for the couple to walk around the corner before he approached Queensland Funeral Home. The man with a cane was just then getting behind the wheel of his late-model Buick on the corner. He seemed to be moving better, now, but JP shook off the thought as he pulled on the heavy door to the funeral home.

Entering the quiet, cool foyer, the reporter was glad he took time to slip on a jacket. He sometimes wore a tie but a sports coat was typically too dressy in his coastal hometown. He noticed, though, that styles were more conservative even this short distance inland. As the door swung shut behind JP, Mr. Funeral Home Director emerged, introduced himself as Charles Durnham, assistant director and asked how he could help.

"Well," JP hesitated, "it's about Miss Irma Hodge."

As he struggled with what to say next, all his rehearsing in the pickup now a total waste, Durnham swept his right arm down the hallway and started walking without making a sound. He reached the first door to his right, turned to face JP and again extended an arm, this time his left. "Miss Irma Hodge," Durnham said. As JP entered, the man silently retreated, presumably to leave the visitor with his grief.

The reporter balked, started to call out to Durnham and stopped himself again. He felt a bit like an intruder even though he knew there was nothing wrong with him viewing the body of a woman he had never met.

"Maybe this will help me get to know her better," JP said softly as he eased into the room. On his left was a lectern that held an open book beneath a sign that said, "Please Sign Register." He delayed the decision whether or not to leave evidence of his visit.

A magnificent casket sat against the far wall of the room. Half of the lid was propped open. Instead of advancing, JP Weiscarver stood quietly and still, carefully surveying the room.

On a small table next to the register book was a green vase that held an assortment of fresh cut flowers. It wasn't until then that he noticed there were no names in the book. He realized that she had not been there long, which further made him believe he watched Michael Hodge drive away just a couple of minutes earlier.

Perhaps twenty chairs were spaced around the side walls in groups of two, three and four. A couple of generic paintings, the sort one may look at without seeing, hung on the walls. There were also two sets of heavy drapes that may have had some purpose he could not determine, but they at least helped the thick carpet absorb sound.

JP was approaching the other end of the room before he realized it. There was a spray of carnations over the bottom half of the casket. A couple of other easels held flowers off to the right and he drifted toward them. He recognized the names on both as being neighbors he met yesterday. He presumed that many more flowers would arrive today, once everybody learned of the death and that her body was in an out-of-town funeral home.

Irma Hodge's final earthly home seemed quite nice, but the reporter was aware that he knew nothing about judging a casket. The exterior was a highly polished metal and the interior seemed to be richly padded.

The interior also held the body of one Irma Hodge. He recognized her from photos he saw in Pat Baird's Lifestyles folder. Barely. He remembered hearing comments about how someone lying in a casket might "look so lifelike," something he never had been able to relate to. He never knew this lady in life, but he certainly did not think she currently looked as if she was about to rise and speak.

To the left, above the head of the corpse, was another easel. It held an attractive frame around a studio portrait of Miss Hodge. JP noticed that they dressed her in the same purple blouse … or dress, he could not be sure … she wore for the photo. Even her hair was similarly prepared. She was also wearing a necklace that he assumed to be pearls, just like in the photograph. But she no longer had on the matching earrings.

"She looks so natural, doesn't she?" and the question shook JP from his study. He turned to see an elderly couple speaking to one another and he quickly and quietly excused himself. On the way out, he found Charles Durnham in a small office and asked about funeral services.

"Three o'clock, Sunday afternoon," Durnham replied, "here in our chapel."

"Do you have a list of family members?" Weiscarver asked, trying to not sound like a reporter.

If the question surprised the assistant director, he did not show it as he pulled a folder from a holder on his desk and flipped through a couple of pages. "Biographical information has been prepared by the family and sent to the printer; it will be available in time for the services. In fact, you could probably come by late tomorrow afternoon and find one in the viewing room. Anything else, sir?"

He then gave JP a small smile that effectively said, "That's the best you will get out of me on that issue."

But the reporter pressed one more time. "Can you tell me how to get in touch with her son, Michael?"

"Certainly," the man replied. "You may leave a message with me and I will deliver it to Mr. Hodge tomorrow."

Tomorrow, JP thought. Of course, the family often receives visitors the evening before the funeral. That, plus the survivor information, will likely be available in the full obituary, which will surely be in Saturday morning's Odds and Ends. In fact, the obit desk should have it this afternoon.

"Thank you for your help, Mr. Durnham," JP said. "I may do that."

He started for the office door, stopped and turned back. "Mr. Durnham," JP said, "you did a wonderful job with Miss Hodge. She looks so natural."

FRIDAY – 1:29 P.M.

Two blocks from the funeral home, JP pulled into a Dairy Queen parking lot. The noon rush had passed, but there were a few patrons in the restaurant wiling away the early afternoon. He needed something cool to drink, a restroom and a place to jot down notes from the past twenty minutes.

He wasn't halfway through his root beer before he finished making notes and confirmed what he already knew: there wasn't much with which to work. Meanwhile, most of the diners had slipped out the door.

"I don't know what I expected to find here, but this wasn't it," JP mumbled around the plastic straw.

Hoping to learn something new and maybe locate some sort of inspiration, he dialed up O'Hanlon's desk on his cellular phone. She sounded a bit winded when she answered on the third ring.

"How did you know I was here, big guy? I'm just now unloading all my junk." JP smiled at her reply and considered the possibility that he called Jennifer because he knew she would lift his spirits.

"Couldn't very well go on without checking in with Task Force Leader O'Hanlon," he said with a mockingly official tone. "Actually, I'm hoping that you will have something to save us from a totally wasted afternoon; I'm floundering about Queensland with no apparent purpose. Tell me you're hot on the trail of something."

"All right, I'm hot on the trail of something," she said. "Seriously, I have nothing that's very serious, but there are a couple of items of interest. Neighbors mentioned that Miss Hodge had a home health aide calling on her the past few weeks. They thought it strange because she had seemed to be, and had claimed to be, in rather good health, as you already have been told."

"Interesting, maybe," JP agreed, "but quite possibly just an eccentricity she could afford."

"I ran it by Sergeant Bellew to see how he'd react and it was kind of strange. Two or three neighbors told me they saw the aide, who apparently came two or three times a week, but Miss Hodge had never mentioned it. In fact, one lady said she asked about her – the aide, that is – and Miss Hodge called it nothing and wouldn't talk about it. The neighbors decided she was embarrassed that she needed help."

"You mentioned Bellew …"

"Yes, well he didn't want to talk about it, which makes me think they're concerned, but he finally said they had not been able to track down this aide. It seems to me that wouldn't be too complicated if she worked for some home health care company or one of Miss Hodge's doctors."

"Could she be freelancing?"

"I suggested that to Sergeant Bellew and, like I said, he didn't want to say too much about it, but he allowed that was another possibility."

"You mentioned there were a couple of interesting things," JP said.

"Oh, you'll love this. Were you aware, Weiscarver, that she was not living alone at the Hodge mansion?"

"What? You're kidding. Dear old Miss Hodge had a boyfriend?" He whispered the question for fear an employee behind the counter would hear the mention of the Hodge name; there were by now no other customers in the restaurant.

"Sorry," Jennifer said between laughs, "but apparently not that interesting. He seems like a shadow character, the type of fellow most people don't see, but they say he's been living in what amounts to the servant quarters out back for decades."

JP was sipping thoughtfully on his soft drink, contemplating possibilities.

"What's his story?"

"He's the gardener."

"At the risk of repeating myself, you're kidding, aren't you? I mean, toss in a butler and a pool boy and we'll have ourselves a good old-fashioned murder mystery."

"At the risk of stating the obvious, Mr. Weiscarver, we do have a murder mystery," O'Hanlon said.

After disconnecting, JP continued slowly lowering the level of his beverage while weighing the new information. He could understand Irma Hodge not wanting to talk about needing home health care, not caring to discuss her medical concerns. And there's no motive for an aide to kill her unless it was robbery and police seemed confident that nothing of value was taken.

The gardener, though, was indeed intriguing. He's been living in a hovel out back for decades while the lady of the manor had that big old mansion to herself. I don't know it's a hovel, JP thought to himself. The man might have been very well cared for, but he could also be looking forward to the reading of the will. A loyal servant was often rewarded upon his or her master's death.

Returning his thoughts to the present, JP noticed a pay phone on the wall and asked at the counter to borrow a phone book.

It's something that has amazed him during his short newspaper career how often he and other reporters would invent ways to obtain information while ignoring the most obvious method. Sure enough, the Queensland phone book had a listing for "Hodge, Michael, 1304 Biscayne Lane." Now back in full reporter mode, he dropped a coin into the telephone, opting to use it instead of his cellular phone, just in case the man had Caller ID.

"Hello, is this Mr. Hodge? Michael Hodge, son of Irma Hodge?"

It was and he recognized the name of JP Weiscarver, commending him on the sidebar in the morning paper. "You sure did latch onto the most important part of her life, those stupid animals."

Not an auspicious beginning, but Hodge did agree to see JP in his home without asking why. JP was thankful for that because he wasn't sure he could answer such a question without it sounding like, "Oh, I'm hoping you will slip up and somehow indicate that you are responsible for the death of your rich, estranged mother."

FRIDAY – 2:12 P.M.

Hodge's directions took the yellow JP-mobile across downtown Queensland, over two pair of railroad tracks that threatened to remove the fillings from the driver's teeth, and to a trailer park on the outskirts of town. When Hodge first said to look for a trailer park on the right, JP mentally substituted the term "mobile home park" and then considered "manufactured housing." Using correct terminology, even politically correct terminology, was an area where he tried to discipline himself.

"This," he said aloud as he turned into the community's circular drive, "is definitely a trailer park."

Nothing there seemed to be younger than the reporter, including the rust on the axles, most of which no longer had tires and those that did had ceased to hold air. JP eased down the pot-holed road, searching for the Confederate flag that Hodge said marked his trailer.

Even before he saw the flag, apparently used in lieu of drapery in the window above the trailer's towing tongue, JP recognized Michael Hodge. He was, indeed, the same man escorting the woman down the funeral home steps and he was directing his visitor to park between two old station wagons, one brown with its windows rolled down and the other a color that was once white and which sat on cement blocks.

"Mr. Weismann," Hodge said as the reporter stepped from his pickup, "welcome to my home. Did you find it OK?"

"It's Weiscarver," he answered, "but, please, call me JP. Yes, your directions were perfect, including the hint to take the smoother railroad crossings in the center lane." That last comment was to be nice; if the outside lane was any rougher, JP didn't want to experience it.

Inside the ancient mobile home, JP accepted Hodge's offer of iced tea and waited until his host was seated before starting to talk. For the second time today, he had no firm concept of what he wanted to say, so he said so.

"Mr. Hodge, to be honest with you, I'm not too sure why I asked to come by. It's not something we usually do, bother the family during a time of grief, but your mother's story is so captivating that, well, I guess I was hoping to learn something that would help tie it all together."

"Did you know Irma?" Hodge asked.

"No, I never met her. Of course, I had heard of her and had seen her name in the paper a lot, but our paths had never crossed."

"Why do you say she's so … what did you say, capturing?"

"Captivating. Same thing, I guess. It's hard to say. Well, you for one. Obviously, her old friends knew she had a son, but I bet a majority of people, like me, who only knew her from what they read in the paper, where she was called 'Miss Hodge,' appropriately, well, it's going to surprise them when they read her obituary tomorrow and see she's survived by a son."

"And a granddaughter."

"Was that your daughter leaving the funeral home with you? Uh, I was just arriving and saw you coming down the steps but didn't realize at the time it was you."

"Yeah, that's Maggie. She's taking it kinda hard. She'd only recently gotten to know Irma some and I think she was hoping to make up for the relationship I didn't have. That's silly, though, but maybe it's because her mother died several years ago."

"I'm sorry, Mr. Hodge," and JP grew even more uncomfortable.

"Oh, we were already long divorced at the time. You see, I didn't want to make my mother's mistake and have a kid outside of wedlock, so I married when I was seventeen. But it didn't last too long. New mistake. I hope Maggie learns from both of us."

JP took a long drink of tea, unsure what to say next, but Hodge didn't mind taking the lead.

"So, you went by to see Irma? They did a good job."

"Yes, and I liked the photo; that's a nice touch," and with that, the reporter was ready to get down to business.

"What kind of memories do you have of your mother while growing up? It must have been somewhat different, maybe even awkward."

"I don't know it was so awkward. Different, yeah," and Hodge seemed to drift back in his thoughts as his body eased deeper into the old, soft sofa. "Even though Irma was mite strange, I had a perfectly normal mother and father. You know about the Moores, don't you? Robert and Midge?"

JP made eye contact and nodded as he opened his notebook to the first blank page.

"As they raised me, they had me call them Uncle Bob and Aunt Midge, but as I learned what was really going on, I started calling them mother and father. They liked it. That was the same time … oh, I was probably eight … when I started calling my birth mother by her given name, something she seemed to appreciate, which pissed me off to no end."

The reporter smiled at the comment.

"Mr. Hodge, do you mind if I tape our conversation? I really don't know for sure that I'll even be able to do a story, but just in case," and JP made himself stop talking before he said too much.

"Heavens, no, you go right ahead. I ain't got nothing to hide or to fear anyone hearing. Anyway, my mother and father gave me a right good upbringing. Irma, for what it was worth, helped them out some financially, at least until I graduated high school."

"Did you go to college? What kind of work do you do?"

"Nope, no college, but Irma said she would pay, at state college, anyway. I wanted to go to a good cooking school, you know, become a chef, but she wouldn't go for that. So, I just said, screw the money, and got a job in a restaurant and started working my way up, learning as I went along."

"Still in the restaurant business?"

"Yeah, I'm the chef – the cook, really – at Madison's over on Fifth Street, been there a couple years. Old man Frankston is gettin' ready to get out of the business and he's willing to sell it to me and finance some of it, but I gotta have a pretty good wad of dough up front to get started."

"I bet it must be expensive setting up a restaurant," JP said in an effort to keep Hodge talking along the line of money.

"Actually, Irma loaned me the dough a few years ago to buy into a café, but that didn't go good. I had a lot to learn and my partners were more interested in throwing away money to impress their friends than serving up a good meal. We lost our shirt."

"But now…"

"I think I'm ready. Frankston does. Mom and Dad do. But Irma wouldn't hear nothing about giving me another shot."

"You asked her?" JP queried, trying to be nonchalant without being too obvious.

"Sure. So did Mom and even Maggie. Just last week, Maggie thought Irma might have a change of heart, but she stuck to her guns: 'No more money for my bastard son.'"

JP squirmed a little bit and jiggled his tea, causing the ice to clink in the half-empty glass.

"Let me ask another question, Mr. Hodge. And I know I may be treading on personal ground, so feel free to not answer. Do you expect to gain anything, or maybe everything, from her estate?"

"To tell you the truth, I've tried to not think about it ever since she died Wednesday night. I expect something but nothing monumental. Maybe a collection of those you-can-do-it self-help books and twenty bucks for a haircut." He shook his head. "She never liked the way I cut my hair, not from my earliest memories."

"What if she were to leave all of it to you?"

"Nah, can't see that happening. She was always so caught up in her clubs and charities and whatnot, she'll leave the meat to them. I'll be lucky to get a scrap or two."

"Does that bother you?"

"No way, got used to it a long time ago."

They sat quietly for a few seconds and JP sensed that Hodge was struggling with something. The reporter patiently waited.

"Look, I'd be tickled pink if she left me a heap o' money. I'm OK if she don't. But," and he was still and it was quiet enough that JP heard music from a passing car. "But, I sure 'nough wish that she leave a nice reward to the Moores for all they done for her. And I don't suppose Maggie needs it, but I'd like it if Irma left her something, if for no other reason than because the girl was friendly to her the last few months."

"You mentioned earlier that Maggie was taking it rather hard. Had the two of them become close?"

"You know," Hodge said, "I can't really say, but I think so. Maggie volunteered to pick out Irma's clothes and all for the funeral. It was her idea to match the picture and she was a little upset that she couldn't find some of her jewelry." He seemed to be debating whether he might be crossing into dangerous territory and JP was mentally forming a response, but the older man gave way and continued opening up to his new acquaintance. "I've been telling myself that Maggie and Irma might form a special bond, something that would do 'em both good."

"How do you mean?"

"Well, Irma never had nobody around, except that crazy old gardener and her society creeps. Well, all those stupid animals. Sure, I didn't care for her, mainly because she gave birth to me and then threw me out with the bathwater, but I didn't never hate her. I'll swear on a stack of Bibles to that, JP."

"You said it might do them both good."

"Oh, Maggie, you mean. Yeah, like I said, her mom died when she was about twelve, so the girl didn't have a natural mother to help her through those tough years. I think it's harder on a girl than a boy, you know? Well, Mom – Midge – helped out, but it never seemed to really take. I did all I could; I really think I made a good dad, but…"

"Are you and Maggie close?"

"Not really, not the way I'd like. We get along fine and all, but we don't have no real bond, you know? I think there was some time she blamed me for her mom's death; you know how a kid can do. I provided for her but not the way she wanted all the time. Actually, and don't print this, but it's crossed my mind that this whole thing might make us closer."

"Does she still live with you?"

"Heavens, no. She moved out soon as she could. She kinda likes doing things her way."

"So, where does she live? What does she do?"

"She's," and Hodge stopped as if remembering something. He then covered his tracks. "Listen, she don't really like me talking about her. Maybe you can strike up a conversation with her at the funeral Sunday. You are coming, aren't you?"

That caught the reporter off guard.

"Well, I hadn't really thought about it. It will probably depend on how things work out."

Hodge nodded as if that answer was suitable, though JP knew it was an incredibly weak offering.

"You mentioned the gardener earlier. What do you know about him?"

"Know? Nothing. Well, he's been there long as I can remember and I've probably talked with him a half-dozen times. He does seem to be decent and real dedicated, though I don't know why. I don't imagine she paid him much more than room and board."

"Could he be in her will?" JP asked and then, almost without thinking, he added, "Could he have killed her?"

The second question once again brought an eerie quiet to the room.

"Killed her. Murder," Hodge said softly. "I knew that would have to come up sooner or later."

"Listen, I'd understand…" JP started saying, but Hodge interrupted him.

"No, no. It's something I've got to come to grips with. Even though I don't really feel like I knew Irma, even though she often did me wrong, she still gave birth to me. And it's hard to think about someone just killing her. Maggie just won't hear it. She won't let us talk about how Irma died."

It was quiet for a long minute before Hodge addressed the questions.

"I don't know if he might be the type to kill someone. He always seemed harmless enough. Would he be in her will? Hadn't thought of it, but he could be. Like I said, he'd been with her a coon's age."

"One last topic, Mr. Hodge," JP said as he finished off the tea. "What do you know about your father?"

Michael let loose a laugh, as if he had all day been in search of a reason to do so.

"That one's easy, JP. Absolutely nothing."

Weiscarver waited because he knew "absolutely nothing" could not be the complete story.

"Oh, I've asked," Hodge finally said. "Over and over again. And I believe Mom and Dad don't know nothing more than me. I finally pissed off Irma by asking so much. Not only did she never tell me nothing, but she made sure her friends kept quiet if they knew something, which I'm not sure they did."

JP stood up and stuck out his hand and said thanks.

"Hold on, there, buddy," Hodge protested. "I can't let you leave without meeting my folks. They just live next door and they're expecting you."

FRIDAY – 2:57 P.M.

It was as if JP was a long-lost relative when the Moores welcomed him into their mobile home, one that was much neater than Michael's and smelled of baking bread.

"We read your stories so much that we feel like we know you, JP," Midge gushed as she offered an oatmeal cookie. "Do you mind if we call you JP? That's what we call you all the time anyway. I ask, 'Hon, did you read JP's story today?' He always has because he reads the paper while I'm whipping up breakfast, don't you, Hon?"

"Hon" simply nodded while offering JP sugar for his iced tea, which he declined. Having a glass of tea wasn't an option; it was simply handed to him. Bob Moore proceeded to dump two overloaded spoonfuls of the sweetener into his glass and commenced a drawn out stirring campaign while his wife looked at the reporter, who suddenly remembered there was a question hidden in her last statement.

"Oh, please do call me JP. I get nervous when people call me anything else."

"My dear, but you did a wonderful job this morning," Midge took off again. "Over the years, Irma seemed to rely more and more on building relationships with her animals while losing contact with people, well, with us, anyway. Isn't that so, Hon?"

Bob never broke stride with his spoon. Even JP had already figured out that answers were seldom required, at least from her husband.

"You know, Cletus – that's her father – never allowed pets around the house and one of the first things she did when he died was to buy a registered Siamese cat. Do they register cats? Whatever, it was the prettiest thing. Called it Cleo, even after she found out it was a boy cat. Can you believe that? Of course, we haven't been to her house in years, but there were bunches of cats and dogs then. And the fish, can you believe all the beautiful fish? I'm surprised she didn't have pet goats in that huge back yard of hers. Couldn't you just see that?"

She took a sip of tea and JP jumped in to try and redirect the conversation.

"Mrs. Moore, I was talking to Michael a while ago about his father. I've got to ask, do you know anything about who his father was? Did he maybe work for Cletus Hodge? Might you have met him or seen him in the early days?"

"He was a scumbag, I know that," Bob mumbled. Midge ignored him.

"You gotta remember that we never met the Hodges or knew nothing about them until after Michael was born. I'd heard rumors that the fellow worked at the docks. Well, I finally asked her one day, this was when things were still going pretty smooth between us, something like, 'Well, tell me about Michael's father.' I had practiced just how I was gonna ask 'cause I knew it might upset her."

"What did she say?" This question came from Michael and JP wondered if he had ever heard this story.

"That's the funny part. She heard me; I know it. I mean, we had been chatting away about Michael, sitting in the baby's room. She was in one of her more maternal moods and she was holding Michael. Well, I asked the question, just like I had practiced it, and felt like I kept it from sounding too nosy or threatening. And she just sat there. I mean, she didn't flinch. I waited a minute and said something else, about dinner or the weather, and she joined the land of the living again. I knew then that the subject was taboo."

JP nodded his head during a few seconds of an uncomfortable quiet, then shifted forward in his seat.

"I know your relationship with her must have been a bit, well, strained, but you probably knew her about as well as anybody. Do you have any idea who would want her dead and why?"

"Maybe," came a voice from the hallway behind JP, "just about anybody who knew the old biddy, just to do the world a favor."

"Charley, did we wake you, dear?" Midge asked while straining to get up from her chair. "I probably got too loud, going on about … oh, this here's JP Weiscarver from the Odds and Ends. He's the one who did the story about Irma in this morning's paper."

"Sorry to butt in on your conversation like that," a somewhat more subdued Charley said while offering his hand. "It's just that I've watched that witch living high on the hog while my folks here did so much for her without never receiving nothing."

JP could not refrain from working out the multiple-negative statement and thinking that Charley, probably unbeknownst to himself, might have actually managed to say what he intended.

"So, Charley," JP said while balancing the glass of tea and shaking his hand, "Miss Hodge's violent death doesn't surprise you?"

"Well, can't say I'm not a bit surprised, but it seems somewhat just," he replied. JP's eyes sought out Michael without turning his head and could not discern any reaction to that statement. "What do you mean, violent?" Charley continued. "I thought your story said she OD'd or something."

"It wasn't my story but was the police reporter's, and it quoted the police as saying she was poisoned," and JP paused a bit, contemplated whether or not to bring up the information received this morning about the

Suxamethonium overdose, and decided against it. He still had a promise to Sergeant Bellew in effect. "As for violent, I guess I tend to think anytime someone dies at the hand of someone else, regardless how it is achieved, that it is an act of violence."

The reporter thought he could read a bit of embarrassment in Charley's demeanor. Maybe he was just a blowhard.

"Seriously, Charley, do you really know of any reason someone would kill her?"

"I can't honestly say I haven't thought about it," Charley finally said. Again, JP saw no reaction from Michael. "I mean, look around here. My folks at one time were living in that castle taking care of her little problem – sorry, Michael, you know I love you as much as I despise her – and then they were kicked out on their poor-white-trash butts – sorry, Mom – so Irma could live the high life without nobody in the way.

"Now, Mom and Dad are barely getting by financially, living in this dump of a trailer park. Their health is worse than their bank account, but they don't have money for doctors. And there ain't nothing to make us think things will get better unless Irma dies and actually leaves them or Michael something in her will."

Everyone was quiet, even Bob with his iced tea, as Charley obviously steamed toward boiling point, but before exploding he quickly arose and headed back toward the hallway, stopped and said, "Well, I guess this is the only way of finding out, huh?"

After the back bedroom door closed, clinking sounds again emanated from glasses around the living room. JP took a long swallow and announced his need to return to Oldport and the office. Midge gave him a hug as he left and Michael walked him to his pickup.

"Don't go reading too much into Charley's ranting," he said. "I can guarantee you he'll come out in another 10 minutes and apologize to everyone; that's just the way he is."

Shaking his head, JP dismissed any need to be concerned, but it occurred to him that neither Michael nor the Moores seemed to see that Charley could be making himself into a suspect.

A suspect, Weiscarver thought as he started driving back toward the coast. Isn't that what he came here for, really? Michael, Bob and Midge all could have reason to benefit financially from Miss Hodge's death, but none of them seemed likely as candidates for murderer. Charley, now, it's possible that he could have pulled off something in order that the others would profit.

Wait a minute, JP thought. Does Charley live with his folks? Now the reporter chastised himself for not thinking to clarify that issue. Does Charley have a job? Maybe he too would gain quite a lot if his parents inherited any large sum. Or Michael, for that matter, because JP was sure that Irma's son would take care of the Moores even before he bought a restaurant.

As JP drove through downtown again, he once more saw the man with the four-footed cane, slowly exiting the Dairy Queen with an ice cream cone in his free hand.

FRIDAY – 3:42 P.M.

Using his cell phone, JP checked in with Jennifer since he never told her where he was going. She lectured him about going off on what could have been a dicey interview without letting anybody know.

"Yes, Momma," he finally said, thus stilling that discussion.

He had her transfer him to Pam Gipson, the regional reporter who covered Queens County, whom JP asked to try and discretely learn anything about Charley Moore.

On a whim, he stopped by the Oldport County Animal Control Department and asked to see Juan.

"Any luck placing your ark-load of beasts?" JP asked when he saw his new friend.

"Tell me, first of all, if you had any luck sleeping last night," Mendoza countered.

"Hey, Bubba and I are tight. He seems happy and he slept all night. We played some this morning and, well, what can I say but that things have started off great."

"Your story lit up our phone lines here today," Juan said. "Our field officers only left on emergency calls because it's taken us all to handle the phones and to process the adoptions. Not only have most of Miss Hodge's pets been placed, but several of our other residents also have found new homes. Thank goodness all her cats and dogs had already been neutered so we didn't have to take care of that.

"Oh, and you'll love this. There's a new dental office opening in town. Three or four dentists are going together with their different specialties and opening a joint office. They had already installed a huge fish tank and they adopted all the fish … probably saved them a fortune and definitely saved us a whale of a headache."

JP just shook his head. "It still amazes me sometimes how well people respond to a need once they're aware of it."

"Speaking of which," and Juan flashed his grin again, "expect to hear from me next time we're overstocked with pets seeking homes."

It was almost 5:00 when JP walked into the newsroom and, first of all, he had to update Pat Baird on Michael Hodge. Listening in was Lydia Murray, who said she also had an interesting interview.

"OK, it wasn't as interesting as yours, but Mrs. Selma Brewster, also a Palmetto Club honoree, seemed to think there were people who were jealous enough of Miss Hodge's money and the attention it gave her to 'do her in,' as Mrs. Brewster put it."

"Were her sources of information any more traditional than little green men?"

"It wasn't so much information as it was opinion, I believe, sort of like your example of Charley Moore. Mrs. Brewster believed there was a number of people who thought Oldport would be a better place without Miss Hodge in it. In fact, she gave me every reason to believe she was a member of that group."

"We have to remember that saying she was not good for the community, even saying that she deserved to die, does not necessarily mean Mrs. Brewster had anything to do with the murder," JP replied while giving his chin a workout with his thumb and forefinger. Kind of like Charley Moore, he thought.

"True, and I didn't mean to insinuate that she did," Lydia said, not at all ruffled by the comment. "However, there is another interesting aspect to her situation. She was in line to receive the Palmetto Club's Future Builder award, considered the organization's second-highest honor. In other words, she was the first runner-up to Miss Hodge."

"JP," Pat spoke up, "you admitted to a slight awareness of the club yesterday. You were correct in that it mostly serves as a way for well-to-do women to do well by the community, but a person's position within the organization carries no small amount of prestige by itself. These awards are only given out every four to ten years. The reason to spread them so far apart is to give weight to their importance. So, someone not awarded anything this fall won't have a another chance for at least four years. It's been seven years since the last awards."

"I don't think Pat means to suggest that the awards mean so much that someone would actually kill for one, but ..." and Lydia left the thought suspended.

"Will Mrs. Brewster likely receive the Woman of the Year Award now?" the reporter asked.

Pat fielded that one.

"It stands to reason, though I don't know it's actually in the bylaws. I would think the four remaining winners – there are five in all – will each slide up a notch and someone new would be picked for the fifth award, the Palmetto Frond."

"What do you think, Lydia?" JP asked. "Do you think there is any way Mrs. Brewster could do it?"

"She doesn't seem to have the personality for it, but I did have to reassess my initial read on her once she invited me into her library for our interview. The walls were covered with hunting trophies, many of them big game. I asked if her husband hunted and she said he did but that his trophies were in the den. 'I killed every one of these beautiful creatures myself,' she said. She then quickly asked me to not print that because she was afraid it did not fit the Palmetto Club image."

JP next swung by the regional reporter's desk and learned from Pam that Queensland cops grudgingly admitted that Charley Moore was "known to them," police parlance for just what it insinuates, they knew him because they had dealt with him.

JP and Jennifer slipped into one of the glass-walled meeting rooms in an effort to minimize interruptions.

He updated her on what he had found in Queensland and outlined his feelings about each of the people he met. O'Hanlon started off recounting her afternoon by revisiting the home health care issue.

"I saw Sergeant Bellew just a half hour ago and he said they still haven't found any leads on the aide. They seem to be rather interested in her, but it occurs to me that he might be playing that up to me as a smokescreen."

"What do you think he wants to screen you from?" JP asked, slightly perplexed by the attitude he sensed from his partner.

"I don't know, maybe Mr. Saunders."

"Who in the world is Mr. Saunders?"

"Oh, you haven't heard his name yet. George Saunders is the gardener. Sergeant Bellew says they took him in right away and questioned him. You see, Mr. Saunders is the one who found the body, so I guess that means he has access to the house. Anyway, the cops are not holding him, but I couldn't get them to swear him off as a suspect either."

"So, where does it come in that you're suspecting a cover-up?"

"I … I guess I'm getting frustrated and, well, ticked off that they knew about this gardener and had talked to him from the get-go and never bothered mentioning it. You know, I kind of feel like Bellew's not being totally upfront with us on this."

"Whoa, let's do a reality check here, OK?" JP said, trying to use his smoothest voice. "Keep in mind that this is an ongoing investigation, so they're not going to just up and volunteer information like that. Did you ask who found the body? Did you ask if anyone else lived on the property?"

"No to the latter, but I did ask who found her … and," Jennifer stalled while flipping pages in her notebook, "here it is … he said 'a worker.' I pressed him on it but he said they were not ready to release more than that."

Her voice trailed off a bit and she added, "OK, I see what you're saying. We dig up our own information and ask them questions about it."

"Yeah, but we're not limited to dealing with the police. You talked to others about the gardener, as have I once you told me. These folks probably know more about him than the police can tell us. That's reporting, my dear. You beat the bushes, learn what you can, use some of it to help you learn something else, then sift through it to figure out what is fact and which of that is pertinent to the story."

"I know, I know … Lord, grant me patience, but do it right now."

With that levity, they were able to segue into an analysis of their information.

"I do feel like we're working on a movie script here," Jennifer finally said. "Let's see, for suspects, we've got my favorite, George the gardener …"

"George, George, George of the garden," JP chanted until Jennifer heaved her pen toward him.

"And my favorite so far is Charley Moore, Miss Hodge's son's adopted brother, so to speak," he said.

"I still think the cops seem to be leaning toward the aide and I can see why. She could probably inject something without Miss Hodge putting up a struggle."

"Hey," JP blurted out, "do we know where the drug came from? I mean, it's probably not something you buy on a street corner."

"Bellew said they're checking that out, but it was obvious he didn't expect a lead to turn up there because the batch number or something was removed from the bottle."

JP scribbled some notes.

"Back to our suspect list," Jennifer said. "How do you explain Michael Hodge? He certainly stands to gain a lot, but you said you don't rate him a prime suspect. I had the impression this morning – was that only this morning? – that you pretty much figured Michael did in his mother.

"Give me a break, here, O'Hanlon. That was before I talked to the fellow." JP bounced the tip of his pen off the notepad and rubbed his chin while he thought. "Maybe the guy snowed me, but my gut tells me he just doesn't have it in him to kill anyone, let alone his mother."

"OK, but his name stays on our list."

"Naturally. And the Moores should stay there, too, but I really doubt any involvement on their part."

"That leaves the mysterious father," Jennifer said. "It seems the cops know nothing more than we do about him."

"Well, I couldn't turn up anything in Queensland. In fact, Michael said his attempts to learn about his father seemed to be the catalyst for the gap between him and his mother. He wanted to know about his father, understandably, but never got any information. And Mrs. Moore didn't know anything. I can't help but feel like he did his thing, took a payoff from the old man and lived up to his promise to disappear. He probably married some gal on the West Coast and lived a normal life."

"Probably," she said, "but maybe he ran out of money and has been trying to milk her for more. For now he stays on the list."

"You're the boss," JP said, flashed a toothy smile and leaned back in his chair. He jumped when Chad Brooks, a sports writer in for the evening shift, knocked on the glass wall, pointed to JP and held up two fingers – call on line two.

Jennifer wasn't surprised when she heard him mention Sherry's name into the phone. It was later than usual for both of the reporters to be in the office without having an evening event to cover. But she was surprised when she saw it was almost 6 o'clock. She had her notes in one stack and JP's in another by the time he hung up the phone.

"Are you in trouble for being out so late, Mr. Weiscarver?" she teased him. She knew JP was five to six years older than she was but was surprised when she first learned his girlfriend was about her own age.

"Maybe I am," he replied while shuffling through his stack of papers. "She backed out on our movie date for something work-related."

"At least, you have a life to be canceled. I go through the day with the knowledge that it's just me and the television for the evening. Some nights I sit and actually wish for something to come over the police scanner."

"Shoot, I can make you feel even worse," JP shot back as he began returning to form. "I even have someone waiting for me at home and Bubba's not going to come up with some lame excuse for not spending the evening with me. Say, why don't you bring your without-a-life self over to my place? I'll have a pizza delivered and introduce you to my new roommate."

FRIDAY – 7:49 P.M.

The pepperoni and mushroom on a thick crust arrived just as Jennifer parked her car on Dolphin Street and she hurried up the sidewalk carrying a small plastic chest with a six-pack of beer on ice.

"Hey," JP cried out as he handed the pizza money and tip to the teenage driver, "I do have a refrigerator, you know."

"No, I do not," Jennifer said after casting a smile at the departing boy. "I've heard stories about you bachelor types living on nothing but peanut butter and take-out." Then she caught sight of the ferret, sitting in a recliner with his front paws on the arm so he could peer over the side.

"This must be Bubba," she gushed as she set the chest on the coffee table and approached the three-pound creature that was studying her so intently. She could not have known that he was giving the same passionate attention just moments earlier to the delivery boy and then the pizza box. "May I pick him up?"

"If you don't, he just may jump into your arms. Y'all get acquainted while I serve up dinner. I'm going all out for company, using plates for the pizza and glasses for the beer."

The topics of Bubba and ferrets in general dominated the dinner conversation. By the time the two reporters had their fill of pizza, Bubba was asleep on the sofa next to Jennifer, oblivious to the police scanner squawking away from JP's bedroom.

"He seems to approve of you," his new owner said. "I hope he comes around to think of Sherry as fondly. They haven't exactly hit it off yet, but they haven't spent much time together either."

"How did you two meet? You and Sherry, that is."

"Not your usual encounter," JP said. "It's been almost a year ago. I was walking on the beach and saw a crowd forming near the water and, well, you know, I had to go see what was happening. Apparently, this guy had some kind of problem while swimming and he went under. Friends pulled him ashore and this good-looking babe in a two-piece bathing suit was giving him CPR. The EMTs rolled up about then and took over."

"Did the swimmer make it?"

"No, but we didn't know that at the time. I mean, they didn't give up until some time after he got to the hospital."

JP pulled another beer out of Jennifer's ice chest and decided to skip the glass and he took a pensive sip straight from the bottle. His guest sat silently, watching his eyes as he recalled the day in question. She knew his mind was seeing details he could not convey and it was obvious that it was having an effect on him.

"I still can't say how or why things worked out the way they did," JP said. "There was something about her that hit me. You know, I've worked plenty of accident scenes and shootings and drownings, and I've interviewed scores of witnesses and victims and family members, but it was like I was out of my element, watching from above or something, an out-of-body experience."

Bubba lifted his head, looked at Jennifer through half-open eyes and snuggled more tightly next to her leg as she scratched his ears.

"Maybe you would say it was voyeuristic, but I hung back and watched Sherry as she gave way to the emergency squad. As she did so, she was relaying information to them and I could tell she was medically trained because it was evident she knew what to say and how to say it.

"But then she just melted in among the bystanders who watched the man carried toward the ambulance. I slipped back away from the crowd but stayed where I could watch her. She returned to her beach chair and sat down and I could tell she was crying. After a while, I finally approached her and said something, I don't remember what, and she looked up like she was hoping to find a friend and, for the first time, it occurred to me that she might have known the guy."

"Oh, no, was it her boyfriend?"

"That wasn't really the point, but, no, she didn't know him. I mean, I was so caught up watching Sherry that I lost focus on the victim. I remember asking her then if he was a friend and then I asked why she was crying. 'He's not going to make it,' she said. I suppose I just stood there giving her my famous dumb look. She said that her CPR was just buying time but that she knew there was no spark left in him."

"That would be tough to handle," Jennifer said while reaching for her second and last beer. She poured it into her glass.

"We sat there and talked a bit. I think she welcomed the opportunity to kind of work it out. Eventually, we made plans to meet for dinner at a restaurant just down the beach, the White Cap, and we sat there and talked until they finally turned out the lights and we took the hint and left."

"That's sweet … well, except for the guy drowning, of course."

"Yeah, the fact that we met over a dead man is an outlawed subject, but it will make a great story for the grandkids."

"Grandchildren? Are you making permanent plans?"

"No, not really, I just meant …"

"I know what you mean," Jennifer said. "It's just a saying."

"The funny thing is that we really didn't start off on a romantic relationship. We found that each of us was interested in what the other had to say and that we could spend hours talking. Eventually, romance developed and I'm kind of partial to that way, liking someone before dating them and falling in love."

"And it had nothing to do with that bikini she was wearing?"

"Well, I noticed and noted that she looked awfully good in it, but, really, what grabbed my attention was the way she conducted herself in that situation. She impressed me."

"Does she still impress you?"

"Yes, she does. She's quite a study. But, what about you? Is there any Mr. Jen out there you haven't told me about?"

She took her turn to think a bit before answering.

"No. There has been an occasional boyfriend but never anything very serious and there's been nobody since coming to Oldport. But that's fine for right now because I'm still concentrating on work. Things will happen when the time is right; I'm a big believer in that."

"I'm with you. Things do seem to have a way of working out. Take the murder of Miss Hodge. The cops, or maybe we, will come up with a motive and a murderer, sooner or later."

There was a brief pause and Jennifer finally laughed.

"Wow, that was some smooth transition from love lives to work," she said, wagging a finger at his confused face until he started grinning.

"It was bound to come up sooner or later. After all, it's what we have in common," JP said. Deepening his voice and gradually rising out of his chair, he proclaimed, "The strongest bond is that we are both warriors for truth, justice and the American way."

Jennifer scooped up the ferret and looked him in the face. "I've learned something of immeasurable value about your roommate, Bubba," she deadpanned. "He's an incredibly cheap drunk."

SATURDAY – 8:12 A.M.

Bubba was waiting for JP's eyes to open Saturday morning, notably later than their first morning together.

"Hey, thanks for letting me sleep in on my day off, Bub. Do you mind if I call you Bub, maybe just occasionally? I didn't intend to sleep late, but it felt good."

The conversation seemed to excite the ferret, who was dancing around the floor as his new owner eased out of bed.

"Hey, you were the perfect host last night, Bubba. Now, tonight, I plan to have Sherry over for one of my famous grilled steaks and I would love it if you could be just as charming for two nights in a row. As enticement, I have some fresh grapes for you and there will be more tonight if you win the heart of my gal. Deal?"

Bubba playfully nipped at JP's ankle. "I'll take that as a yes and a contractual arrangement."

During breakfast and the morning routine, the reporter continued chatting with Bubba, mostly about Irma Hodge, most notably the various "suspects." The ferret slowed down and JP spied him heading into his closet bedroom.

"Hey, thanks for your assistance, buddy. You helped me make up my mind. While you hit the sack, I'm going to amble over to the Hodge mansion and see what I might find."

Even though JP had decided what he wanted to do, he wasn't sure how to do it. If he just parked in the Hodge driveway and walked to the door, it would probably put George on the defensive. What door should he go to? Is George living in the mansion now? Where are his quarters? Walking around to the back to hunt down the gardener would feel a bit like trespassing and might be treated that way. If the man did kill his employer, he's not likely to be the kind of person you should surprise.

Meeting him casually would be ideal, JP figured, but he knew that might take a while. Well, it's not as much a long shot as most people. The man is a gardener, after all, so he probably spends a lot of time outside.

OK, JP had a plan. He put on casual walking clothes with pockets to carry his notebook, recorder, pen and telephone. He thought about jogging but decided that would minimize his chance to gaze across the grounds and try to spot George. He filled a plastic bottle with water, donned a John Deere baseball cap for a little sun protection and drove the pickup to a city park only a couple of long blocks from his target. After stretching a bit and reviewing his plan, he set out with a slow, steady pace, slow enough that he could survey the area well, fast enough so that it did not appear that was what he was doing. Or, at least, that was what he hoped.

He maintained a deliberate stride down Alligator Way as he passed the Hodge mansion, keeping his eyes busier than his head but detecting no movement. There was an occasional person out but nobody seemed to take notice of a morning walker.

A short distance later, he took a left on Turtle Crossing and made a block in order to make a return trip by the house. As he came into full sight of the grounds, he kneeled to undo and retie his right shoelaces and the stalling paid off. Surely, that was George who came around from the back of the house pushing a green wheelbarrow. JP went to work on the left shoe to give George time to get closer to the street and he then resumed his course.

"Mornin'," JP said as he neared the man who stopped the wheelbarrow next to one of the numerous flowerbeds, this one covered with yellow flowers the reporter did not recognize. The man gave a humble nod, as one might expect from a lifelong servant. JP stopped walking to indicate that he intended to hold a conversation. The man looked a little more closely.

"You have beautiful grounds here," JP said. It was no lie; they were without a doubt the best in the area.

"Thank you, sir," the man mumbled as he picked up a plant from the wheelbarrow.

"Do you take care of this huge lawn and all these flowerbeds yourself? And, please, call me JP." The name did not seem to register on the man, who looked to be in his 60s. His skin was weathered by a lifetime of working outside. He had that lean, hard look of someone accustomed to physical labor.

"My name's George Saunders," he finally said. "Nice to meet ya. Yeah, I've made and kept these grounds for nigh on 35 years, every danged plant in the place and a great many afore 'em. Are you a gardener?"

Ahh, JP thought to himself, this just might work.

"Never really tried, Mr. Saunders. Frankly, I don't know beans about growing things, but I do recognize something as attractive as your yard here."

George thanked him again and indicated he was ready to return to planting even more of the yellow flowers, as if gardening was the only topic he found interesting.

"To be honest with you, Mr. Saunders, I walked by here in hopes of seeing you." George was all of a sudden interested in his visitor again. "My name is JP Weiscarver and I'm a reporter for the Oldport Odds and Ends newspaper. I did a story a couple of days ago about all the pets stranded by Miss Hodge's death."

He was glad to see George nod his head as if he knew the story. He was even happier to read in the gardener's body language that he was now receptive to discussion.

"I've come to really regret not knowing Miss Hodge before she passed," JP continued. "The more I've learned about her, the more complex her life and death seem. You must have known her well if you worked for her for 35 years."

"Yes, sir, I did, most likely better than anyone short of her daddy. Heck, prob'ly knew her better than the old man did."

"Do you live in Oldport?" JP asked, even though he knew the answer.

"No, I mean, yeah, but I live right here, with Miss Hodge. Well, I didn't live with her. I stay in a house out back. Guess you'd call it a mother-in-law house. It's small, but it's all I need. It's nice enough. Miss Hodge took good care of me and, well, I took good care of her."

"Man, I guess that puts you in a touchy situation. I mean, you stand to lose not only a job but your home, too."

"Nah, I ain't worried. Miss Hodge always told me I'd be taken care of if anything happened to her."

"Sounds like you two did have an extraordinary relationship. I should have considered that and extended my condolences when I first met you."

"Thank you, sonny. You know, you're the first person to do that."

JP began to feel a little guilty about trying to work the gardener for information but then remembered that George had to be considered a possible suspect.

"Listen," George spoke up. "It's getting late enough into the morning now that I can make an excuse to break for a drink. Care to join me?"

It seemed a bit early in the morning for iced tea, the usual mid-morning drink around Oldport, but JP deduced that his host might have been at work for quite a while. He followed George around the large Hodge home to the gardener's house, acknowledging to himself that it was not wise to follow a possible killer into his lair but listening instead to his reporter's gut.

The house was small and simple but actually had plenty of room for one person. The kitchen JP followed George into was an offshoot of the living area. One doorway on the opposite side of a brown sofa presumably led to the bath and the bedroom.

"As one bachelor to another, George, I've got to say that you have fixed up this place very nicely," JP said as the elder man reached into one of the painted cabinets above the sink.

"No, no, I didn't do none of this. If it's green and growin', I can make somethin' beautiful out of it, but none of this … what do you call it, interior decorating? Nah, Irma did all this." Then he slammed an empty shot glass in front of JP and produced a half-full bottle of whiskey.

"Whoa, when you said 'drink,' you meant drink. I, uh …"

"I'm sorry, young man, I wasn't thinking. You see, Miss Hodge and me usually had a little nip every morning, 'cept, of course, she drank somethin' a little more feminine. But if it's too early for you, I've got a soda in here."

JP quickly decided that having a drink with the old man might go a long way toward cementing their newfound friendship.

"Who cares?" JP said. "It's Saturday, hit me."

As the two visited, it became obvious to JP that Irma and George had come to depend on one another through the years. Makes sense, he thought to himself, two people living alone so near each other with some sort of relationship already established, that they would tend to grow closer together, even if it wasn't in any kind of a romantic way.

"Tell me, what was Miss Hodge like? Was she good to work for?"

"To tell you the truth, JP, it wasn't work that kept me here so long. She was good, a good woman," George said as he poured his third small shot.

"How do you mean?" JP continued to sip slowly on his first drink, not that his host noticed.

"First of all, she took me in when I had nothing, when I was nothing. And it wasn't 'cause I was a great gardener … I am now, but I didn't know diddly-squat back then. She let me learn, try things, and she was patient. She was good to talk to and she told me things she couldn't get no one else to listen to and … and."

JP quietly waited while George gathered his composure.

"And I'm gonna miss her," he said, pouring out the final contents of his glass into the sink and putting away the bottle.

"But what about you?" JP asked with genuine concern. "She told you that you would be taken care of, but, well, you've got your work, your home, it appears your everything riding on that. Do you think she's going to leave the house to you?"

"I won't lie to you, JP. I've had a couple days to think about it and I wouldn't mind if she did. I've been thinking that I might just stay here where I am and maybe rent out the house to some young family for a decent price and then I could still keep the grounds. Wouldn't that be a hoot?"

"What about her family, her son and granddaughter?"

"You know, I really want to like the boy, Michael, 'cause he didn't get treated right when he was little. But, on the other hand, he ain't exactly gone out of his way to treat her motherly, you know what I mean? Irma will do him right, she'll leave him a nice piece of money, I reckon, but maybe not the house."

"And Maggie?"

George looked puzzled. JP wasn't sure if it was the liquor or the name.

"Is that the name of Michael's girl?"

"Yes, sir, I believe it is."

"You see, I hadn't even heard the name and I never saw the girl. I knew that Irma had been seeing her granddaughter, but she just barely mentioned it around me. So, I don't know. I hope not, 'cause I feel like the brat had that very thought in mind when she started coming around. Oh, maybe I'm just being a cranky old fart."

Regardless, JP wanted to keep him talking.

"You say you never saw the granddaughter. What about the home health aide who had been visiting Miss Hodge?"

"You hit on somethin' there, son. I couldn't figure that out. I mean, Irma talked pretty freely about her health to me, but she never told me nothin' about why she needed doctoring help. And when the gal would come, Irma would ask me to leave. Well, I finally writ it off as female problems, you know what I mean?"

"Guess so. Was she here the night Miss Hodge died?"

"Nope. Well, not that I know of. I had gone to the feed store to get some ant killer and it took a while because my beat-up old truck was causing problems. When I got back, I came inside my place to eat dinner. I always went up to the house after dinner and Irma and I would have an evenin' drink together. That's when I found her. Did they tell you I found her? You know, I believe that's when I'm gonna miss her the most. I loved those nightly visits with her."

JP weighed his words and decided to shoot straight.

"You loved her."

"Yes, sonny, I did and I'm not ashamed to say so."

SATURDAY – 4:19 P.M.

It took JP three circuits through the supermarket before he picked up everything on his shopping list. The conversation with George Saunders kept playing through his mind, the gardener's suspect status waxing and waning.

As JP was deciding between French bread and dinner rolls, he was mentally listing the reasons George might have had for killing Miss Hodge. By the time he was checking the carton to make sure none of the medium eggs were broken, he was reviewing a list of little things that did nothing to suggest any foul play by George.

He was pondering different cuts of red meat when he felt a presence over his right shoulder.

"You really should pay more attention to your surroundings," he heard in a familiar voice. "You never know when there might be poison-tipped darts flying around."

"Maybe not, Sarge, but I do know that's not as funny as it might have been a few days ago. In fact, I was just puzzling over a conversation I had this morning with the person who may have been Miss Hodge's closest friend."

"OK, I'll bite," said Tad Bellew. "Who might that be?"

Bellew sidestepped several opportunities to offer up more information about the case as JP told of his chat with George. Well, the reporter didn't quite tell everything, but he did relate the admission from the gardener that he was in love with his late employer. A slight nod of the head by the police officer indicated to the reporter that he was aware of that already.

"Just between us," Bellew said, "my impression is that our investigators don't put much stock in Mr. Saunders as a suspect."

"Just between us," Weiscarver echoed, "in whom are they placing stock?"

"That's just it. There isn't anyone in particular. Therefore, quite naturally, the gardener stays on the suspect list."

"With?" the reporter prodded.

"Well, I don't know JP. You know they don't make me privy to that kind of information. But I have a good idea of one name on their list."

JP moved half a step closer and dropped his voice to encourage the sergeant to take him into his confidence.

"Who?"

"Why, you, my boy," Bellew said, louder than he actually intended. Dropping his voice to match JP's, he added, "After all, you are the only person we know of to have had a bottle of Suxamethonium outside of an operating room."

SATURDAY – 6:45 P.M.

JP just had time to clean the house (beginning with placing evidence of Friday night's beer and pizza in the trash can outside – no point in having to explain, he thought) before Sherry arrived.

"Welcome, welcome to a land of relaxation and charm, far removed from the cares of the world, hospital emergency rooms in particular," JP gushed as he opened the door, hoping he wasn't overplaying it too much. He had no idea what was bothering his girlfriend, but his wish was to help her return to her normal state for the evening.

"That sounds wonderful," she said. "To do my part, I 'accidentally' left my pager in the car."

"And, believe it or not, I 'accidentally' turned off the police scanner. Now, we'll pray we don't hear any sirens that cause us to wrestle with our consciences."

"Do you need help in the kitchen or do you most of all need me to melt into this recliner for a while?"

"Melt away, Florence Nightingale. What about a glass of wine before dinner?"

"Make it half a glass. Too much before dinner and I might melt myself to sleep."

"Are you still not sleeping well?"

"Not for days now, but last night was better. In fact, I..." she started but then she let out a short shriek.

"JP Weiscarver, this beast of yours almost gave me a heart attack. I think he snapped at me."

Her host broke into a deep laugh.

"If it's any consolation, you gave him at least as great a fright with your scream. I'm sorry. I should have thought to remind you about Bubba. Truth is, even after only two days, we are right at home with each other."

With Sherry's wine poured, JP gathered the ferret into his free arm and sat on the sofa near the recliner.

"Bubba, this is my very good friend, Sherry. She will come around here at times and you should grant her all the courtesies you would expect me to bestow upon your very good friends. Now, say 'hello' to Sherry."

When JP's grip relaxed, the rodent jumped to the floor and skedaddled away.

"Well, looks like I should apologize about my roomie."

"Please don't," Sherry said. "It's a thing with me and animals. Put me in a trauma situation and I can get the best out of injured children, scared parents and egotistical doctors. But put me in a room full of lovable puppies and they'll all attack me. Hey, this wine is really good. Don't tell me you actually bought something that didn't come in a box. What a surprise."

"Only the best goes with this culinary masterpiece. Speaking of surprises, I have something for you."

JP fished the earring out of his pocket and handed it over. "Recognize this?"

"Hey, thanks. I missed it the other day and remembered taking it off when I used your phone to check messages. These earrings were a gift from my grandmother. She never liked any of my jewelry and said, 'A lady needs at least one nice set,' when she gave them to me. She also gave a matching necklace, but that only comes out in extremely special circumstances; it's a bit heavy and imposing for my tastes."

"You've still not told me much about your family."

"Nor you yours. Maybe we can schedule a weekend I'm off to do a joint genealogical session."

She's right that she should take it easy with the wine, JP thought, for it seemed like she was feeling it already.

"My grandmother died some time ago," Sherry continued. "She was living in California at the time. Quite an amazing woman but not one her grandchildren got very close to."

"You know both my folks still live up north, but what about your parents?" JP asked.

"My mother left us when I was too young to remember. My dad is out West too, Oregon the last I heard. Seriously, my family history is not suitable for a romantic evening."

"Medium on your steak?"

"You know it. If the offer still stands, I think I'm OK to have the other half of that glass of wine after all," she said with a slight giggle.

"I hope you don't mind me bringing it up," JP said as he poured the wine, "because I know what you said the other day, but it's all I've been working on the last three days, the death of Irma Hodge, that is…"

"Oh, JP, I'm sorry to have overly worried you. I just reacted badly when you first brought it up. I was coming off an exceptionally stressful day at work, we lost a patient because his family waited too long to call an ambulance, we were short-handed, all that kind of trouble."

"Any time you want to talk about those tough days, feel free to lay it on me. I know it often makes everything easier to assimilate if you can present it to another person. I guess that's why I'm so often talking about work to you. You sometimes comment on it in such a fashion that it helps me look at it from a more appropriate perspective."

"You're absolutely right, my dear reporter man, and I'm glad to lend you an ear. And I'll keep your offer in mind; it's just that I don't usually process like that, but I do appreciate the gesture."

JP quietly tended to the cooking for a couple of minutes before he decided to forge ahead.

"Well, then, I've got to say that I have become captivated by this story and I am grateful you'll let me talk about it. It just doesn't fit any patterns you would expect in the homicide of an elderly heiress."

"Explain it to me," Sherry said, satisfying JP that she really was open to discussing the subject, even during a "romantic evening."

"First of all, you would expect the violent death of such a person to either be part of a robbery, an inheritance scheme or just a crazed assailant looking for someone he could assert power over. The method of death effectively rules out the first and last. It had to be someone who had personal access to her."

"You mean, like family? That's disgusting."

"Believe me, when someone has money, sometimes even surprisingly small amounts of money, there are people who will turn on even the nearest of kin. She gave enough people plenty of reason to not care if she lived or died. I talked to some of those people yesterday and, while they didn't seem too upset by her death, they gave me absolutely no impression they cared enough to kill her."

"OK, catch me up here. I've heard people talking at work, but I haven't actually read anything. Sorry about that. How did she die?"

"At first, they thought it was just natural causes because she was found in a peaceful manner in a chair at home. It wasn't until tests showed a drug that police started looking at it as a homicide."

"Did they never consider it may be a suicide?"

"Briefly, by what I understand, they considered suicide or even that she accidentally injected something besides her insulin. Without getting into information I've sworn to keep private for the time being, I believe that even if she did it, then someone else will be culpable for providing her with the drug that killed her."

"So, who did you talk to yesterday? Do you mean relatives of hers? I didn't even know she had relatives, the way people were talking."

"Apparently, only the old-timers remembered that she had a son. In a nutshell, she had him out of wedlock and did not want to be bothered with motherhood, arranged for a couple to care for him and even eventually encouraged them, somehow, to move to Queensland. She provided for him but wasn't much of a mother. But that's it, no siblings, no other children, though there is a granddaughter she's only recently gotten to know."

By now, Sherry was setting the table and trying to help out in the kitchen.

"That was my first thought," JP continued, "the displaced son and the couple who raised him, mainly because none of them ever received much of the wealth that Miss Hodge was sitting on. Like I said earlier, though, either they're all very good actors or there wasn't anything about them to suggest they had the capacity to do such a thing. On top of that, none of them seemed to have any strong suspicion they stand to inherit anything."

"Sounds like a narrow suspect field. Have you considered the butler?"

"Cute, but you'll be surprised to find out that I talked to him just this morning."

"You're kidding, right? Nobody has butlers these days, do they?"

"Actually, he was the gardener, but he lived in a separate house on the property and had been working for her for almost 35 years. As a matter of fact, he's still living and working there. A real interesting fellow and, I suspect, probably the one in the best position to inherit anything substantial. I got the feeling they had quite a spiritual bond, judging from the way he talked."

"So, now he's your prime suspect?"

"You're gonna think I've gone soft, but, no, I don't think he could have done it. I'm sure he was deeply in love with her."

"Sounds to me like you've got your work cut out for you. Unless, of course, the cops actually solve it before you do."

"OK, point taken. Let's eat."

Dinner conversation drifted around everything but work issues, particularly about the entertaining antics of Bubba, even though he was sedate this evening. As JP served up slices of store-bought key lime pie, he again mentioned Irma Hodge.

"I visited the funeral home in Queensland yesterday and viewed the body of Miss Hodge."

"JP, you didn't. Really? Why?"

"Actually, I hadn't intended to. I was only trying to find a way to contact her son, Michael, but I was glad I did. I don't know; it just gets too easy to separate yourself from a story, but seeing her lying in that casket made it real and somewhat personal."

"Wow, guess I didn't realize just how involved you get, but I think it's time to shift the conversation to more pleasant topics."

"Sure, I'm sorry. Just one last thing. They did something I thought kind of nice. They had a framed studio photograph of her on display and her granddaughter had dressed Miss Hodge the same as in the photo."

"Interesting, but tell me, what do you know about this granddaughter?"

"Not much at all. Michael doesn't seem to want to talk about her. It's just that she had been seeing Miss Hodge recently. Maybe I'll get a chance to see her at the funeral."

Sherry almost spilled her wine as she jerked around.

"You have got to be kidding me. Are you crazy? Why in the world would you go to the funeral? Wouldn't you feel like, I don't know, a bit of a voyeur?"

"I would have felt odd and I never would have thought about going, but Michael seemed to really want me there. I can't explain it. Maybe my story about Miss Hodge's pets touched a nerve and made him realize he will miss his mother. Maybe he figures there won't be anyone there he knows. Maybe he did kill her and is trying to throw off suspicion. I haven't actually decided yet, but I'm leaning toward going. Are you working tomorrow? We could go to church, have a nice lunch and go to the funeral. We'll sit at the back and slip out right away."

"As tempting as that sounds, JP, I'm afraid I'm scheduled. For now, let's drive to the beach for a moonlit walk and I'll try to convince you how obsessive you're sounding over this Hodge woman."

SUNDAY – 10:09 A.M.

JP briefly considered skipping church and then he locked gazes with Bubba. The reporter couldn't help but feel there was a plea behind the ferret's black eyes.

"Bubba, how did you so soon decide to become my conscience? All right, I'm going to church and then you and I can discuss whether I should go to the funeral."

It was well before time for the service to start and he was sitting alone pretty much in the center of the sanctuary, his gaze directed at but not quite focused on the stained-glass windows behind the pulpit. The little church would not likely see itself half filled on the autumn morning, but its seams were tested every winter when the snowbirds flocked in from the north.

The building itself was at least 40 years old, but the church had been around since early in the 20th century. JP had heard old-timers tell stories of the hurricanes that had hit Oldport County over the years but how the tropical storms had never done extensive damage to this building nor any of its predecessors.

JP was still lost in his thoughts when the widowed sisters Irene Plimpton and Mary Jane Woodall scurried over to comment on his Irma Hodge story. They were always complimentary of JP's work and of JP himself: "If I was only 40 years younger," Irene had a habit of saying.

The sisters were also known to be aspiring matchmakers and occasionally inquired about JP's status, as Mary Jane did again.

"No, Mrs. Woodall, I'm not really available. I've had a pretty steady girlfriend for the past few months."

"I don't recall seeing her with you, dear boy," Mrs. Plimpton pressed. "Do tell me she's a good girl."

JP suppressed a laugh and simply smiled.

"Yes, ma'am, she is a good girl. Actually, she came with me once, but she's a nurse in the emergency room at the hospital and, being new and at the bottom of the totem pole, she works most weekends."

That satisfied the sisters and they skittered a couple of pews forward to visit with the Bagleys, who happened to have a single son who graduated college last spring. The tolling of the church bell eventually chased them back to their usual seats.

JP had a small amount of difficulty staying focused on the service as his mind continued to bounce between Irma, Sherry and his list of suspects. But he managed to tune in while the pastor read the text from the fourth chapter of Genesis, upon which he would base his sermon, entitled "Am I?"

"Now Cain said to his brother Abel, 'Let's go out to the field.' And while they were in the field, Cain attacked his brother Abel and killed him.

"Then the Lord said to Cain, 'Where is your brother Abel?'

"'I don't know,' he replied. 'Am I my brother's keeper?'"

Murder and deceit has indeed been around forever, JP thought. It was the first time it had occurred to him that the original homicide had been brother-on-brother, which made it even more difficult for him to fathom.

"'Am I my brother's keeper?' was Cain's response," said the Rev. John Barker. "It was obviously a rhetorical question. Cain knew the answer, thought he knew the answer. He wasn't responsible for his younger brother, who as a shepherd had earned the Lord's favor."

"'Am I my brother's keeper?' Cain asked. 'Yes,' was the Lord's answer. 'Yes, indeed, we are all keepers of our brothers and sisters.'"

JP lingered in his seat as the postlude played and people trickled out. Before the sermon started, he had pretty much convinced himself that he was obsessing over Irma Hodge, that he was getting too involved, that it wasn't really his concern.

As Margaret Edmonds said a couple of days ago, the newspaper's function and his job were not to play detectives. He was to report what happened.

Then what was nagging him so?

"Am I my brother's keeper?" echoed in his mind.

Yes, I am, he thought. And even though the chances of me helping are incredibly slim, I must continue looking and asking questions. I can't help but feel like I have a role to play in this.

SUNDAY – 1:44 P.M.

Following a quick stop by the house for a sandwich and looks of encouragement from Bubba, JP Weiscarver was parked outside Queensland Funeral Home a quarter hour before the 2 p.m. service. Already, people were entering the chapel and JP forced himself to join them before he had the chance to give it too much thought.

After signing the register, he picked an end seat toward the back, a place where he could watch people and maybe not attract attention. When he was prospecting for information, he always wanted to be the proverbial fly on the wall and would make a concerted effort to not draw attention toward himself.

It was no trouble remaining alone. It's doubtful anybody in Queensland knew the reclusive Miss Hodge, except for her son, her granddaughter and the Moores. And it appeared that the 45-minute drive from Oldport discouraged many of her friends who might have attended at home. Considering that and Miss Hodge's quiet lifestyle, the two dozen or so who attended was a respectable number. JP did recognize the couple he saw viewing the body on Friday. He was pretty sure the woman was wearing the same dress.

He figured out too late that he chose the wrong side of the chapel to sit on because the family room was on the same side and therefore totally out of his line of sight. The service was brief, the message delivered by a minister who obviously did not know Irma Hodge. And now he never will, JP thought, just like me. The reporter wondered if the minister also found himself wishing he had known the woman.

At the end of the service, JP joined the line filing past the open casket, but he was mainly concerned with watching people's reactions and getting a glimpse into the family room. There he saw only five people – Michael and Maggie, Bob and Midge Moore, and Charley. Maggie was dressed all in black and still wore her veil. Michael had on a reasonably nice, dark suit while the three Moores were in what were probably their best clothes but not what would seem most appropriate for a funeral.

JP turned his gaze upon Irma for the second and last time. What was this strange attraction he felt toward the woman? She did look good, he decided, noticing above the casket the same photo. Under his breath and barely moving his lips, he promised to take good care of Bubba. He then nodded farewell to a lady he had never met and followed the line out the side door.

Within a couple of minutes, the family members emerged. Midge looked as though she had shed a few tears. Michael was quite somber but definitely not moved to watery eyes. Maggie was nestled under his left arm, quiet and almost seductively hidden behind heavy black lace.

"I'm glad you made it, JP," Michael said as he extended his right hand. "This here's my daughter, Maggie."

As JP turned his eyes toward her, she dipped her knees, slipped from under her father's arm and crawled into the family car for the trip to the cemetery.

"I'm sorry," Michael said as she closed the door. "She's always emotional, more so now, and she probably thinks I'm trying to play matchmaker, something that really upsets her."

"Don't be silly. I can empathize with her. I wouldn't want a stranger butting in at my grandmother's funeral."

With that, he extended condolences one last time, declined the invitation to view the graveside service and started home, his mind racing again, even without gaining any new information. As he pulled out of the parking lot, he saw the same old man, propped on his four-footed cane, watching people leave the funeral home.

SUNDAY – 3:13 P.M.

En route home, JP wanted to talk to someone and he knew Sherry would be at work, so he dialed in Jennifer O'Hanlon's number.

"Hey, Weiscarver, I was just thinking about you. Have you had a nice, relaxing weekend?"

"Well, actually, no, and I have a confession to make. I have been digging around the Hodge story without touching base with task force leader."

He gave Jennifer a rundown of his conversation with George the gardener, his encounter with Sergeant Bellew and then mentioned the fact he attended the funeral.

"You what?"

"That's pretty much the same as Sherry's reaction. There was a possibility – unrealized as it was – that I might pick up something and, strange as it sounds, I knew Michael really wanted me there."

There was a bit of silence, so JP continued.

"But, out of all that, the one thing that keeps cropping up in my mind is the aide. George obviously felt the same. He said Irma wasn't ill and I believe he would know. The aide just doesn't seem to have a reason for being there. Cops can talk to Irma's doctors, I guess, but they won't give me any information. I wish I knew better how something like that worked."

"Pardon me for interrupting your soliloquy, Mr. Investigative Reporter, but aren't you married to a nurse?"

"Ha, ha, ha. But you're right that I should pick Sherry's brain. I'm reaching heavier traffic now, so I'll talk to you later unless you're holding back any other wonderful ideas."

By the time JP settled in at home, he figured he could catch Sherry on her break. Joe Baker answered the phone and said Sherry hadn't come in yet.

"She called about the time I got here, said she had something come up but that she would make it a bit later," he said. "Listen, got a resident who needs help and I've got to run."

As he hung up, the reporter's brain considered that maybe he had been taking too much for granted. Just because the neighbors had seen someone with a medical uniform enter the house doesn't mean it was a home health aide or that it was a professional call.

It certainly would not be difficult to make something that looked like appropriate attire. In fact, a uniform could probably be rented from a costume store, borrowed from the theater's wardrobe, handed down by a late aunt. None of that addressed motive for killing Miss Hodge.

Or maybe it really was an aide but one who was selling cosmetics or Tupperware on the side. Of course, JP knew that Miss Hodge owned more than three dozen dogs, cats and birds. The visitor might have been shopping for a pet, or tending to a sick animal, or trying to find a home for one, or, or…

"Or maybe it was really a Great Dane in a uniform," JP said out loud, frustrated by his deteriorating hopes of figuring out what happened to Irma Hodge.

"Bubba, I wish you weren't so secretive. Surely you know what happened."

Instead of offering any assistance, the ferret simply snuggled up closer to his new owner, who decided he should check on his girlfriend. At her home number, all he got was her cheerful voice on an answering machine, so he dialed her cell phone.

"Hey, handsome," she answered on the second ring, "thought I might hear from you about break time."

"You know you can't hide from this reporter. Yeah, Joe told me you had something come up and I thought I should make sure you didn't need any help."

"I lied to Joe a little bit. Honestly, I just wasn't feeling well, but I didn't want him to know. The last thing you want is to have a shift full of nurses fretting over your health; it's enough to drive a person crazy. But I'm better and am headed in to finish my shift."

"What about getting together after you get off work," he suggested. "My mind has become a pinball machine and it would help to have someone to bounce thoughts off of."

Sherry made him wait while she executed a left turn.

"I don't think so, JP, just don't believe I'm up to it tonight."

"That's probably a good idea, anyway," JP said to the ferret after disconnecting. "It will give the two of us a little quality time together and maybe you can help me puzzle through this homicide. What am I saying? When I've got something eating at me, what do I do? I go to the beach. Come on, Bubba, it's time for you to meet my therapist."

When JP first moved to Oldport, he couldn't stay off the beach. The magical connection of the vast Gulf of Mexico with the North America continent, its always-changing yet always-constant nature, drew him to it. He would swing by the beach on the way to work, carry a sandwich there for lunch and watch the reddening sun slip over the horizon at night.

With time, he did not have to maintain as much physical contact, but the spiritual nourishment was still there. Whenever anything weighed heavily on him, JP found gravity pulling him to the beach, where his mind discovered freedom to work things out, whether it was with him sitting on a bench, lying on a towel or splashing in the surf.

Not knowing how Bubba might react to open spaces, JP slipped a harness and leash on the ferret, even though he had no intention of letting him romp around only to carry a bucket load of sand home in his gray coat.

Instead, JP carried his new buddy down the beach, just out of reach of the lapping surf.

"I hope you like it, Bubba, because this is where I am more like myself than anywhere else … though that does not necessarily mean I make any more sense." For perhaps 200 yards, JP quietly strolled, the ferret snuggled in the crook of his arm.

It was autumn, JP's favorite time of year, especially in Oldport. Even though he accepted the summer heat and humidity without fussing, relishing the cooling breeze that usually rolled in off the Gulf of Mexico, it was still refreshing when the temperature started to ease its way down in the fall. It was still plenty warm enough for a bare-footed stroll and splashing in the water.

But the greatest relief was the decrease of tourists. He knew tourism was important to many area businesses that bought ads in his paper and helped pay his salary, but it was nice when traffic slowed down in the fall and one was able to run into a convenience store and still find it to be convenient.

JP was roused from his soul-cleansing by a ferret that apparently achieved and tired of its nirvanic state more quickly.

"Did Irma bring you to the beach?" the reporter asked Bubba. "I doubt it, not with that house full of dogs and cats. Was she even the beach-going type? Please tell me about her. Anything. But most of all, who killed her and why."

He stopped strolling and pulled the ferret's muzzle to his nose. "Money sure seems like a good motive. Or maybe it was unrequited love. Old George the gardener sure seemed to have the hots for Irma. Did she spurn his advances? Maybe they weren't really as close as he makes it seem. Or maybe a double suicide was the intention and then he chickened out."

He started walking again.

"Family always stands to benefit from a well-to-do estate, sometimes even if the dearly departed didn't exactly have that in mind. Michael sure didn't seem to be caught up in the idea of gaining money, but maybe he's just playing it cool.

"I can't buy that, Bubba. I know it's not unheard of for a man to kill his mother, but I just can't accept that story, especially after getting to know Michael. I tell you, if he did kill his mother and was then able to conduct himself as he has, then he must be the scariest man alive. I don't think he is.

"It seems the same arguments can be made for the Moores, though they have the added incentive of providing for their two sons. Charley, now Charley's another topic. He could certainly blow his top and off someone, though I'm not sure he would really have the guts and I thoroughly doubt he has the brains and means to carry out murder by Suxamethonium.

"The elusive Maggie's an unknown. I wonder if the black attire and the veil is just for the death of her grandmother or if she actually dresses like that all the time. Maybe Southern chivalry has rubbed off on me, but I have a problem picturing a young lady doing in her grandmother.

"Of course, the great unknown is the home health aide, if indeed one really exists. The means would be there, supposing she or a friend has access to Sux, but a motive is elusive. Hmm, unless one of the aforementioned hired her to do it. Would this little old lady have been a victim of a hired killer? That's just one more idea that doesn't make much sense.

"What are we leaving out? There's always the possibility of a loose cannon, such as a neighbor upset at never having the best yard on the street. Don't overlook the possibility of someone not appreciating Irma's decision to not support some benefit or maybe she undermined somebody's effort to with the gardenia club's presidency. And, to be perfectly honest with you, the Palmetto Club is more than a little scary.

"It could be Tad's right. Maybe I did it just to write a first-person story about the life of a murderer."

JP noticed that his rider seemed to be getting heavy eyelids and he headed to a bench facing the ocean. While the ferret slept, the reporter's mind continued racing over the bits of information he had gathered about Miss Hodge. She obviously loved animals, but a few decades ago she couldn't make time for her only child. Maybe she had loved a man once, whoever Michael's father was. Maybe she loved the gardener. It's possible she never loved any man, never found anyone who could replace dear old dad. There hasn't been a bit of evidence, though, to lead one to think she had cultivated a deadly enemy. Money can do that without anyone realizing it, he figured.

Eventually, his mind touched on the morning's sermon from Pastor Barker as he recalled the resolve that built up in him. A few moments of introspection proved that the resolve remained, in spite of the frustrations JP had been experiencing. The ferret stirred only slightly as its human pillow pulled a cell phone out of his pocket and dialed Jennifer O'Hanlon.

JP's eyes were not really focused on the horizon, where the sun setting to his right seemed to melt into the deepening blue sky with gradually diminishing pink and red hues. He responded when the phone was answered.

"Jen, I really want to find Irma Hodge's murderer."

MONDAY – 7:32 A.M.

When JP arrived early the next morning, Jennifer already had her notes spread out over the same conference room table they occupied Friday night. Her partner was still sorting through his when Pat Baird slipped in, carrying two cups of coffee.

"I'm not about to inquire as to what you two kids are doing in here this time of day, but I feel compelled to point out that it is an incredibly poor location for a romantic tête-à-tête, not to mention bad timing since the boss will be here soon."

She never gave them a chance to respond, talking from entry through deposit of coffees to exit. The other two could not see the impish smile on her face as she shut the door behind her, but JP knew it was there. Jennifer would learn soon enough about Pat's wonderful sense of humor, but for now she just stared at the senior reporter, not sure if she should be embarrassed, angry or entertained.

"Moving along," JP said while raising his coffee mug as in a toast, "did you experience any epiphany overnight?"

"For now, I thought we should prioritize our hit list. Friday, we made it a point to leave everyone but Bubba on the chart, so maybe we should narrow our focus on what we feel are the best candidates. Then, at a respectable hour and on the assumption that the police department has been as diligent as you over the weekend, I will pop in on Sergeant Bellew and casually try to find out what they're thinking."

JP let loose a subdued laugh.

"This tells you how bad my tunnel vision has been. It has not crossed my mind that Detectives Smithson and Robbs might solve this case before we do. In fact, I have barely considered their investigation."

"So little faith in our ..." Jennifer started before being cut off.

"No, nothing like that. I don't really know them, but my point is that I've been taking the approach that I must solve the murder myself."

"And that's not our job, is it? But does that make it wrong? I mean, it's not our job to fight fires, but if one broke out in the newsroom, you and I both would be throwing coffee on it."

JP was leaning onto the table, rubbing his chin with his left hand and dangling a pencil from its tip, the eraser hovering just above the surface. He let the pencil gently fall and then looked up.

"George Saunders," he said without looking up. "Did I tell you the gardener and I shared drinks Saturday morning? Yeah, we got real cozy, George and I, and I left pretty much convinced that he cared too much for Miss Hodge to have killed her."

Jennifer watched without speaking as JP slowly worked his thoughts into words.

"Did he love her too much?" he finally said. "Let's face it; he was her hired hand, the gardener who lived in a little house in the back. She was the lady of the manor, ruler of the grounds. Is there much of a chance that she would have reciprocated? Publicly, anyway?

"I'm weighing possibilities here," he continued, almost talking to himself. "Unless George was just out-and-out making up huge stories for me ... and there was no need to do so ... then he really did love Irma Hodge. Did she even know? If so, did she accept his advances? Maybe she enjoyed a physical relationship with him but was too social-conscious to allow it to be made public. Maybe she never gave him the time of day and treated him like nothing more than a loyal dog. Maybe she was ready to marry him, but he wouldn't divorce the wife of 40 years that he still supports in the old country."

"So I take it that you feel George should be a prime suspect for us," Jennifer finally said.

"I don't know and that's what's tearing me up. He convinced me the other day that he couldn't have done it, but now I'm thinking the reasons he could not be the killer are the reasons he may be."

"Michael Hodge?"

"Ha. He's just another version of George. I left him Friday dismissing the possibility he could have killed his mother. Shoot, he even talked me into going to the funeral. Nice guy. Simple fellow. Then again, he could have killed her. He certainly has plans that could use the money. Man, I feel like all my super reporter senses are seeping away as if Pat's been spiking the coffee with kryptonite. But George is at the top of my list, as of ..." and he looked at his watch ... "7:44 a.m."

"OK, it's George Saunders for you. For me, it's the home health aide."

"I can't argue against that."

"Which is the problem, we don't know beans about her," Jennifer said while scratching the word "aide" on her yellow legal pad. "Maybe that's what raises my interest. Mr. Saunders lived there and was her gardener forever. Michael Hodge was her son, estranged though he may have been. The Moores raised her son. Even their son ... what's his name?"

"Charley."

"Even Charley is known to us. But this angel of mercy is so ethereal. Why is it nobody knows of her? Of course, there's also the whole issue of Miss Hodge dying because of an injection of a substance normally used only in medicine."

"You know, Jen, it's not a requisite that there be only one killer. George told me that Irma never explained to him the presence of the aide, but maybe he and the aide were in on it, like he connected her with Irma or maybe the aide was really supposed to be calling on George. Neighbors said Irma had been healthy, right?"

"Right, but there is another possibility."

JP leaned forward during the pause while she collected her thoughts.

"I can envision a scenario, JP, where a young, upstart reporter passes herself off as a home health aide and convinces a wealthy woman she's ill, all in hopes of ... hey, where are you going?"

"More coffee. Lots more coffee."

MONDAY – 9:09 A.M.

Sergeant Tad Bellew seemed even more upbeat than usual when Jennifer walked into his office.

"Please tell me, Sergeant, that your cheerful disposition is because you folks know who killed Miss Hodge. I mean, puh-lease."

"Wish that it were true, Miss O'Hanlon, but this jolly Monday a.m. countenance is the direct result of a weekend that caused me being called out only once – a nasty street fight that your weekend reporter picked up Saturday. But your plea sounded as if it is based on concerns that might slightly transcend the pursuit of justice."

"No, no ... oh, shoot, gimme a cup of coffee, would you?"

Jennifer realized that she was a little concerned about JP's tenacity and told the police officer in general terms what had been going on. With the patience of a counselor, he listened, periodically nodding his head.

Topping off her cup, he smiled. "It does my heart good to see the concern you have for your partner, Miss O'Hanlon. You know he and I have become good friends while working with each other these several years. Take my word for it; be concerned if JP Weiscarver is not passionately pursuing some great truth. This is what makes him tick. Don't worry that he'll blow a fuse or something. I did for a while, until I deduced that is simply his modus operandi."

Thanking the sergeant for the advice, Jennifer shifted back to reporter mode.

"Well then, what can you tell me about this homicide? What progress are you making?"

"Fill in the blanks," he said. "It's the standard continuing investigation line. Even though I had a free weekend, I can guarantee you others in this department have been carefully pursuing any leads they have while trying to ferret out others. There is nothing unusual about this. If you're lucky, you walk in on a smoking gun with someone screaming, 'He had it coming.' Most of the time, though, it is a series of tedium until something happens.

"You go over the crime scene, evidence, witnesses, potential suspects, possible motives – anything that might help – and then you start over and do it again. And again. And again, until something pops up. Maybe a story changes, someone remembers something or thinks to say something that they had previously though insignificant. You can spend hundreds of hours without moving forward and then find a loose thread, pull it and everything begins to unravel. As far as I know, the detectives are still looking for a loose thread, or the right loose thread."

By the time the PIO finished, the young reporter had decided to open up to him a bit about what she and JP had been talking about, the possible suspects and motives. Bellew nodded throughout and arched an occasional eyebrow.

"You know, Miss O'Hanlon, that I am not involved in the investigation and that detectives are often afraid of telling me things they don't want to read in the paper. Sometimes, it's as if I know nothing more than one of your readers, but I do hear things and I am fully qualified to think for myself. That said, it seems the two of you have progressed very sensibly. Your instincts seem sound, but I could not confirm any of them even if I did know, which I don't.

"Here's my point. As good as you or I might be at sifting through what we know, we are hampered by what we do not know. There could be some incredible forensic evidence or key statement that condemns or exonerates any of our suspects. Now, my real point. Leave the cop work to the cops. They're good at it and they have all the tools on their side. Besides – and this is something I hope you will find more persuasive than Weiscarver ever has – keep in mind that whoever we're seeking has already killed once."

MONDAY – 9:15 A.M.

Shortly after Jennifer left the Odds and Ends office en route to visit Bellew, JP Weiscarver started out, only to be hailed into the office of the city editor.

"Missed your byline this weekend, Weiscarver," grumbled Stanley Hopper.

"Gee, that's touching, boss."

"Listen, I know you're getting deep into the Hodge story, can tell by the way you act, but don't forget we put an issue out every day. Tuesdays, for example."

"Loud and clear, boss. I will do everything I can to come up with something for tomorrow."

Knowing that was the best he would get without more effort than he cared to expend, Hopper waved the reporter out of his fishbowl and toward the street. The commandment from above did not alter JP's destination, but it did give him an idea. He wanted to talk to George Saunders again. It might be easier to do if he was working up a feature story on the recluse gardener.

After all, there were several interesting aspects to the man in addition to being a colorful character. He had been gardening the same ground for almost 35 years, his living at the job was a throwback to days thought to be long gone and there was the suspicion that his boss was recently murdered.

If George would consent to an interview, potentially probing questions might slip in unnoticed.

George seemed glad to see JP when he walked up to the little house out back and immediately invited him in.

"You're just in time, young man," the host said as he reached into his cabinet.

"Isn't it a bit early, even for you, Mr. Saunders?"

"Well, it does seem that I been hittin' the ol' bottle a tad more often and more quicker these past few days, that's for sure," George said while placing one shot glass on the table and lifting another toward JP as an invitation.

"Not for me, sir. I'm working today and it might raise a few eyebrows, and a few questions, if I come in with alcohol on my breath, especially before noon."

"Can you visit a tad, though, before you go back to work? I ain't had nobody to talk to but cops since I last seen ya. And what's with this 'sir' and 'Mr. Saunders' stuff. I thought we was past that."

"To tell you the truth, George, I've been thinking about you since we talked," JP said, happy that at least that wasn't a lie. "It occurred to me this morning that you would make a good story. You're an interesting fellow. I would like to tell our readers about you and show photos of your flower beds and such. What do you say?"

He quickly agreed, opened a can of Dr Pepper and set it in front of JP without asking.

"I woulda gone along with 'bout anything, JP. I tell you, those cops came by a bit after you Saturday and spent all day here askin' me the same ol' questions over and over. Then it occurred to me that they must've thought that I'd done the killin'. I mean, I ain't got no education and I know I don't talk too good, but I'm not stupid. They kept tryin' to trick me up, askin' the same question different ways. But I ain't stupid."

Anxious to get George off the defensive, JP asked how long he had known Irma Hodge.

"Ah, we go way back, back to when I, uh ...," and he paused to throw a shot down his throat. "I think I told ya I'd worked for her almost 35 years."

"Yes, I believe you did. How did you get into gardening in the first place?" Gardening was always a safe subject, JP decided.

"Well, my boy, it ain't that I had any real experience. But when I come back to Oldport, Irma kinda took pity on me, I guess, and gave me a chance. She said she had hated the way her dad let the grounds go. I read every dang book the library had on plants and dirt and fertilizer, you name it. And I spent hours at the feed and seed store talking to anyone who knew anything about growin' plants, even if it was just okra or cotton. I learned good."

"Where did you come from?"

"Not like I would know," George said with a grunt. "My old man left home afore I got off all fours and my mom spent the rest of her short life on the road. I don't reckon we never spent two months in the same place. She died when I was 15, but I still kept on movin' 'cause that was all I had known. That might of had somethin' to do with me bein' so perfectly happy here all these years, ready to settle down."

JP scribbled a bit longer on his pad, partly thinking about what to ask next.

"What happens now, George?"

"That depends on her will, I guess, but I ain't worried."

"Why?"

"She told me I'd be taken care of if she died, not that I ever really figured that would happen before I kicked the bucket. If not, well, I've gotten pretty good at gardening these past 30-odd years." He laughed and JP joined him.

"Tell me about your relationship with Miss Hodge."

"I've done that."

"Pretend we didn't talk Saturday and start at the beginning. It will help the story."

"I don't know that I should do that," George said softly. "I mean, she never would have me around with her friends and I'm pretty dang certain she didn't tell 'em about us. I just don't know."

"Let me ask you what I did the other day. Did you love her?"

"Well, yeah. Yeah, I did. I guess I can say that."

"Did she love you?"

"Aww, I don't think it would be right for me to say."

"Were you and Miss Hodge lovers?" JP asked without missing a beat.

"What? Holy cow, boy, I ain't gonna go there. What kinda question is that?"

"How did Miss Hodge die?" JP asked in a quick redirection. There was a moment of silence.

"What do you mean?"

"It's something I've got to ask, George. Do you know what killed her? Do you know who killed her?"

George looked down, saying nothing.

"Did you kill her?" JP pressed.

Still the gardener did not reply, but the reporter saw sobs roll through his weathered body. JP was on full sensory alert, carefully taking in everything.

George sat on the opposite side of the walnut kitchen table, his forehead propped up on his left hand, which was slowly massaging both his temples. The fingers of his right hand slowly played with the empty shot glass before releasing it to dab at watery eyes. The mid-morning sun filtered through the kitchen window for a delicate effect, one a photographer would have loved to help accentuate the old man's wrinkles. Outside, birds were singing. Inside, the refrigerator motor kicked on.

Finally composed, George looked up and looked right through JP, who managed to not flinch. He stared back.

"Mr. Saunders, did you kill Miss Hodge?"

MONDAY – 11:51 A.M.

It was almost noon before JP pulled his old, yellow pickup away from the Hodge estate and his mind was busily sorting out the information he received. He decided he could use some help getting things in line and put a call through to Jennifer's cell phone.

"Did you learn anything new from Sergeant Doughnut?" he asked.

"Not really, but I gave him an outline of our thinking and he endorsed it, considering what he knew. Then he gave me the warning about not getting too involved, just like you told me he would. How did you fare?"

"George and I had a good talk. He doesn't know anything, he says, but he definitely has his suspicions. Listen, do you have any lunch plans? What about reviewing all this with me?"

"Sure, I'll have an interview room set up by the time you get here," Jennifer readily agreed. It struck her that morning that she was learning a lot during the sessions she and JP spent analyzing their research.

"Better yet, Jen, why don't I pick up a couple of burgers and you meet me at J.M. Qwilleran Park, just so we're not interrupted. Oops, I've got another call. On the way out, would you tell Hopper that I'll have a feature for him by deadline?"

Without waiting for an affirmation from Jennifer, JP switched over to the incoming call without checking Caller ID and smiled when he heard Sherry's voice.

"Hey, lover boy, it's lunch time and Quickie's had a bucket of chicken on sale for eight bucks ... want to join me? I'll be at my apartment in about 10 minutes."

"I have a working lunch scheduled already, but I'm sure we can squeeze you and your bucket of chicken into it. Jennifer and I were meeting at J.M. Qwilleran Park to review notes, if you can stand to be around shop talk through a meal."

"If I must, then I suppose I can sacrifice, especially if it gives me a chance to meet this Jennifer girl you've been talking about so much. I also picked up a quart of iced tea. Do you think she'll go for chicken and tea?"

"My dear, a rookie reporter will eat or drink anything that's free."

Weiscarver was first to the park and located a somewhat isolated picnic table that was visible from the parking lot. Qwill, as locals referred to the park, tried to optimize the small number of trees that are generally found along the Gulf coast by concentrating picnic areas anywhere two or more trees congregated. Two different areas of playground equipment sat in open spots between the tables. On this Monday, a school day, only one mother was pushing a toddler in a baby swing.

JP was concentrating on his notes from the George Saunders interview, filling in blanks and making more legible entries while it was all fresh on his mind. His thoughts were caught between pen and paper when Jennifer O'Hanlon broke in.

"Hamburgers? Don't I remember you saying something about picking up hamburgers? If you don't start taking better care of me, Mr. Weiscarver, I just may insist on you getting a new date."

Her playful mood was interrupted by another voice chiming in from behind her.

"I suppose I could pick up that role."

"Jennifer," Weiscarver said, suppressing a grin, "meet Sherry. Sherry, Jen."

Jennifer began stumbling over herself apologizing and explaining but Sherry cut her off.

"Believe me, Jennifer, I understand," Sherry said. "You couldn't work with JP as much as you do without having his smart-alecky nature rub off on you just a bit. I completely hold him to blame. To prove it, I brought deep-fried fowl as a peace offering."

Realizing the chicken would keep them from taking notes, the reporters put off talking about the story while eating.

Exhibiting the lack of tact endemic among many reporters, Jennifer decided to get Sherry's story of how she and JP met.

"It was 11 months and 10 days ago ... not that I'm counting," Sherry promptly replied, giving JP a playful jab in the ribs. "I was sunbathing on the beach, enjoying a day off, when this guy I didn't know had a medical problem. Not JP but another guy. While I was tending to him and waiting for the ambulance, a bit of a crowd gathered and I guess you already know that a crowd is a flame to a reporter moth.

"After the ambulance left, everybody went about their business and, I guess, this handsome guy here decided to make me his business. He's a quick operator, I'll tell you. We went out to dinner that night and he hasn't let me see anyone else since. Actually, I've wondered if maybe he can't get anyone else."

JP watched his co-worker's reaction, hoping she would realize that Sherry did not like to talk about the man drowning. She maintained her composure and tossed out a follow-up question that surprised them both.

"Quick operator, eh?" Jennifer said. "Are you two about ready to announce wedding plans?

Sherry and JP looked at each other briefly and he took over.

"We haven't talked too seriously about that yet. The truth is, she's right, I can't get anyone else and I'm afraid if I spook her too early, she'll run off and leave me to become a bitter, old, bachelor reporter."

"The truth is," Sherry seemed to mock JP, "we haven't discussed it at all. Anytime I bring it up, I get to watch him do some kind of tap dance until he finds something else to talk about."

"Well, I think that marriage has become a weakened institution and I, we, want that old-fashioned relationship, the 'until death do you part' kind of marriage," JP said. Then he grinned and shook his finger at Jennifer. "But you know what? You're a good interviewer. You handled that question beautifully and then, the best thing of all, you knew to keep quiet and give us time to say more than we probably meant. Yep, you're good."

"And there's your tap dance," Sherry said and then flashed a huge smile.

"That's enough of that, then," Jennifer said. "It's fine for you two lovebirds to coo over each other, or whatever you're doing, but it's a little strange with me being here. Besides, don't we have work to do?"

"I'll clean up if you don't mind me sitting it on your session," Sherry said. "I was thinking it might be nice to see the reporter side of JP for a change."

"That's reassuring," answered the junior reporter. "I wasn't too sure he had anything but a reporter side."

Taking his cue, Weiscarver updated Jennifer on his interview and Sherry closely followed every word, a fact JP noted gratefully.

"So, once George got control of himself, he answered my question directly, 'No, there ain't no way I coulda killed her. I really did love her and she loved me. No, sir, I did not kill her.'"

"Do you believe him?"

Weiscarver chuckled. "Yeah, even though I'm working myself out of suspects, yeah, I do believe him."

"So, did he offer up any ideas on who might have done it?"

"Yes, as a matter of fact. He has apparently spent a lot of time thinking about it and he's convinced it's the recently arrived granddaughter."

"You've got to be kidding!"

At the outburst from the previously quiet girlfriend, JP and Jen both turned toward her.

"I'm sorry, but, I mean, a girl killing her own grandmother? How could she do that? And why?"

"Let me take the why, first," Weiscarver said. "Money. Our dearly departed Irma Hodge apparently still controlled a sizeable amount of moola. People do worse for less, I can assure you. As to the how..."

JP glanced at Jennifer, who simultaneously shrugged and nodded, which her partner took as encouragement to share the unrevealed information.

"I'm sure you're familiar with Suxamethonium."

"Sure. Well, I know what it is and that they sometimes use it in surgery, though it's not something I use in my job. Why?"

"That's what killed Miss Hodge," Jennifer injected.

"But you don't buy that off the shelf," Sherry said. "Do they know where it came from?"

"No," JP answered. "I take that back. They might know, but they haven't told us, which would not be surprising. Tell me, Sherry, would it be easy for someone to sneak a vial out of the hospital?"

"Well, I don't know," she stammered, clearly flustered with the idea. "Why would someone at Oldport County want her dead?"

"I didn't mean there, specifically. I was really asking how easily someone could steal a drug like that."

"Of course it could be done; you know that. How easily? I guess someone could get it without too much trouble if they had access to it. Now that I think about it, I suppose I could get some if I had the nerve to try."

The reporters waited while Sherry thought it through and eventually continued.

"The drugs are inventoried and signed out, but a day or two could pass before it was missed. Actually, I don't know for sure that they inventory that often. It might be longer. If so, dozens of people might have access."

"It would be nice to know what Smithson and Robbs learned from the hospital," JP murmured and both women could tell he was deep in thought.

"Wait a minute," Sherry said after several seconds, "how do you know that Suxamethonium killed her? Did the cops just tell you and then ask you to keep it a secret?"

"I'm impressed," Weiscarver said. "Good deductive reasoning. Actually, I found the empty bottle. No, that's not true. Bubba found it. Apparently the bad guy left it behind and my ferret friend stuck it into his pillow."

"Did they find any fingerprints on it?"

"I'm guessing not, except mine, of course. Someone who knows enough about Sux to use it to commit a murder would probably be smart enough to wear gloves and would likely have ready access to those, too. All of that makes the mysterious aide a great suspect."

"I don't know about that," Sherry said. "If she's a home health aide, she will have access to gloves but shouldn't be performing major surgeries at home; I don't know that she could get the drugs."

"So, where does this leave us?" Jennifer finally piped in. "This morning, you were leaning toward George Saunders but he talked you out of it. You might recall that the aide was at the top of my list. Would Mr. Saunders have made me change my mind, too?"

"We talked about her and George did not like her as a suspect, though I think his main logic was that she was too cute and too nice."

"Does that mean the granddaughter was an ugly witch?" O'Hanlon asked.

"Quite the contrary," JP said. "Wait, I haven't seen her face yet, but she looked fetching under a veil." Sherry threw half a biscuit at him.

"George never saw the granddaughter," he continued. "For some reason, maybe the grandmother's doing, he was never there when she came by. Plus, Miss Hodge wouldn't talk about her to him."

"Then what makes him believe the granddaughter ... what's her name?"

"Maggie. Maggie Hodge, I guess."

"What makes him believe Maggie killed her grandmother."

"Frankly, I believe his first suspicion is rooted in the fact he never saw her. He likes to judge people eye-to-eye. Of course, then there is the fact that she only recently entered the old woman's rich life and that she could very well stand to inherit a sizeable amount of money."

"Or her dad would."

"Listen, I'm going to run over to Queensland and see Michael Hodge again," JP said while getting his papers together. "Jen, would you tell Stanley I won't have that story after all? You could promise him I'll have it tomorrow, but he wouldn't believe you. Sherry, what about dinner tonight at my place? I'm thinking about cold chicken."

MONDAY – 1:40 P.M.

Weiscarver decided against calling ahead. By this point, he was afraid to trust his usually reliable "gut" and decided against possibly tipping his hand. His gamble paid off as he found the brown station wagon parked outside Hodge's trailer and within five minutes the reporter was stirring iced tea while sitting on Michael's couch.

"JP, I really appreciate you showing up yesterday," Michael said as he pulled an old kitchen chair into the living room. "Here, I was going to mail this to you," and he handed his guest an envelope.

Weiscarver glanced at the envelope, on which was scrawled, "Thanks for caring." He tried to emit a gracious thanks as he put it in his pocket unopened.

"Michael, I'm afraid this isn't really a social call. We've been puzzling over who might have killed Irma. Well, there's just no easy way to say this, but I'm looking into the possibility that your daughter might have been involved."

"Maggie?"

"Yes sir. Let's not get carried away here. I'm no cop and there is absolutely nothing formal about this. I'm just a guy asking questions of a lot of people and I would like to ask you some."

Michael Hodge was deflated. "Why would Maggie..."

"Michael, focus on me, all right? I'm not saying that she did, just that it is a possibility and I want to ask you some questions. Will you help me?

"Of course, JP, but I'm sure you're wrong. She seemed so happy to have finally gotten to know Irma."

Weiscarver accepted the open door and barged in.

"You told me you don't see Maggie often. Where does she live?"

"Now, that's a corker of a start. You see, I don't really know and now I know even less. OK, I believe she was living somewhere in Oldport County, but I never knew where. She dodged the question anytime I asked. I figured she just wanted to protect her privacy. Well, and here's the funny part, she called just 30 minutes ago and told me she was moving, said she was going to Mexico maybe, said that she'd try to let me know where she was some time. And here I thought maybe we were getting closer through all this. How does that grab you?"

"Forgive me, Michael, but it raises suspicions. Maybe she's running away in an effort to hide from the police."

"No," Hodge almost yelled. It was obvious that possibility had not occurred to him. The father would be the last to suspect.

"What does Maggie do for a living?" Weiscarver asked in an effort to keep things moving.

"Uh, she's worked in retirement homes, but I don't know for sure that she has a job. Man, this is all making me sound like such a bad father, but it's hard when they're grown and on their own, you know. I was so proud of her when she got a job and all, but it seemed later like that was the final straw, what gave her the power to totally separate from me."

"Was she ever married?"

"No, I'm pretty sure not."

"You told me the other day that Maggie volunteered to pick out Irma's clothes for the funeral. Was there anything odd about how that came to be? I don't know what I mean. Did she seem to force the issue?"

"No, no, but heavens, I don't know, I was just glad she said she'd get it done. So much was going on and I was getting kind of swamped by it that she just offered to help. She also picked out the flower spray with Mom's help."

JP continued writing for a few seconds and then took a drink of tea.

"OK, Michael, so you don't know where she lives and, anyway, she told you she's moving but not where. You don't know where she works, if she works, but she has worked in a retirement home in the past. You don't think she's been married. Does that sum it up?"

"It don't sound too helpful when you put it like that," Hodge said. He sat for a moment, his mouth half-open as he gradually formed the next statement. "JP, Do you think my little girl murdered her grandmother?"

"No, not necessarily, but it does all look suspicious. In fact, have the police talked to you about Maggie?"

"Not a word. I figured they talked to her themselves."

"Probably so."

"Maybe that's why she's leaving. JP, what are we going to do?"

After convincing Michael everything would be all right, which JP didn't really believe was true, and declining a half-hearted invitation from his host to visit with the Moores next door, the reporter slowly started the 45-minute drive back to Oldport.

On a whim, he pulled into the Dairy Queen drive-through and ordered a chocolate malt for the drive home. While waiting for the order to be filled, he heard a noise and was startled to see a somewhat familiar old man standing at the passenger window of his pickup.

"You that reporter, ain't ya?" the man asked.

"Yes, sir, JP Weiscarver. Who are you?"

"Never you mind; it ain't important. But I got a piece of advice for ya. Keep to writin' about stray dogs and you'll be happier." With that, he turned his back to JP's stammering questions and walked away, balanced on a four-footed cane.

"Sir," the reporter called after him to no avail.

"Sir," JP heard echoed in his left ear. "Sir! Here's your malt and I put napkins and a straw in the bag."

By the time JP circled the restaurant and pulled onto the street, his anonymous advisor was nowhere in sight.

MONDAY – 3:15 P.M.

Back at the office, JP arranged a session with Stanley and Jennifer.

"We need to make this quick, kids, 'cause I've got a budget meeting in 15 minutes, where we'll talk 'bout reporters with actual stories written," Hopper started.

"We've been stacking up mounds of circumstantial evidence that is beginning to point to Miss Hodge's granddaughter as a prime suspect," JP began.

"Such as?"

"The motive is simple enough," inserted Jennifer. "She stands to inherit or at least have a chance to get her hands on a sizeable wad of dough."

"As for means," JP said, "I just learned this afternoon that she has worked in retirement homes. That might make it easy to pass herself off as a home health aide. And then there is opportunity. Several people know that she was visiting Miss Hodge, but I haven't talked to anybody who met her. Even George, the gardener, has not seen her."

"What else?"

"It's all circumstantial, just suspicious stuff, but the biggest thing is her secretive nature. Her father does not know where she lives or works, nor does he know her phone number. Meanwhile, I cannot find a Maggie Hodge anywhere, like she has tried to stay off the radar. Then she calls her dad this afternoon to say she's suddenly moving off, but she won't tell him where."

"Good grief, boy, we'd all be in jail if it's a crime to keep a secret from our parents."

"But it's more than that, Stanley. He doesn't know for sure whether or not his daughter's been married. He laughed when I asked if he knew any of her friends. And I'll tell you one other thing that's been eating at me. I have seen her twice, walking out of the funeral home on Friday and at the funeral itself yesterday and both times she was wearing a veil."

"Old-fashioned, maybe," Stanley started, but Jennifer interrupted him.

"No, Mr. Hopper, it's not that. This gal will be about my age and I can tell you that no normal woman that young would be wearing a black veil to view her grandmother's body. I think JP's right, that she was trying to hide from something."

"Then why even show up?"

"Motive, remember the money."

"OK, boys and girls, you're right that this is very interesting, but I don't see a story. Surely you're not wanting to accuse this unknown person on the front page of the Odds and Ends. I'd say you might rattle the cops' cage a bit and see if they release anything. Other than that, find this killer granddaughter. Just don't do anything stupid."

As the city editor headed to his budget meeting, JP and Jen split up to analyze what they had and Lydia quietly slipped into JP's guest chair.

"Would you like to hear the next installment about our poor little rich girls at the Palmetto Club?" she asked.

"Certainly, and by the way, your story on Mrs. Brewster was well done," JP said, glad to be able to encourage her some.

"Thanks. Well, today's interview was with an apparent supporter of Miss Hodge. Janiece Ferguson was totally aghast with the idea that someone would kill a Palmetto Club Woman of the Year. It was as if she was practicing a eulogy, listing all the things Miss Hodge had accomplished, the fact that she had previously won two of the lower club awards and that she maintained such exquisite grounds at her home. Mrs. Ferguson even mentioned your story, except she made it sound like Miss Hodge ran a home for wayward children instead of merely having a bunch of pets."

"Do you think she was protesting too much?"

"I couldn't help but entertain that thought. In something of an offhanded fashion, I asked, 'Nobody in the Palmetto Club could have killed her, could they?' I swear, JP, it was as if she was acting a part. Her mouth dropped open just a bit, her left hand went to her chest and her right hand to her cheek. 'Oh, I never thought of that,' she said. Then she started talking about Selma Brewster. It was so obvious that she wanted to steer me toward that line of thought."

"Next question," JP said, "is whether she was trying to point out a possible killer or was she trying to direct attention away from herself."

"I suggested she call the police department about her suspicions and she assured me she would."

"Any oddity about Mrs. Ferguson? Interplanetary travel or intercontinental beast slaying?"

"Nothing at all," Lydia said and then let slip a giggle. "No, her spare time is taken up with her hobby. Years ago, when her now-late husband had problems with his feet, she took special training in pedicure. She enjoyed it so much, she started having friends over to massage their feet and trim their toenails. Apparently, she has developed quite a following. She never charges for it, she quickly assured me, because she's not licensed to do so, though she never refuses a gift of a pie or a trip to the theater."

"You're right, that's not all that odd, really."

"Hold that thought. She collects the toenail clippings. Really, she showed them to me. She has them tucked away in a special carrying case, catalogued and cross-referenced by shape, size, color, defects and I don't know what else. She even has a special collection of clippings that look like different objects, such as a salamander."

"I'm developing a whole different impression of high society women."

MONDAY – 4:02 P.M.

JP took Hopper's advice and headed next to Tad Bellew's office. Since it was late in the work day, the two got down to business right away.

"Sarge, what can you tell me about Maggie Hodge?"

"Nothing you don't already know," Bellew answered with a noticeable sigh. "And I sincerely doubt you can say the same thing."

"Do I detect some frustration?"

"Dang it, Weiscarver. OK, this is strictly between the two of us, but I think our detectives got a little careless. Yes, the granddaughter is looking like a great suspect, but they haven't even talked to her, can't find her."

"Do they know she was at the funeral?"

"Oh, they do now, but they just got cozy or lazy or something. And now they're going crazy trying to track her down."

"Would they be aware that she's leaving town, maybe already gone?"

"I doubt it. What do you know?"

JP related his conversation with Michael Hodge, all of which the sergeant said he would promptly relay to the detectives.

"You're doing good work, Weiscarver, but watch your step. I'm thinking maybe we ought to deputize you since there's a good chance you'll find this killer before our detectives do."

JP decided to call it a day and headed home, where a bounding bundle of fur was sure to perk him up. He and Bubba frolicked around the house for 20 minutes before they crashed on the sofa, cuddled up next to each other, and dozed off. In fact, Bubba did not even budge an hour later when the doorbell rang.

MONDAY – 7:07 P.M.

"Who could that be, Bubba?" JP asked while picking up the ferret and heading to the door. "Oh, I forgot that I asked Sherry to come over." He quickly ran a pocket comb through his brown hair and opened the door, Bubba squirming in the crook of his arm.

"Hey, sweetie," Sherry said as she leaned above Bubba's slightly bared teeth to give JP a kiss. "Are you ready for leftovers?"

"Sure, I'll grab a couple of beers. Should I open a can of beans or something?"

"Nice try, JP, but I know vegetables are not required in your diet. Let's just eat."

She scooted his junk to one side of the dining table and asked, "Hey, is this for me?" holding up the card given JP by Michael.

"Go ahead and open it. I forgot about it. Actually, it's ..." but he was cut off by Sherry's cry.

"What kind of sicko would do that?" she said, dropping it on the table. Sure enough, a card was in the envelope, but there was also a photo of the late Miss Irma Hodge, laid out in her coffin.

Mumbling apologies, JP quickly stuffed it back into the envelope and vowed there would be no conversation tonight about murders, dead people or anything else work-related. Remarkably enough, there wasn't.

TUESDAY – 7:05 A.M.

JP Weiscarver was downright cheery as he prepared for work Tuesday morning. After a pleasant evening visiting with Sherry and forgetting about work, he even turned down the police scanner in favor of a good night's sleep. He awoke early, prepared bacon and eggs for breakfast instead of the usual corn flakes and was reading Chad Brooks' column, where the sports reporter once again took issue with "the deterioration of baseball, thanks to the designated hitter."

Meanwhile, Bubba was bouncing on JP's bare left foot, which the reporter ignored until he felt something slice between his toes. Looking down, he saw that the ferret had the envelope from Michael Hodge and had almost removed the card and photo.

"Thanks, Bub, I forgot about that again," and he pulled the card out.

"Dear JP, Thank you so much for the tender story about my mother's pets. But I especially thank you for attending the funeral. It meant so much to Midge and Bob to see you there and I was glad, too. Here's a photo we took just before the funeral. Don't feel like you have to keep it, but I thought you might want to see. Thanks again. Michael Hodge."

JP extracted the photo next and shook his head. People are funny, he thought. He just could not imagine sending photos of his dead mother to a near stranger.

As he looked more carefully at the image, something caught his eye. He stared at the photo for a couple of minutes, slowly massaging his chin.

"Listen, Bubba," he said, "I've got to get dressed and get to work. Thanks for showing me the card and photo."

TUESDAY – 9:18 A.M.

"There you are, JP, I was about to call and wake you," Jennifer teased as her mentor entered the newsroom.

"Yeah, I should have checked in with you, Mom, but I stopped by PD and visited with Tad again this morning."

"What did you learn?"

"Basically, he thinks we're on the right track and I believe he's a bit put out that Detectives Smithson and Robbs have not done as well, particularly that they haven't found Maggie Hodge. Anyway, I talked with the detectives this morning and updated them on what we know and what I think."

"Weiscarver," Stanley interrupted. "Any excuses today for not having that feature?"

"Not yet, boss, and I'm working on it right now – the story, not the excuse."

"Right," the city editor grunted as he stared at the reporter's blank computer screen.

"And I was just telling Jennifer about talking with the cops. Seems they think there is an outside possibility they'll have an arrest later today."

"Who?"

"Let's just say that I am regaining confidence in my reporter's nose."

"Keep me posted," Stanley said as he headed to his fishbowl.

"You didn't tell me that," Jennifer said.

"I was about to, but we really need to keep it to ourselves."

"Maggie?"

"They seem convinced, but I don't believe they really know where she is. Anyway, I must get started on my Gardener George story. Oh, and Tad's got a winner for you. It seems some loser tried to rob a convenience store last night in a novel disguise. Apparently, he didn't quite get the idea of using a stocking to disguise his face and he entered the store with a pair of pink women's panties pulled over his head."

"You have got to be kidding me."

"They have tapes from the security camera, though I didn't see them."

"Did it work?"

"No, he left frustrated. The clerk couldn't quit laughing long enough to open the register and produce the money."

TUESDAY – 2:45 P.M.

With his feature story filed well before deadline, JP decided to spend the rest of the day working the telephone, touching base with various contacts he had not seen in a while and trying to come up with a good story idea, but his first call was to Sherry Miller.

"I've been thinking about you all day," JP said. "Last night was just what I needed: bad food, good company and talk that never brought up work. Let's do it again tonight."

"Young man, what will the neighbors think?"

"That I'm extremely lucky. I'll order pizza, we'll pop a couple of tops and make it two in a row."

"It's my turn to buy and I don't get paid until tomorrow," Sherry said. "Why don't you come to my place and I'll cook up something?"

"You overlooked the 'bad food' ingredient in my perfect evening. No, it's my treat. And let's do it at my house; I'm determined to get Bubba to accept you."

JP then visited Lydia Murray's desk to see if she had encountered any revelations in her next Palmetto Club interview.

"A little Palmetto Club conspiracy seems to be taking shape," she said, tickled to have a visit from the ace reporter. "Mrs. Charlotte Vanderpool took off on the same tangents today as Mrs. Ferguson did yesterday. I mean, they were preaching the same sermon. I said something like, 'You know, that's identical to what Mrs. Ferguson said," and the lady fell apart."

"I never knew you were such a tough interviewer," JP said, which elicited a titter from the young writer.

"Well, I just let her talk and soon enough she told me that Mrs. Ferguson had solicited her help in planting the idea that Selma Brewster might have poisoned Irma Hodge. Mrs. Ferguson apparently figures that, with Irma dead and Selma suspected of murder, she would slide into the coveted Woman of the Year spot."

"I've heard a preacher or two mention that coveting can lead to bad things, but these ladies are redefining it. Do you know if either of them passed on their suspicions to the police department?"

"I know where you're headed and I got around to that, too. No, it seems that our conniving ladies were at least smart enough to not file a false police report. She also told me she was not the one who called our publisher in the middle of the night with the tip that Miss Hodge had been murdered. No, I did not mention the call but she volunteered that she did not make it. I guess they were hoping we would be dumb enough to do the dirty work for them."

JP noticed that Lydia took pride in saying "we."

TUESDAY – 6:52 P.M.

It was the same pizza delivery boy who dropped off the pie last Friday – was that only four days ago, JP thought – and he was returning to his vehicle with a generous tip when he crossed paths with Sherry as she arrived. He stopped, noticing it was a different woman, turned and looked past her at JP, to whom he gave a gap-toothed smile and a thumb's up sign.

As Sherry entered the door, Bubba made a threatening noise and scampered off.

"JP, I don't know if that little creature of yours will ever accept me."

"No, I'm not so sure either, but I have a theory about it."

"This I've got to hear. Do tell."

JP delayed his story until they were seated and he served his guest a slice of spinach pizza, Sherry's favorite. His he took from the other half of the pie, sausage and mushroom.

"Do you love me, Sherry?"

"I do; it's that rodent of yours I'm concerned about."

"There's something I have to say. Afterwards, you'll either have to work at loving me again or it just won't matter."

Sherry simply looked up, her mouth full of pizza and a large question mark covering her face.

"I lied to you about not talking about work tonight," JP continued without touching his pizza. "I have come across things ... guessed at things

... heard things that have me deeply disturbed and we need to talk it out."

Sherry had finished chewing and placed the rest of her pizza on a plate. "Go on," she said.

"I know so little about your background, nothing to speak of concerning your parents or grandparents. I've never met any old school chums, not to mention relatives. In some ways, you've been as elusive as ... Maggie Hodge."

He looked up and saw no reaction to Maggie's name.

"Maggie Hodge is in medicine, too. I learned that yesterday. She has, or had, a grandmother with a pair of earrings just like those given you by your grandmother. Those are mere coincidences, though, nothing to make a big deal out of. But there are others.

"It wasn't surprising that you didn't want to go to the funeral with me Sunday; that's understandable. But then you were absent from work during the time of the service. Meanwhile, Maggie was there wearing a veil that completely obscured her appearance. When I spoke to her, she left without a word. And I couldn't help but find myself watching how she moved. Frankly, I thought she was sexy. Maybe she reminded me of you.

"I told you that when I first saw Irma Hodge in the funeral home she was dressed identically to a portrait on display there, except the earrings were not on the body, but I didn't mention that. I later gave you the earring that Bubba found and, after that, they appeared on Miss Hodge in time for the funeral."

He sat for a moment looking across the table for something, a signal of denial, anger, anything. Finally, he spoke, slowly.

"Tell me this is just an unbelievable string of coincidences," and JP drew out a pause before adding, "Maggie."

As he stared at her, his girlfriend of 10 months took another bite of pizza and chewed thoughtfully, washing it down with a large swallow of beer. She was a picture of composure.

"First, let me answer your earlier question again. I do love you so much. Nothing changes that. I don't guess I ever had a real boyfriend before you, nobody I dated exclusively for more than a month or two. You're the first person to hold my interest. You're the first person in my life that I'm always looking forward to seeing again.

"I love the way you make me feel special. I enjoy getting 'nothing' phone calls from you, when your only reason for calling is because you want to hear my voice. I love the way you sometimes obsess about your work and how you are so dedicated to the craft.

"Now, I have something to tell you, too, JP. I'm moving, as soon as I get paid tomorrow. Somewhere away from here. I'm thinking about the Pacific Northwest. You always hear about it being great living conditions. I already have my clothes packed and in the car. I was planning on pulling out as soon as possible in the morning."

"Why?" JP asked without budging.

"Why what?" she said around another mouthful of pizza. Speaking as if she was discussing the choice of topping, she added, "Why did I choose the Northwest or why did I kill my grandmother?"

JP nodded and raked the cold beer bottle across his forehead before taking a sip.

"She wasn't my grandmother, JP. She was the bitch who ruined my father's life, who through that act ruined mine and my mother's."

This was a different look at his girlfriend. Each word increased her level of anxiety.

"Do you know why nobody ever saw her granddaughter at her home?" Sherry continued. "She insisted that I come in my uniform so nobody would suspect anything. She didn't care about me any more than she cared about my father, far less than she cared about that stupid ferret or any one of her disgusting dogs and cats."

"So you did kill her? I can't believe it."

"Oh, yes, and I wouldn't have believed it either, not until I spent many days with her, not until I saw for myself just how heartless she was, what a user of other people she was. In the end, it was easy. I started giving her her shot when I was there. She liked that because she could not do it well. Last Wednesday, I took a vial of Sux from the hospital, palmed it as I filled the syringe and she never knew what happened. Give me credit that I didn't make her suffer like I should have."

"What now?" JP asked.

"I must leave. Even the idiot cops will figure it out soon enough. For what it's worth, you're the reason I haven't left already. Well, you and my check. Come with me. You're a great reporter; you just proved that. You can find a job. A good nurse always has work and I am a good nurse."

"Sher ... what do I call you?"

"Sherry. Let's bury Maggie Hodge right here in Oldport as we leave town. We'll leave now, tonight. Forget about my check."

Silence permeated the room. The ferret was still, silent but alert. Suddenly, he started looking around.

Sherry twisted in her chair as the front door opened and, simultaneously, two men appeared from JP's bedroom, one in plain clothes with a badge and a gun fastened to his belt. The other was in a policeman's uniform. She looked across the table at the reporter, who finally picked up his first slice of pizza.

"They're with me, Maggie. It's Sherry Miller that I'll be burying tonight and then I'm headed to Queensland to try to explain to your father what went wrong."

"Maggie Sue Hodge," said the man in the dark suit while the uniformed officer applied handcuffs. "You are under arrest for the murder of Irma Hodge. You have the right to remain silent."

WEDNESDAY – 7:55 A.M.

"Hey, Weiscarver, killer story this morning," called out one of the advertising sales reps as the general assignment reporter crossed from the front office to the newsroom of the Oldport Odds and Ends.

"Aw, go sell your soul to somebody, you Neanderthal," Jennifer piped up before turning to JP. "I am so sorry. I cannot imagine what you're going through."

"I can't imagine why you're even here," said Pat Baird as she handed him a cup of coffee. "I'm sorry, JP."

"Hey, look on the bright side," he said, unconsciously pulling the coffee mug close to his chest, "at least I didn't marry a murderer."

An uncomfortable silence settled over the trio. The younger pair was probably waiting for Pat to say the right thing, she thought, so she did.

"You want to tell us about it?"

"I should be able to do that. After all, I've been up all night thinking about it. You know what really brought it together in my mind? Crazy, really. It was watching Maggie move. You remember, Jen, me telling you about when Sherry and I first met?"

"Yeah, the beach drowning. You said she impressed you with the way she handled the situation."

"I said impressed because I don't know what else to call it. Just seeing her move touched me somewhere deep inside. Watching Maggie, even under that black veil, touched me the same way. Yesterday morning, it became obvious to me that Maggie and Sherry were the same person. I mean, it was like a light turned on; I can't explain it."

"Surely, there was more than that," Jennifer said.

"Of course, but I didn't see any of that until the light came on."

JP recounted all the pieces of circumstantial evidence and how the photo with the earrings on Miss Hodge's body made him face what his ferret had been trying to tell him. Three more writers and an editor gravitated to the area during the retelling of events.

"Bubba was on top of it from the beginning," he said. "Had he not hidden away that vial, the cops might have never tied Maggie into it. And Bubba never cut Sherry a bit of slack, every single time she was in the house."

"Are you aware, JP dear, that you're still calling Maggie by both names?" Pat asked gently.

"Uh-huh. That was one of the things I decided while not sleeping last night. I really believe they are ... or at least were ... two different people. The girl I saw crying on the beach for not being able to save a stranger is no way the same one who calculated means to take her grandmother's life. For now, anyway, I choose to have fond memories of Sherry."

The older woman placed her hand on his shoulder.

"Pat, I was entertaining thoughts of marriage," JP said, his voice finally cracking a bit.

It became quiet again. Jennifer broke it this time.

"Then, after all that, you came in to write a solid news story. Why didn't you call me in to help, especially since you gave me a shared byline?"

"Hey, we were a team and you were the leader. No, this story was one I needed to write. I hope you understand."

Archie Hanning cut in: "I tell you what I don't understand. How did all your circumstantial evidence work its way into an arrest?"

"Oh, that. I guess it is a tribute to my charm. I convinced the detectives that Sherry might very well be their suspect. They wired my kitchen table yesterday. Before Sherry arrived, one of the detectives and a uniformed cop hid out in my bedroom and another pair was listening in a van parked on the street, just like in the movies.

"I would like to say that I cleverly manipulated Sherry into spilling the beans, but she waltzed right into it after I accused her of being Maggie. She thought she could talk me into joining her on the lam. By the time the cops walked in and took her into custody, she laid out how she did it and why. The district attorney is going to love this case.

"Oh, one other thing and you're going to appreciate this, Pat. It seems that George Saunders, the gardener, worked on the docks for Cletus P. Hodge 40-something years ago."

"You don't mean..." Pat started.

"I do mean. He said that he was the father of Michael, but Miss Hodge wanted to keep it a secret. They resumed their relationship after Cletus died and apparently kept everyone from knowing about it. George tells me he plans to contact Michael once things settle down a bit. And, as for the estate, he says her will is supposed to leave the house and a quarter of her investments to him, half of the investments to their son and the rest to various charities. That should set up Michael's restaurant and take care of the Moores just fine."

"Speaking of the restaurant," Pat chimed in with a more cheerful tone, "we got an interesting call just before you came in this morning. One Bertram Frankston, owner of Madison's restaurant in Queensland, said he owed you an apology."

"How's that? I don't believe I know the guy," the rather tired reporter replied.

"He mentioned that, but he said Michael Hodge works for him and he was afraid you were trying to pin Irma Hodge's murder on her son. That's why he verbally accosted you at the Dairy Queen Monday."

JP cut loose with a deep laugh. "The old man with the cane. I saw him talking to Michael and Maggie outside the funeral home. I'm glad to know that because I had written him off as one crazy dude."

"You've been through a lot," Jennifer asked. "What's next for you?"

"Hey, we've got another paper to get out tomorrow," JP said. "I think I'll let you handle the Hodge story from here on out. But I've got to come up with something new and different for the boss man."

"You got that straight, Weiscarver," Stanley Hopper bellowed from behind his surprised reporter. I've paid you the past week for, what, three stories, all on the same subject. Got something nice and easy for you. Received an anonymous tip that the county judge has been directing county money into a program that benefits only three people, all of 'em his in-laws. You ready to come off vacation and go to work?"

"Yes, sir, boss, but I might want to start taking my ferret on all my interviews. He seems to think we're a team."

2 THE REPORTER AND THE HURRICANE

A pair of Wolof fishermen, who all their lives eked out a living pulling fish from the Atlantic Ocean off the shore of their native Senegal, eyed storm clouds approaching from the east.

It was nothing new. They had many times weathered August storms rolling off Africa's Sahel savanna belt. Their tiny fishing boat was not much to look at, but it could withstand almost anything the sea threw at it, riding swells under the deft guidance of its owners.

This storm was different, however, surprising the fishermen with its ferocity and overtaking the vessel before its occupants could react.

Though their bodies would not be recovered, family and friends knew the two died at sea as, indeed, it was always suspected they would. But no one considered the possibility the men were only the first of hundreds to fall prey to the storm.

AUGUST 5, 11:13 A.M.
Nine Months After Irma Hodge's Death

As a reporter, JP Weiscarver made considerable effort to maintain an even keel during an interview, but Jeremiah Forge made that difficult.

"Every home, even those without a direct view of the Gulf of Mexico, has a floor-to-ceiling glass wall view of the interior of the complex, including the vision that is our namesake," Forge gushed as he opened the curtain.

Vision is right, Weiscarver thought, as he tried to take in the image.

Forge, general manager of the soon-to-be-completed Oldport Cascades Condominiums, stood silently as his guests' eyes slowly worked their way up and down the twenty-story waterfall. The carefully selected vantage point on the fourteenth floor presented the massive structure in all its grandeur.

Forge went on to explain how the cascade was designed to offer a series of waterfalls around the slightly tapered circular structure.

"There are actually five separate water paths wending their ways down and around the column," said Forge, strategically positioned for the best chance to be included in the frame of photographer Cole Thompson's camera. "Not only does that give the cascades a full effect but it also allows us to shut them down one at a time for maintenance without it being too noticeable."

Oldport Cascades Condominiums, scheduled for a grand opening November 1, just in time for many of its owners to flee northern winters, was breaking new ground in the small coastal city of Oldport. Tourism had always been an important part of the local economy, but most rooms were in small family-owned motels that offered primarily a place to sleep while resting from all of the outdoors activity.

This new concept – new to Oldport County, that is – offered high-class condos for individual ownership. Some people would live in their units fulltime. Others would live there in the winter and rent them out during the more lucrative summer tourist season. For some, a condo would be a pure investment, maybe a personal vacation spot, maybe a place for a business to entertain clientele.

Of course, not just anyone could make an investment to the tune of $1.4 million ... the cost of the least expensive unit.

"Every residence has its own private, oversized balcony, most of them with a view of the Gulf," Forge continued. "The discerning homeowner will appreciate the stainless steel designer appliances nestled among granite countertops in a gourmet kitchen. Every bedroom has large walk-in closets. Baths offer selections with a shower, tub, walk-in tub, hot tub or a combination.

"We've already talked about the infinity-edge swimming pool outside, the indoor pool, the spa and fitness center, four lighted tennis courts, valet parking, concierge service and, well, what further questions do you have?"

It was obvious to both Weiscarver and Thompson that Forge was ready to wrap up the interview and while they found the building fascinating, they were ready to move on, too.

"All of the physical features are impressive," JP said as they approached the elevator, "but I'm particularly bowled over by the 'smart homes' technology, like adjusting lights and air-conditioning from a remote location. Or the fact that you just authorized the express elevator by scanning your thumbprint."

"Security is of considerable importance to us, as you might guess," Forge said. "If someone spends $3 million on one of our finer residences, he wants to feel safe reaching his home. Or her home, of course. Those utilizing the property rental aspect of Oldport Cascades will have access to only the public elevators and even those will require a key card; property owners will have their own elevators accessible via a card or thumbprint, as you've noted."

Cole Thompson eased into the conversation, something he had a habit of doing that JP appreciated, though some reporters found it irritating.

"One thing that I've been wondering about as y'all have been building this, is the wisdom of constructing a 25-story, glass-walled building where a hurricane will eventually hit," Thompson said.

Ouch, thought JP, that was direct, but he did not detect even a flinch from Forge.

"You are correct, Cole, that any place on the coast of the Gulf of Mexico will sooner or later see a major hurricane. The fact of the matter is that people like you want to live here and others wish to vacation here. Property owners are willing to take the chance a damaging hurricane will not occur anytime soon, maybe not for a hundred years, and, to be frank, insurance companies are willing to take that gamble with them."

"What preparations for hurricanes have you made?" JP asked.

"You're right, JP," Forge said. "That is what I should be talking about. While a Category 5 hurricane offering a direct hit on Oldport might cause catastrophic damage, our structure has been designed to exceed the top standards of coastal construction. It can weather most of what Mother Nature decides to throw at us. In fact, I'm told it is secure enough to use as a storm shelter in even the worst hurricane."

By then, the trio had reached the massive front doors, currently propped open for crews carrying in kitchen appliances – "designer" kitchen appliances, JP thought – and Forge extended his hand, glad to complete the interview. He felt his time was better spent with reporters from larger cities, especially from up north, where he expected to make a sizeable portion of his sales, but he knew playing the public relations game with the locals was important. The last thing he needed was for the local population to turn against him any more than they would with anyone constructing a building eight times larger than anything else in town.

As the two reporters walked toward JP's 11-year-old yellow pickup, Cole stopped and looked out over the Gulf.

"What's up?"

"JP, I'm a simple photographer. I don't know anything about construction and all, but I've seen hurricane damage before and when I look at the ocean sitting right there, I think there's no way to protect a building from something like Hurricane Camille or maybe even a smaller storm like Katrina."

"Like the man said, odds are we'll never find out."

AUGUST 5, 1:01 P.M.

After grabbing a fast-food lunch, JP and Cole were entertaining much of the news staff at the Oldport Odds and Ends with good-ol'-boy descriptions of the magnificent condominium they toured.

The Odds and Ends was a small regional newspaper covering nine counties and with a circulation of almost 35,000. Any time from 7 a.m. until 1 a.m., someone was in the newsroom, but the population usually peaked after lunch as reporters and photographers aimed at a 4 p.m. deadline.

Pat Baird, the Lifestyles editor, contributed to the conversation several tidbits obtained from her numerous contacts around town, adding that various high society circles were anxious to take advantage of the condo's meeting rooms.

Cole eventually aired his concerns about the safety of the structure during a major hurricane, opening a discussion about past storms.

Pat flagged down city editor Stanley Hopper as he crossed the newsroom and reminded him of Oldport's worst hurricane.

"Yeah, 12 or 13 years ago; I hadn't been here long," he said. "Hurricane Michael. It was nothin' remarkable by historical standards, but it sure made an impression on me. Small Category 2 at landfall, so things coulda been much worse."

"We're headed into the heart of the season now and have had only two named storms, both tropical storms that died at sea, so maybe this will be a slow year," Pat said as she turned toward her desk.

"Funny you should say that," chimed in Christine Finney, who as news editor was constantly monitoring dispatches from the wire services. "There's a tropical wave west of the Cape Verde islands they say has potential for development."

"The television networks love those Cape Verde storms," Hopper said with a grunt. "They can sensationalize them for days before any land is threatened."

Christine nodded. "I'll post the usual brief just to let our readers know it's out there. One thing I learned after moving to the coast, people love tracking tropical storms."

AUGUST 7, 10:21 A.M.

JP Weiscarver was going through e-mail, deleting various offers to increase sexual performance or to secure wealth, all the while hoping to come across an idea for a story. Summer doldrums hit newspapers, too, as everything slows prior to the start of school.

"Hey, JP, your tour of the Oldport Cascades must have been interesting, judging from yesterday's story."

He turned from his computer screen to greet Lydia Murray, a young typist in Lifestyles who admired JP professionally and made no secret of her plan to earn a reporter's spot someday.

"Yes, Lydia, it's an amazing structure; hard to imagine something like that right here in Oldport."

"Have you caught much flak from readers?" she asked, trying to choosc her words carefully. "I mean, I know a lot of people are fearful of the changes the Cascades might lead to in town. Well, in fact, I've heard a few comments about, uh ..."

JP spoke up to relieve the girl's agony.

"It's OK, Lydia. You'll learn quickly enough in this business that someone will disagree with your story that says the sky is blue. I always want to know what people are saying, but I feel a lot of what I hear isn't what they're really thinking. So tell me, what have you picked up on the street?"

"A lot of it ... most of it, in fact ... is just people not wanting to see things change. You know, this isn't why they moved to Oldport, it's never again gonna be as good as it was, northern money is gonna ruin life here, that sort of thing."

"That's a never-ending song and one I addressed with plenty of comments from members of the community. The more strongly opinionated among them feel the newspaper's job is not to give both sides but to campaign ferociously for their side."

"Yeah, I'm with you on that, but one line of objections did catch my ear a bit," Lydia said. "Two different guys told me they didn't like what they saw in how the building went up; they're afraid it's not safe."

"Any specifics?"

"No. My impression was that they knew something about construction but didn't feel they knew enough to be highly critical of such a large project. So, I'm not sure if their concerns are valid or merely a grasping of straws."

"Good observations. Let me know if you hear anything interesting."

As Lydia walked away, JP clicked on the next e-mail and promptly called her back.

"Thought you might want to hear this," he said. "A tipster says we might want to look into city inspections of the Cascades. That's all, nothing clear whatsoever, but I'm guessing he's implying some building inspector isn't doing his job."

"At best."

"Yep, I didn't want to say that out loud, but one has to keep open the possibility of someone being on the take."

"Why would an investor drop hundreds of millions of dollars into a project and choose to cut corners?"

"Hard to say, Lydia, except that every cut corner is more profit, but let's not give too much credence to an anonymous e-mail. I'll start checking things out, beginning by replying to my tipster here to see if he offers any hard information. We have a while before the Cascades open, time to get something solid – if it exists."

AUGUST 7, 3:37 P.M.

"So, we've got Pam's feature on the new county precinct park and the back-to-school information," recounted managing editor Ed Roberts. "Any real news?"

"Not that it's anything special," chimed in Stanley Hopper, "but Archie's put together a piece on the city's difficulty in hiring sanitation workers."

"Looks like we'll need it. Christine, anything on the wire?"

"You have your pick of the usual suspects – latest unrest in the Mideast, mud-slinging from congressional members kicking off the summer recess and a wildfire in California. We also have Tropical Storm Clarice well out in the Atlantic, so named earlier today."

"What's the long-range forecast?"

"It's expected to head generally west the next five days, toward the Gulf of Mexico, and they're predicting it will become a major storm, at least a Category 3."

"OK, add Clarice to the list, but don't play it too high. We don't want to seem like network TV."

"Clarice, huh?" said Dickey Simmons, the graphics artist. "I'll get National Weather Service info and put together a map. Maybe we'll throw in 'some fava beans and a nice Chianti.'"

AUGUST 7, 6:44 P.M.

"Mom, I'm home," yelled Lydia as she struggled through the front door with a couple of bags of groceries. "I brought home dinner. Mom, where are you?"

She knew the question was unnecessary. Like always, Lydia found Maxine Murray lying on the sofa watching television. At least, her viewing habits were unpredictable. This evening, her attention was captured by a game show her daughter did not recognize.

"Did you get out any today?" Lydia asked.

"Sure," Maxine said. "I wandered to the back porch and got a frozen pizza out of the deep freeze," barely able to finish because of her own laughter.

"Oh, Mom, you know you should get out around people. You might like it enough to get a job. Heaven knows we could use the money and, to be honest, there will come a time when I'm no longer here."

Drat, she thought to herself, now I've done it. There will be no conversation from her the rest of the evening.

However, the last comment caught Maxine by surprise.

"What do you mean about leaving?"

"Mom, I'm a woman now. In the natural chain of events, I would marry and set up my own household. I know our life hasn't been all that normal in the past, but I still have hope. I must have hope; it's what keeps me going," Lydia said, the final sentence trailing off quietly.

Maxine was taken aback by Lydia's uncharacteristically blunt analysis of their situation, but abnormal was definitely a fair label. Her husband, Lydia's father, left them when the girl was 12. Maxine responded by jumping from homemaker to breadwinner, working hard at low-paying jobs to keep things going.

Until Lydia graduated high school, that is.

Without warning – or without any warning picked up on by the 18-year-old daughter – Maxine dropped out of life and encouraged Lydia to take a job waiting tables at the pizza restaurant.

She did just that for three years and managed to take one or two junior college classes each semester at Oldport Community College. A journalism class whetted her appetite for reporting, but Maxine's newfound neediness dampened any idea of Lydia going off to university.

It was while serving pizza to Pat Baird that Lydia learned of an opening in Pat's Lifestyles department. "It's nothing glamorous," Pat told her. "You will type a lot of boring recipes and wedding announcements into the computer, take birth notices over the phone, pass out forms to the public, that sort of stuff. Once in a while, you might get a chance to write a story, if you demonstrate an ability to do so."

It wasn't that Pat wanted to dissuade the girl from applying, but she had been through too many starry-eyed typist candidates before. Nonetheless, Lydia sold herself to the Lifestyles editor and won the job.

Changing jobs did not have much effect on her home life, however. Maxine appreciated that Lydia was happier with her work, but her only comment was that it meant her daughter would be home in the evening to prepare dinner and that her salary, while not appreciably higher, was steady and did not rely on tips.

Even without a ringing endorsement, Lydia continually shared with her mother any accomplishments at work, particularly when one of her rewrites was published.

Now, though, Lydia remained quiet while preparing dinner, fearful that she had hurt Maxine's feelings. Her mother's silence, though, was because the words had indeed made an impression. Maybe she's right.

Her baby girl was a 23-year-old woman with a career and a chance for a "normal" life. Why shouldn't she have hope for something better than what she saw in her mother?

"You're right," Maxine finally said. "It ain't fair that I hold down a couch all day waiting for you to take care of me."

"Oh, Mom, I just got carried away ..." Lydia started.

"Hush, child. You're right. It ain't like I can't take care of myself or hold down a job. And I got skills, you know. And it ain't like I've gained 400 pounds sittin' 'round here. It's time for me to get off my backside and get a job. And, like you said, it's natural for you to be lookin' for a new life, a life of your own, without havin' to worry about me."

Lydia went back to preparing the meal as both women allowed the proclamation to sink in.

"You know, Mom, I owe you so much for taking care of me and getting me through high school after Daddy left."

She was somewhat startled when her mother spoke because she had moved into the kitchen to open a can of black-eyed peas.

"My darling child, you don't owe me nothing. Having a daughter as loving as you is all the payback a mother needs and is more than many get. Of course, I might need to lean on you again in another 30 or 40 years, but I should take care of myself now. Like you said, it's natural."

"So, what's next for us, Mom?"

"You know that new condo they're opening? I saw in your paper that they're gonna be hiring cleaning crews next week. I'm gonna get me one of those jobs."

The television continued running in the living room, now with news briefs at the top of the hour:

"The National Hurricane Center says Tropical Storm Clarice has reached hurricane status with sustained winds of 75 mph. Hurricane Clarice is still well out in the Atlantic and no immediate threat to anything but shipping interests."

AUGUST 8, 1:00 P.M.

An update from the National Hurricane Center listed Clarice as a Category 2 storm with 110-mph winds. The five-day forecast – with a broad cone of uncertainty, for sure – had the storm plotted for the northern coast of the Gulf of Mexico.

AUGUST 8, 7:00 P.M.

Twenty-four hours after becoming a hurricane, Clarice was upgraded to a major storm, Category 3, with 125-mph winds. Though it still was no immediate threat to land, people began taking notice.

AUGUST 8, 10:00 P.M.

Strengthening at a staggering rate, Clarice grew to Category 4, with 130-mph winds. Night editors at the Odds and Ends made the adjustment to the morning stories before shipping the pages to the press.

AUGUST 9, 8:33 A.M.

As JP Weiscarver slipped into his desk chair to begin the day, he knew better than to get comfortable; there was no doubt he would be summoned into the city editor's fishbowl as soon as Stanley realized JP was there. Even though Hurricane Clarice was considered a television toy two days ago, things changed as the storm gained strength.

Just a few hours earlier, the storm reached Category 4 with winds holding at 130 mph. That's impressive and Clarice was already the talk of Oldport, not a storm to be ignored any longer.

"Weiscarver, c'm'ere," Hopper yelled as the reporter turned on his computer terminal.

"What's up, boss?" JP sang out as he plopped onto Stanley's pea green sofa.

"Don't get comfy; you won't be here that long. It looks like this blankety-blank hurricane won't let us ignore it. Instead of doing whatever junk it is you normally do to fill your day, put together a story about ... oh, I don't know ... something 'hurricany.'"

"The first thing readers need to do is learn what to do. I'll pull the preparation checklist we ran at the beginning of hurricane season and amplify its more important points. I'll localize it by talking with local retailers. How's that?"

"Sounds like you've been thinking about it already," Stanley mumbled as he waved JP out of the office. "Of course, that's why you're getting the big bucks."

"Yeah, let me know when those big bucks start, will you?"

AUGUST 9, 10:04 A.M.

"May we talk on the record?" JP asked Rafael Ventura, manager of Oldport Supply Store, once the burly and bearded man answered the page to the customer service desk.

"Certainly, it's our part in helping people prepare for life on the coast."

"Though Hurricane Clarice is headed in this general direction, it's probably three to five days away and highly unpredictable. I guess I'm saying the odds of it hitting here as a major storm are still rather long, so how does a store like this prepare for that?"

"As you would likely assume, we have detailed plans that have already rolled into motion for just such a situation. Our suppliers are part of that plan. For them, this is a greater threat because they supply stores all over the South, so they have a good idea that storm preparation materials will be needed somewhere. They already have warehoused items ready to roll and even have trailers in strategic locations ready to roll wherever needed."

"Are you stocking up already?" JP asked.

"Indeed we are. We've ramped up our stock of lumber and plywood for boarding up windows, as well as screws and nails. We've loaded up on plastic sheeting, flashlights, batteries, insect spray, ice chests, propane gas, weather radios and even bottled water. We're ready to roll."

Ventura excused himself briefly to help a young employee who was trying to explain techniques for boarding up windows to a customer.

JP looked around at what were probably more customers than usual for the store but definitely nothing like a crush of people. All gave the impression of calmly going about their business, nothing of any looming fears. He knew things would get much more hectic if the storm closed in on the region.

He then noticed one couple, probably in their 20s, who were carefully reviewing a brochure, making notes about different things and seemingly taking considerable care discussing each item. He started to approach them, but Ventura returned.

The store manager also saw the couple and mentioned the brochure.

"We realize the Oldport population changes rapidly and many people who live here now have never been through a hurricane. We have brochures offering advice and checklists to help them prepare. The brochures are available year-round, but people tend to pay little attention until something like this happens. We now have them readily available at entrances and elsewhere around the store. Our staffers have all received extra training to help customers decide what they need to do."

He handed a copy to JP and it occurred to the reporter for the first time that he, too, needed to consider making preparations for Clarice. And I have to do that while covering a potentially huge story, he thought.

"Mr. Ventura, something like this obviously puts a strain on you personally. How do you manage to take care of your own home?"

"I follow my own advice, JP. I have material in storage already precut for my windows. My family puts together a hurricane survival kit every June. We make a party of it and, in December, we move food items into our pantry and reconfigure the kit for winter survival."

"A winter survival kit?"

Ventura issued a laugh befitting his size. "You wouldn't fall for that in this part of the country, would you? That's what we call it, but we're really stocking up on supplies for Christmas, New Year's and Super Bowl. In addition to supplies, we have a detailed plan. Already, my wife is making early preparations like securing loose items outside, making sure we have gasoline in the vehicles and for the generators, contacting family inland to make sure they can receive us if we evacuate and so on. If Clarice continues to approach us, we'll take more serious actions, culminating in boarding up the house and evacuating the coast."

Rafael Ventura recognized that the reporter seemed overwhelmed, something he often saw in amateur handymen.

"Tell me, JP, do you have a plan?"

Somewhat surprised by the question, Weiscarver laughed nervously and said, "No, I guess not. I've merely been writing about what people need to do. I guess I always figured, since it's only me and a ferret, I would just stock up on groceries and top off my tank. Now, I'm thinking I might return this evening as a customer."

After getting Ventura's permission to send a photographer by later for photos, JP thanked the manager, who made it a point to extract from the reporter a final promise to make personal plans for a hurricane. JP then headed deeper into the store in search of the couple he spotted earlier. He found them considering an emergency generator.

"Excuse me. My name is JP Weiscarver," he said, handing each a business card. "I'm a reporter for the Odds and Ends newspaper doing a story about hurricane preparations. I might be totally off the mark, but I'm guessing this is your first potential hurricane."

The surprised couple looked at one another and she laughed.

"And we thought we were being so smooth," the man said, "blending in with the old-timers. Actually, we moved here just last week from the Midwest"

"If it helps, you probably are not that obvious; I was just on the lookout for someone like you," JP said. "Oldport is, as the name might imply, a deeply rooted community of families who have been here for generations. However, there is a large and rapidly growing contingent of people like y'all who are new to the area. If you don't mind, I would love to chat with you a little about your plans."

The couple introduced themselves as Joseph and Suzette Lundgren and arranged to meet at their home at 3 p.m.

AUGUST 9, 11:47 A.M.

An almost empty newsroom first caught JP's attention as he strolled in, but he then saw a large number of people stuffed into Stanley Hopper's office.

"Just in time," Stanley grumbled as JP entered, as if it were a scheduled meeting. "We're starting local angles on this hurricane, whatever its name is, with something O'Hanlon's out working on now concerning emergency preparations and, Weiscarver, what did you come up with?"

"I visited with the GM at the supply store, a carpenter for home preparation tips and a gasoline retailer about fuel availability. I've pulled the good old hurricane checklist to run inside."

"Good, that'll give us two stories to acknowledge to readers we indeed know there's a storm a'brewin'. Dickey, I assume you'll keep us up on the latest maps and any other of your graphic artistry. Let's plan ahead a bit, just in case this, this ..."

"Hurricane Clarice, boss," JP inserted.

"Just in case this Hurricane Clarice actually deserves our attention. What else ya got, smart-aleck?"

"I'm meeting this afternoon with a couple who just moved here from the Midwest last month," JP said. "They will probably provide a good look at the worst-case scenario; newcomers are only familiar with what they've seen on television networks. I really don't know how that will play out, but they seemed worthy of a story. I thought I'd check in with the animal shelter, see what they plan to do."

"I'll complement the newcomers' story with a look back at Hurricane Michael," Pat Baird chimed in. "I know plenty of people with stories to share."

"I can talk to the power company and find out how it's preparing," contributed Archie Hanning, the city beat reporter. "They will be involved if the storm hits anywhere nearby, even far away if it does major damage."

"Lydia's not here," said Pat Baird, "but she called to say she wants to do a story about those who do not have safe options."

"Meaning?" the city editor asked.

"Think Hurricane Katrina, Stanley," Pat almost chided. "Even here in Oldport, there are people living in houses not worth boarding up, in flood zones and without transportation."

"Good call," he responded, "but can she handle it?"

Pat nodded and looked toward JP.

"Hey, boss, she's shown promise. She's local and from a, shall we say, not-well-to-do family with contacts that often fall beneath our radar. Finally, she's never been shy about hitting me up for advice."

"Give her a go-ahead," Hopper said to Pat, "and we'll designate Weiscarver as her mentor. OK, that gives us a start. Get photo ideas to the photographers in time for them to work on 'em. The rest of you drum up some ideas for future editions so we can gear up if necessary and, one last thing, don't get your feelings hurt of Clarice turns north or peters out and we don't run any of 'em."

AUGUST 9, 12:15 P.M.

Jennifer O'Hanlon created a bit of a stir among the younger – presumably single – firefighters as she approached Station Four. The men didn't say anything or act inappropriately, but there was something about them.. Jennifer calls it strutting, a noticeable change in how young males stand, walk and talk when an attractive young female is in the area.

Before Jennifer had a chance to speak, the shift lieutenant stepped out of the station's large bay door and the guys settled down.

"I take it you're the reporter I'm expecting."

"Yes, ma'am, guilty as charged. Jennifer O'Hanlon. Chief Branden said you and your crew would be the perfect people to visit with."

"I hope we can help you out. I'm Lt. Angela Webb. The rest of the crew joining us is Dominic, Miguel, Billy and Oscar."

The six of them found spots around a large dining table in the kitchen.

"We just cleaned up from lunch, senorita, but I could heat a quick plate of leftovers," suggested Miguel before taking his seat.

"Drop the accent, amigo," said Oscar. "The only things Hispanic left in him are his name and a few Spanish words he remembers from junior high classes."

"He's operating under the illusion that women find Latinos attractive," interjected Billy. "You're too smart to fall for that, aren't you, Jennifer?"

Angela was about to intercede when Jennifer took control.

"What I am, Billy, is too smart to answer that question. As for the original offer, I cheated and had a mid-morning breakfast burrito, so I'm good, thank you. Y'all do have an early lunch, though."

"It's something we do at Station Four," Angela said, "but not at every station."

"It's something we do now that she's in charge," Dominic said, earning a dramatic stare from his officer, "... and we like it that way."

"As you are aware, Jennifer, we never know when we'll have to rush out, so I like eating early, just in case."

"Oh, I understand," the reporter replied. "That was my excuse for having the burrito this morning."

With the insinuated threat that a fire or ambulance alarm could interrupt the interview the same as it can a meal, Jennifer placed her digital voice recorder on the table, pulled out her pen and tablet and started talking about the fire department's role in a hurricane.

It was apparent each firefighter had given thought to his or her role in a major tropical storm. They talked to the reporter about training for high water rescues, fighting fires in hurricane force winds, and preparing for any number of things one would not even think of preparing for.

Angela explained the department would transport some of the fire engines and ambulances to safer spots inland, from where they will return after the storm, the logic being that equipment would be spared from a serious situation.

"Most of the personnel will stay behind, though, so we'll have plenty of manpower," Oscar said. "I'm too important to the department to put at risk, so they'll have me drive one of our engines to safety."

For that comment, three different items were hurled at him.

Jennifer left the fire station feeling like the community was better prepared than she had thought.

AUGUST 9, 1:02 P.M.

After adopting his pet ferret, Bubba, last year, JP kept in close contact with Oldport County Animal Control Department and had formed a friendship with Juan Mendoza, whom the reporter easily located after slipping in through the back door.

"Hey, Mr. Weiscarver, I figured you'd be out over the Atlantic in a Hurricane Hunter."

"And you, Mr. Mendoza, I assumed would be out tying down seagulls."

"Those we'll leave to Mother Nature. We have enough to take care of here."

"How do you prepare?"

"Are you working on a story, JP?"

"I'm always working on a story, but, I'm sorry, I should have made that distinction. So, put to good use that master's degree in European literature and give me a few quotes to use."

"I never should have told you that. OK, our shelter, funded generously by tax dollars and contributors, was built with hurricane survival in mind. We're only a couple of miles away from the coast, but this area of the county is 35 feet above sea level, well above a tidal surge.

"During a tropical storm, some volunteer employees might ride out the storm in the center. However, if it is coming in as a hurricane, policy calls for the center to be secured and all personnel gone no fewer than twelve hours prior to anticipated landfall."

"Those are interestingly specific parameters," JP said. "Is there..."

"Yes, as a perceptive person like you might guess, there is a story behind it. I'm told that several decades ago ... don't know when, exactly ... an employee and a community volunteer lost their lives while riding out a rather small storm at the dog pound. Twelve hours is an absolute minimum, meant to give employees time to prepare at home or to evacuate, but that's arbitrary. Should Clarice live up to her early billing, we'll do what we can for the animals and get everyone out earlier than that."

"What can you do for the animals?"

"The most important thing is to have them in this building. We feel it will protect them from most any storm-related issues, even power outages. There is a baffled venting system designed to facilitate fresh air flow without damaging winds or driving rains getting in. I understand it can generate some spooky sounds, however. Were we not so well prepared and in such a safe building, we would probably take advantage of emergency pet shelters that will be put together well inland."

"Do you have power generators onsite?"

"We do, but they will not run during our absence; that could prove dangerous."

"So the animals can be alone for quite some time."

"Yes, though each is left with adequate food and water, it will not be comfortable for them should we be gone for a matter of days. That should not happen, though, because we have several people who will make the animals a priority after a storm."

"Do you have any advice for pet owners?"

"Sure. First of all, do not drop off your pet here."

"You're kidding."

"I wish I were, but every time something like this happens, we see an increase of animals abandoned at our gate. We will be hard-pressed to take care of them all and, if we've already left, they would be on their own. If you're staying home for the storm, arrange to get your pet indoors and not just in the garage, where the floor is lower and more subject to rising water. Make sure you have food, water, meds and means to clean up after your pet. Keep in mind the storm could be a frightening experience for Fido, too.

"If you're evacuating, check ahead with your destination to see if pets are accepted. Most evacuation shelters do not take pets, but you might find kennels in the area or an emergency shelter like I mentioned earlier. Call the animal shelter or even pet supply stores where you're going and see if they can connect you with someone who can take in your family friend."

"What about leaving the pet behind?"

"That's touchy and we have no official position, but I could understand that a pet might be safer here than traveling and ending up lost in a strange environment. I'd rather not explore that possibility now, however, if you don't mind."

"What about livestock?"

"Ranchers are already doing what they can to move cattle to higher ground. Many horses are shipped to pastures well inland. Fowl present some problems. They're difficult to ship out, though I understand some fryers are being sold early. The family with a few hens will not likely have a sturdy structure for them. The chickens, dumb as they are, seem to survive well, but you may not find them at home after the storm."

"Or you may find someone else's chickens in your yard."

"True; hadn't thought of it that way. One last thought, because you know I have to preach this sermon whenever I can: Please have your pets neutered or spayed before they have offspring you do not want. Having fewer unwanted animals in distress makes it easier to care for them all."

"Don't worry, Juan, I'll work that in somewhere."

"Tell me, JP, what plans do you and Bubba have?"

"Why is it all of my interviews today come back to point out how ill-prepared I am for Clarice?"

AUGUST 9, 1:47 P.M.

Keeping his visit with Juan short, JP decided to forego stopping by the office and instead found a shady spot for his pickup at J.M. Qwilleran Park. There, he turned on his notepad computer and finished piecing together his story about the retailers' plans. After logging into the newspaper's system and filing the story, he put in a call to Jennifer O'Hanlon, the cops beat reporter assigned the story about emergency preparations.

"Oh, JP, I was hoping it was Sergeant Bellew; I'm waiting on a callback from the police department," Jennifer said, talking even faster than normal, as she tended to do when on a deadline, particularly when things were not going as planned. Tad Bellew was JP's favorite and most reliable contact when he had the cops beat.

"Since we're working on the only hurricane stories for tomorrow," JP said, taking the cue to keep it short, "I thought it wise to touch base and see how things were developing. If you would like, I can toss you a quote about the animal shelter's plans and we could use it to tease tomorrow's coverage."

"Sergeant Bellew toured me through the emergency operations center and I checked in with the fire department. I also visited with the mayor and county judge about their stages of activation. I'm just waiting for a fact check from PD and I'll tie up this piece, well before you're done, as usual."

"Thanking you for your confidence, I must sadly point out I've already filed my story remotely, thereby rendering your painful insult erroneous. Plus, I am pressing 'send' on my e-mail to provide a quote you may incorporate into your on-time-if-not-first story."

"Wow, I do see your story in the queue," Jennifer said. "I now stand ... uh, sit ... in awe of your technological wizardry and your ability to occasionally hit a deadline when it's least expected. As for the quote, it may be awkward in my story, but I'll pass it on to Mr. Hopper with your suggestion it might be used to tease next day coverage."

Upon disconnecting, JP took a moment to consider how well he and Jennifer work together; not just anyone "got" his manner, not to mention his sense of humor. It was comforting to know she had his back at the office and he hoped she felt he provided her the same security.

Purely professional, of course, he said to himself as he checked the address he wrote down that morning for the Lundgrens.

AUGUST 9, 2:55 P.M.

JP was impressed by the organization of Joseph and Suzette Lundgren. When he moved to Oldport from his first newspaper job up north, it took the bachelor reporter months to get settled into his new home, even though he had next to nothing with which to outfit the house. The Lundgrens, he noticed, not only had their home looking homey so soon but were already making headway on hurricane preparations.

"Joseph," Suzette yelled toward the back of the house after asking in her guest. "Our new reporter friend is here."

"He's out back cutting plywood for the windows," she explained to JP. "We realize it's a bit premature but figured they would be ready for next time. Care for a brownie?"

"Thanks, and I must say you have settled in quite well. It looks like you've been here for years."

"I wouldn't say my wife is a perfectionist, but the only evidence she's not is the fact she married me," Joseph said upon entering. "When we scheduled a move date, I knew to allow plenty of time to set up housekeeping so I could help Suzette get things the way she needs them before starting work."

"What do you do?"

"I'm an artist."

"He's a teacher."

"I can afford to be an artist because I also teach art."

"I believe I understand," JP said after a chuckle. "Who will enable you in your artistic endeavors?"

"I guess you will, if you're a taxpayer to the Oldport school district. I'll teach freshmen and sophomores at Oldport High School."

"What about you, Suzette?"

"I'm an elementary teacher, but I'm taking off a year or two." She glanced at Joseph before continuing. "We're expecting our first child in early January. I'll do some substitute teaching while preparing for junior."

"Well, sounds like Oldport's getting a buy-two-get-one-free deal. Congratulations, but that does bring an additional element into your first hurricane."

"Yes, sir," said Joseph. "That's probably the main reason behind our zealousness. If we choose to weather the storm, our decisions affect junior, too."

"Plus, we cannot really afford repairing extensive damages, so we decided to invest what we could in preparations," Suzette added.

"The big question for someone so new to the area is whether you intend to stay or evacuate, but it sounds like you've not really made that decision yet."

"Actually, our intention is to stay," Joseph said, "but we do not intend to be bull-headed about it."

"Not bull-headed?" Suzette exclaimed after a laugh. "Your main reason for wanting to stay is to prove to friends back home we didn't make a mistake coming here."

"OK, that and the fact we don't have extra money to run away."

"Let's back up just a minute. You told me you moved here last week from the Midwest."

"Outstate Minnesota," Suzette said.

"Outstate? Is that ..."

"Outstate Minnesota is another way of saying 'not Minneapolis-St. Paul,'" she said.

"Although some people don't like ..."

"Yes, some people like Joseph don't like the term, but they just have to get over themselves," Suzette said while poking her husband in the ribs. "Where we lived was particularly 'Outstate,' well up in the northwest, past the headwaters of the Mississippi River."

"I tell people around here I'm from up north, but it's nothing as northerly as that," JP said. "Are you finding your experience with bitterly cold winters any help preparing for a possible hurricane?"

"I haven't exactly thought of it that way, but it is probably true that I'm drawing on some old survival lessons," Joseph said.

"It has crossed my mind several times," Suzette chimed in. "Laying in for winter meant being prepared to exist on your own for an extended period, possibly without any utilities for a good while, without access to stores and shopping, gasoline, fresh water ... well, you can see where I'm going."

"Makes sense," her husband said. "Substitute a humid heat for cold, rattlesnakes and mosquitoes for wolves, downed trees for snow drifts, and I guess there are considerable similarities. Bottom line is you need to prepare to fend for yourself for a while. However, there are not many winter threats that involve relocating your house from its foundation."

"You've had to jump into this right away. How did you manage to get started?"

"Suzette's an incredible researcher. She actually accumulated preparation information before we moved, so we were not totally blindsided by the threat."

"The checklist and stories in the Odds and Ends were of considerable help, too, but I guess you're an old hand at this."

"Actually, Suzette, that may be the greatest difference between hurricanes and Outstate winters. You were guaranteed cold weather every year, but hurricanes are totally unpredictable. An area might go decades or centuries without a serious storm but may get hit in successive years."

"But I gather that you prepare more often," she said.

"True, good point. Residents are encouraged to make some preparations every year so they can act swiftly. The first summer I was here, many people boarded up for a possible blow and we ended on the dry side – 30 mph winds and a smattering of rain. I understand the worst storm on record was 13 years ago and it really wasn't that bad. As people around here are fond of saying, however, it's not a question of whether there is a major storm, it's a question of when."

"So, you're all prepared?"

"No, but it's working its way up my priority list."

AUGUST 9, 6:32 P.M.

JP made the decision when he moved to Oldport to commit to renting a house instead of an apartment. The small house on the corner of Dolphin Street and Oleander Drive proved perfect for the young bachelor, even though he still had little in the way of furnishings. He liked to think of himself as a good neighbor, based on the fact he was never a nuisance to those around him, most of whom owned their homes.

Two neighbors were chatting on the curb when JP pulled into his driveway and he ambled out to join them, knowing Hurricane Clarice would be the topic and hoping to pick up a tip or two.

"Hey, Jason, Tim."

"Howdy, Scoop, any news on the hurricane?"

"You know how it is, prepare for the worst, hope for the best. Speaking of which, are y'all preparing?"

"Of course," Tim said. "I'm storing up ice in the freezer and stocking up on a fine assortment of beer. When the lights go out, it all goes into my industrial strength ice chests and out comes my fresh stockpile of chips and salsa."

"Unlike you two," Jason chimed in, "I have an investment to protect, not to mention my family."

"So you're going with the whole board up and evacuate procedure?"

"Preparing for it, at least, like you said. I've had plywood put back for the major windows since we bought this place. I just got through checking them out and making sure I have the hardware needed. If the storm gets much closer, I'll board up, shut off the utilities and we'll head to my in-laws, make a vacation out of it."

"Wow, that makes my beer and chips plan sound a little short-sighted. What about you, JP?"

"Why do you think I was trolling for information? I don't really have a plan and you guys only help set bookends to the range of possibilities. I definitely won't evacuate, though, since it may be the biggest news story I'll ever have a chance to cover."

"Are you staying in your house?"

"Man, I just haven't planned anything. I have a pet ferret to take care of and I do need to protect the house, I guess. I'll call my landlord and get his input; he lived here during Hurricane Michael. This is serious stuff, though. I might need to order a pizza and put some plans together."

"Sounds like you're leaning toward my style of hurricane preparations," Tim said as he started home.

AUGUST 9, 7:55 P.M.

The question of whether or not to order pizza never tarried on JP's mind too long. He had quipped that he could never be trusted with deep, dark secrets because captors or tempters would find out what they wanted to know for a tomato pie topped with pepperoni, sausage and mushrooms.

He laughed at the thought. No, he had never called them tomato pies when he lived up north, but he occasionally did here just to mess with his southern friends.

Before calling in the order, he invited Jennifer over for a joint planning session and then upgraded his plans to a large pizza.

When the doorbell rang, JP's pet ferret, Bubba, jumped from his chair and started running dashes between JP and the front door. Bubba was secured in his master's arms before JP opened the door, pleased to find his usual delivery man.

"Hey there, little guy, how's my favorite ferret?" the driver asked.

"He's going crazy at the prospect of company. You should see him run around when the bell rings. I just hope he never learns how to order pizza."

"You can never have too much pizza," he said as he accepted the payment and a generous tip.

"You just gave me a thought, Guy. Are y'all expecting an uptick in business with the possibility of a hurricane strike?"

"Are you kidding? I know we're getting an extra shipment of supplies overnight to prepare for it. In fact, we're already busier than usual. I've delivered to a lot of homes where people are securing their house and are too tired to cook. In fact, we're curtailing deliveries over the next couple of days and requiring more people to pick up their orders, but don't worry, you're on our preferred customer list!"

JP resisted the urge to tear into the pizza before Jennifer arrived but did set out paper plates and napkins to expedite things.

"Well, Bubba, I know you heard what Guy said. I guess that confirms what we've been talking about. We seriously need to think seriously about preparing for a potentially serious storm. Hey, don't look at me like that; I did that on purpose for effect. For a fur ball, you're awfully critical."

The ferret might not have heard the insult because he was barreling toward the front door in response to yet another bell.

"Pavlov would love you, buddy."

As Jennifer walked in, JP handed her the wriggling ferret in exchange for the six-pack of beer she routinely contributed to their pizza get-togethers.

"Sorry it took so long. The convenience store was packed. Seems everyone is stocking up already."

"It may be that there are a lot of people like my neighbor, Tim, who suggested his only preparation was to lay in plenty of ice, beer, chips and salsa."

"You know, that may be a story idea. You hear about hurricane parties."

"The most infamous being the one organized to greet Hurricane Camille."

Jennifer cocked her head as she chewed her first bite of pizza. "Not infamous enough, I guess ... educate me."

"I had heard of it, but I can only provide details because I read up on it last night while researching powerful 'canes. It was August 1969 and they didn't have nearly as much warning. Camille formed near the Cayman Islands and made a beeline through the Gulf of Mexico toward the Gulfport and Pass Christian area. There were barely three days between formation and landfall.

"The hurricane party story is that two dozen people got together to welcome Camille at an upscale apartment complex on the beach. The entire three-story complex was wiped off the foundation by 190-mph winds and a 24-foot storm surge. You'd recognize the before-and-after aerial photos, I bet. Of the 24 party-goers, the only survivor was a woman washed 12 miles inland."

Jennifer sat for a moment processing the story.

"I remember hearing that story told. It's amazing, definitely a cautionary tale about not respecting a dangerous storm. Man, 23 out of 24 people killed is not much of a party. Is the story true?"

"What? Why would you ask that? You just told me you had heard it before."

"Why would I ask? OK, JP, all the alarms are going off now. Why? Because some reporter who seems to have appointed himself my professional guide keeps telling me that stories which sound too good probably are not true. 'If your mother says she loves you,' he likes to say, 'check it out.'"

"Check it out," JP chimed in with the punch line. "My little girl is all growed up; I be so proud of her."

"So it's not true?"

"Apparently not. I continued reading other sites and became convinced that the story probably originated during the hectic hours after the storm – which did kill more than 250 people, including probably eight at that apartment complex – and it was such a compelling story, nobody would listen to pleas for corrections. Survivors from the apartment say there certainly was no party going on."

"OK, but maybe all of that would make an interesting story."

"I became enthralled by it and I'm sure the people of Pass Christian would appreciate it."

"I'll follow up on all of that tomorrow, but I believe we have more personal worries tonight, right Bubba? Oh, sorry, I should have known you would be asleep by now."

The evening's partnership worked well for JP and Jennifer. Each wanted to make proper preparations but didn't want to over-react. With one assuring the other that his or her safety was, indeed, worth the effort, they created action plans.

AUGUST 10, 7:00 A.M.

Those checking the morning news casts heard Clarice made Category 5 status the evening earlier with 160-mph winds and grew overnight, hitting 180 mph of sustained strength. Meanwhile, the forecast track varied little and the slowly shrinking zone of uncertainty made a few Oldport County residents slightly more uncomfortable.

AUGUST 10, 8:19 A.M.

"I see you got a tour of the emergency operations center for this morning's story on cops and fire preparations," Archie Hanning said as Jennifer headed for her second cup of coffee. "Impressive, isn't it?"

"Oh, yeah. I've been in there before, but I've never seen it like this. Things were hopping. You used to cover cops, you know they always have it ready to go in case of something like an explosion or tornado, but planning for something as massive as a Cat 5 storm, and given a few days' notice, they've got everything fine-tuned, ready for whatever Clarice throws at us."

"Wow, sounds like you've fallen in love."

"OK, OK, I know I'm coming across as a homer and as if I've lost my impartial journalistic edge," Jennifer admitted, "but impressive is still impressive."

"Sorry!" Archie yelled, throwing up his hands in surrender. "It was truly a good story and it made me feel safer about living here, not unlike the story I'm working on today."

With the slightest of prodding from Jennifer, he outlined what he had learned about the preparations of the electric company.

For instance, he had never considered the huge influx of workers and equipment that would be involved in simply removing fallen trees and limbs from the equation when it comes to restoring power after a major hurricane.

"Do you know they already have crews heading this direction from around the country? They will position themselves, their equipment and materials in strategic locations far enough away from the coast and will start rolling in to help where needed. It's a two-way street, I've learned. Quite a few folks from here have made winter trips up north to help restore power following horrific ice storms."

"Neither assignment sounds very appealing ... freezing cold or humid heat with mosquitos."

"Add work days that can run 18-20 hours, sleeping on cots and dealing with the inherent dangers of working around electricity and fallen trees ... man, those guys have earned my respect."

"Wow, sounds like you've fallen in love."

"OK, I deserve that. You return to sating your coffee addiction and I'll get back to work on my love letter."

AUGUST 10, 10:01 A.M.

There seemed to be a slightly higher level of concentration around the newsroom as people zeroed in on their responsibilities with the looming threat of Hurricane Clarice.

Lydia Murray, of course, was always quiet and zeroed in.

"Uh, excuse me, JP, but do you have a second."

"By all means, Lydia. How's your story coming?"

"This is kind of a heavy piece for me, so I'm moving pretty slowly. It's a far cry from profiling members of the Palmetto Club."

JP waited as she gathered her thoughts. It had taken him a while to figure out her deliberative style of processing before speaking and then to recognize that jumping in too soon tended to dampen her flow of conversation.

"It seems ... well, first of all, you know I'm looking into people who do not have good, safe options. Well, it seems my pool of qualifying people just keeps expanding.

"OK," she continued, "you start with the infirm, mostly elderly, who are not able to board up their houses or to drive out of town. Add those who are squeaking by on modest, if any, income. If they have a car, they cannot afford gasoline for a road trip, much less a place to stay. Neither can they afford the cost of boarding up their homes, which they probably don't even own.

"Of course, the homeless, those who live under bridges or in the woods on the outskirts of town, they readily spring to mind. Do you force them into shelters?

"Not thought of so readily are people who are not mentally stable or who might be strung out on drugs most of the time. A lot of them might not know what's going on, that there is even a threat. To make it scarier, what about the children who are with them? I mean, the idea of children in such an environment is sobering enough, but to be there with the prospect of a deadly hurricane, well ..."

JP gave her a second.

"How do I cover everyone, JP?"

"That's not your objective. You're to tell what's out there and what's happening as well as you can. The story itself will illustrate that the problem, the need, the whatever, is larger than you can convey. Remember, too, this is a newspaper story, not an investigation. You only have just so much room, probably 15 column inches."

"So, how do I get it all in there?"

"You don't. You pick two or three people representing different needs and get the point across with their stories. You simply outline the broader issues, like you just did to me. Then, put together information for an infographic, telling people where they can find help and maybe what they can do to help, like reporting kids they're concerned about."

"OK, OK, I can do that."

"Go to Dickey right now and give him an idea of what you're doing. Even though your deadline's not until tomorrow, he can get started on the graphic. A graphic also draws more attention to your story.

"Do the same thing with one of the photographers. They're out all of the time and probably have some good ideas."

"OK, thanks," Lydia said. "I feel better. I guess I really knew that, but when I start looking around, there are so many people who need help. But that's true whether there's a storm coming or not, isn't it?"

"You have a curse, Lydia. You not only see the world many of us block out, but you also feel the need to do something about it."

"Yeah, my mom says I was always too willing to take in strays and try to fix my friends' problems. Back to the storm. Are you prepared for Clarice?"

"There you go again," JP almost yelled and they shared a laugh. "Actually, I laid out an action plan last night. I'll pick up some supplies this afternoon and try to get things in order. What about you and your mom?"

"Oh, it's much too early for us to plan anything. We have a system fine-tuned over the years where we put off discussing any potential problem until it's the last minute ... or later. But, working on this story has given me the incentive to bring it up a little sooner. Maybe we'll talk about it tonight."

"Speaking of you and your concerns, have you heard anything else about problems with construction on the Cascades?"

"Nobody's talking about that now, but there never was much said, so I'm not sure it was ever a big deal."

AUGUST 10, 3:00 P.M.

The managing editor was the first to show for the daily budget meeting, where editors outline what's going into the next morning's paper. On his heels was the news editor, Christine Finney, who would lay out the front page.

"I appreciate the early meeting, Ed," she said. "I just have a feeling I'm going to have to fight this layout."

"Yep, a lot to get in there. Everyone here? Start us off with the wire, Christine."

"No surprises there. Hurricane Clarice has held together as a Category 5 since 7 o'clock last night. The forecasted track hasn't varied appreciably; she's still heading straight for us."

"That reminds me," Stanley cut in. "I know you wouldn't do that in print, Christine, but all of us need to keep an eye out for gender-specific pronouns. Clarice the hurricane is an 'it,' not a 'her.'"

"What about quotes," asked Ed.

"Generally, I'd say to go with an indirect quote and avoid the problem. If you've got a great quote, though, then stick with it. I don't want to get too hung up on it, but if we're all the time assigning feminine pronouns, we're just opening ourselves up to criticism."

"Everything else off the wire will work fine on non-gender-specific inside pages," Christine finished.

"OK, Stanley, what all do you have lined up?"

"The lead local would probably be Archie's electricity piece; that affects everyone. It also has a sidebar box telling folks how to prepare their homes, such as tree limbs, cutting off power to protect from surges and in case of heavy structural damage, what to do after the storm, etc.

"JP's interview with the couple preparing for their first hurricane will hit a chord with a large number of people who haven't been through one before. Their comparisons with winter storms make an interesting slant. That story also includes a lot of preparation tips we should highlight.

"Those are definitely the top two. Pat's look back at Hurricane Michael probably would package well with the newcomers, either on front or inside with the jump."

"If you go inside," Ed chimed in, "use a reefer line to plug it from JP's story."

"The other two are more cutesy pieces. Jennifer did a story on hurricane parties, a large part of which debunks the legend of the 'original' hurricane party during Camille in 1969."

"Wait," Ed asked. "Are you talking about the one where there was only one survivor and the building was wiped off the foundation? That's got to be true; I've seen video of Walter Cronkite talking about it."

"Sorry, Ed," Stanley said, giving an uncharacteristic chuckle. "Her story's well-documented and explains what really happened, best we can tell. Cling to that Cronkite memory next time we screw up something."

"Wow, another legend bites the dust."

"Finally, JP did a story about the animal shelter and how it's preparing. Cute, like I said, and worthy of inside."

"Hasn't JP finished paying off that ferret yet?" teased Dickey.

"It might make a good lead for the C section front," Stanley continued. "And, Christine, I pulled a quote to the top that I thought you might use. It seems they always have people dropping off animals at times like this, and the guy tries to point out they really cannot handle them right now."

"OK, is there any non-hurricane news going on?" Ed asked. "No? Stanley, should we save a story or two for tomorrow?"

"No, no, no. Wouldn't want to do that, just in case Clarice takes a big turn and we're left holding useless words. Besides, Lydia seems to be coming along well with her story about the homeless and such and what they'll be facing. That will be ready for use tomorrow. Pam noticed the city and county both are working hard to clear ditches before the storm hits. They had gotten behind on their usual cleanup, possibly hoping to get lucky and save a few bucks. Also, Archie's talking to folks at the school district and the regional transportation district about using their buses to carry folks inland."

"Shades of Hurricane Rita," Ed said. "OK, what's happening in sports?"

AUGUST 10, 5:03 P.M.

JP made sure he was out of the office a little early in hopes of beating the rush to Oldport Supply Store, but he found the store packed. He balked at the entrance, but forged ahead. It's not likely to get any better, he mumbled to himself.

"Hey, JP," he heard above the din. "Is that right? Yeah, JP!"

He finally saw the store manager, Rafael Ventura, weaving through the crush.

"Glad to see you're making preparations," he said. "I'd been wanting to call and thank you for the story. It seems people have taken the warnings to heart and are not putting things off to the last minute."

"Well, you're welcome, Rafael, but I wasn't just trying to drum up business for you."

"That's my point. Sure, it's business for us, but I'm saying your information will probably play a role in saving a few homes and maybe someone's life, just because it clearly stated what needed to be done.

"In that case, thank you very much; I can only hope you're right, if the storm hits here."

"True. If it doesn't, then folks will be mad at both of us. If that happens, and I'm serious, then you should do a story about how preparations were not a waste and I'll give you some advice on how they can store things so they'll last several years."

"I'll remember that, Rafael, but I'd better enter the fray here because it's surely not about to lighten up anytime soon."

AUGUST 10, 5:48 P.M.

"Mom, I'm ... Mom?"

"Don't you be gawking at me like that, child. Well, Lydia, what do you think?

"Wow, Mom, you look wonderful. Why are you dressed up? Where are you going?"

"Nowhere. I've been; I'm back. I've been out most of the day."

Lydia could restrain herself no longer, leaping across the room to give Maxine a robust hug.

"I am so proud of you. Where did you go? What did you do? Did you have fun getting out? Didn't I tell you it would be fun?"

Maxine motioned her bubbling daughter to a living room chair and sat across from her.

"I did what I told you I would do. You probably don't even remember because you've learned to not listen to, certainly to not believe, any promises from me. I applied for a cleaning job at Cascades."

"Wow. Uh, no, no, I remember you saying that, but ... I just ... I don't know what to say."

"You could start with, 'Congratulations.'"

"What? You mean they hired you just like that? I mean, of course they hired you."

Maxine was in full-tilt laughter. Why did it take me so long, she thought, to see my darling child this pleased with me again?

"I was shocked, too, because I haven't worked in years, but I think they're having a hard time getting enough help. I almost danced all the way home."

"Wait, you mean you walked? It's probably two miles. It's hot and humid."

"Believe me, child, those excuses filled my head, but two miles ain't all that far. I left plenty of time, went easy and ... what are we fussin' over fine points about? Lydia, I got me a job!"

"When do you start?"

"First, she said day after tomorrow because I told her I needed a day to get some shoes and a few things. Then she said, wait until this hurricane makes landfall 'cause it was no point starting a new person in the middle of madness. So, when will that happen?"

"That's something I wanted to talk about, Mom."

While preparing and eating dinner, mother and daughter discussed a shopping trip, whether their house was safe in a hurricane, where else they could stay and what they could do with added income.

Through the conversation, Lydia came to the awareness she and her mother fit into the category of people at risk during the storm. Their home was safe from a tidal surge, but it was in a low-lying area subject to flooding in heavy rains. They had nothing to board up windows and the roof looked as if it might cave in if a pelican dive-bombed into it.

"Mom, I don't feel safe here in case of a major storm. What about you?"

"I wouldn't know what else to do, honey. No, that's not right. I know what I'll do. I'll trust my smart, loving daughter. I really don't know about these things, Lydia. You tell me what we should do and I'll do it. Might as well get used to taking orders."

AUGUST 10, 6:51 P.M.

With lumber and other supplies in the back of his little yellow pickup, JP backed up his driveway, cutting into the yard before hitting his landlords' car.

JP had more than once bragged about his landlords. They only expected him to pay rent, respect the property and to keep them informed of any work it needed, which they always promptly addressed. The reporter also knew he got a good deal with rent that was less expensive than a decent apartment.

Of course, the admiration was a two-way street. They were particular about who rented the house because they wanted it protected. In fact, they never advertised the property but found their first renter, JP, through the recommendation of their good friend, Pat Baird.

Wes and Donna Simpson bought the house as newlyweds and raised their only child there. When they lost her in a traffic accident at college 26 years later, they could not bear to stay any longer and moved across town.

As JP parked his truck, Wes was on a ladder by a front window, nailing down a trim board he found to be loose. He had already set up saw horses, run extension cords for the power tools and taken measurements.

"That's great timing. I didn't really expect you to get the shopping done that quickly. Was the supply store not busy?"

"Oh, it was busy, but I left work a little early and, more than anything, I was prepared to get what I needed and get out. I appreciate your advice and especially your help in securing the house."

"Hey, we're in this together. Have you decided if you're staying here or not?"

"Unless something happens to change my mind, I'm staying here. Do you still believe it's safe?"

"Emphasis on belief. I mean, we've never seen a storm like what's out there now. What's the latest?"

"Still a Cat 5 and still headed this way. You've lived here all your life; do storms ever go where they're predicted?"

"We've always tracked everything that threatened the Gulf and I used to say they didn't," Wes said. "Things have changed the last several years as forecasters have gotten much better at factoring in all the elements that affect a storm's track and how they influence each other. They're still not perfect, mind you, but you don't often see storms go way off line anymore."

"If that's so, then we may find out how sturdy this old house is. Not only is Clarice predicted to hold her strength over the warm waters of the Gulf of Mexico, but she has her eye on Oldport."

With Wes guiding the work, the two threw themselves into protecting the house. The elder team member applied his earlier measurements to the plywood, deftly wielding his circular saw. JP was in charge of screwing them into the wall.

Donna Simpson arrived as the two men worked on the final board. After making sure Bubba was put away, she carried in a home-cooked meal, drawing on her memory to find light switches now that the house was darkened by plywood covering the windows.

She filled the last few minutes by surveying the property and picking up a few things that could easily blow away.

"I put your lawn chairs and other items in the den," Donna said to JP as the three of them moved inside for dinner. "Do you have a lantern or two to provide light once the electricity is knocked out?"

"Wait, JP, but you do know to turn off the electricity before the storm hits."

"Yes to both. I have two kerosene lamps, extra fuel, matches, flashlights and plenty of batteries. I also have a good supply of no-need-to-heat foods, a camp stove so I can cook some, gallons of bottled water and even a restocked first-aid kit."

"Sounds like you're ready. How do you guys feel about some of my famous chicken?"

"This is great," JP said. "I'd almost forgotten fried chicken came from anywhere but a store."

AUGUST 11, 1:00 A.M.

Worn out from all the physical activity, JP enjoyed one of his best sleeps in weeks. While he and most of Oldport dozed, news passed through the networks that Hurricane Clarice slipped to a strong Category 3 storm with 130-mph winds.

Forecasters stressed it appeared to be only a cyclical decline in strength and that it would likely build again.

AUGUST 11, 8:02 A.M.

Jeremiah Forge sat in his office at the Cascades fidgeting with his stylish Visconti Rembrandt pen, reading for the third time Archie Hanning's story about electric company preparations for the hurricane.

He had skimmed over the stories about the newcomers and Hurricane Michael, barely glanced at the animal shelter and party articles, and all but dismissed the wire story about the hurricane in favor of later information from The Weather Channel and online.

In fact, he kept The Weather Channel playing in his office in hopes of catching an image of the Cascades in the background. What can I do to get those cameras out front?

But his mind kept coming back to the electric company story. If a storm can cause them that much trouble, how would it affect work on his condominiums?

Finally, project manager Davis Wiley appeared for their scheduled 8 a.m. meeting and pulled the door shut behind him.

"I've been on pins and needles," Forge said, almost whispering even though it was not necessary. "How did your dinner go with the building inspector last night?"

"Not as well as I hoped. He seems to be struggling with a sense of duty or something."

"Yeah, I bet that something is whether or not he can milk more money out of us."

"We've not hit our allotted amount yet," Wiley said after a deliberative pause. "Is it time to up the ante?"

"I've been nursing an idea. We should increase the bribe, but in doing so we must also make him more of a player in this. Right now, he's risking nothing that anyone can prove. Listen to this."

Wiley nodded his head when Forge finished, and went to work to set things up.

AUGUST 11, 1:22 P.M.

"If you're leaving the coast to avoid confronting Hurricane Clarice, you'll drive by many who are staying, some because they have no other option," JP read out loud.

Lydia sat uneasily in the uncomfortable chair JP kept by his desk while her mentor did his final read-through of the biggest story of her career.

That's the very thought that crossed her mind. This could be a breakthrough for her; it could indeed provide the proof she was capable of handling a fulltime reporter job. She tried to force the thoughts from her mind as she watched JP's screen.

"How do you know this fellow's not worried about the hurricane?" JP asked.

"What? Where?"

"Right here, you write, 'Even while the city mobilizes for Clarice, Walter is not worried.' How do you know Walter's not worried?"

"Oh, he told me. So, I should write, 'Walter says he is not worried.' Right?"

"Yep, you knew that. It's one of those little things we keep drilling on as reporters." JP knew as he made the statement that she would take note he included her as a reporter. He did so willingly because he knew how hard she had worked at the craft and, more importantly, because he was confident she could do the job.

Rather than simply taking note, Lydia pursued the topic.

"Not to put you over any barrel or anything, and knowing you don't do any hiring ... well, I'd like your opinion," she finally said. "Do you think I can make it as a reporter?"

JP turned away from the screen and locked eyes with the young woman. He spoke in a soft voice to keep the conversation private.

"I know you can. There is not a doubt remaining within me. This story answers my final concern."

"You were concerned?" she asked.

He laughed softly and dropped his voice another notch.

"Yes, but only because you had not been able to show off your range. I know writing does not come easily for you, but I've seen you work at it and I've seen improvement. You seek the advice of others and you heed it. Each story you've done has shown improvement."

"But you did not know if I could do anything but features?"

"Exactly. Until now. You did some real work digging out the angles to this story, you've revealed some questions and concerns for our area, you've provided answers where they're available and you've given readers the resources they need to learn more and to act."

Lydia stared, soaking in the words she had hoped to hear.

"Yes, I think you have what it takes to make a reporter and, yes, I'd be the first in line to offer you a reference, but now I'm taking this story in to the boss and recommending it for tomorrow's front page."

AUGUST 11, 2:08 P.M.

"Newsroom, this is Hanning," said Archie, the city reporter, as he automatically hovered over a piece of paper with his pen. "I'm fine, mayor, how are you?"

Archie abandoned pen and paper in favor of the keyboard to take notes from Mayor Jeanne Goodrum, a former motel owner who jumped into city politics after selling the business to her son.

"OK, mayor, can't say I've not been expecting this. To recap, the city is ordering evacuation of all areas of town below 25 feet in elevation and encouraging early evacuation of all residents who have concern about riding out the storm. Last point is those who decide to ignore the order cannot expect to have emergency services available to them during the height of the storm."

He typed some more as she gave him an obviously prepared statement.

"Sure thing, mayor. We'll get this onto the Web site promptly and into print for the morning paper.

AUGUST 11, 4:50 P.M.

Davis Wiley settled in at a secluded corner table, ordered a sampler tray of appetizers and a light beer, and watched the door for Fred Franklin, signaling to him when the city inspector walked in.

The two men worked uncomfortably through their first couple of drinks, trying to make small talk about baseball playoff prospects, the upcoming college football season and vacation plans. When conversation turned to the weather, Wiley took the opportunity to talk business.

"You're a local, right?"

"Been in Oldport County all my life," Franklin said.

"Are you concerned about this hurricane?"

"Nah. I mean, I know they can be serious, but it's nothing like what you hear from the media and the forecasters and others who stir the pot to keep people tuning in and buying papers and generally going crazy."

Wiley ordered the inspector a fourth drink even though the effects of the alcohol were already visible. Nothing better than a mark who's a cheap drunk, he thought.

"I understand the media wanting eyes and ears and I guess I understand hurricane forecasters stoking their self-worth," Wiley asked, "but what's in it for the politicians?"

"Same as their reasons for everything," Franklin said, grabbing another buffalo wing. "One, money; two, votes."

"How does that work?"

"The money comes through creating a need. There's a potential for a catastrophe of some kind, so they will make the case for more money in order to prepare for the threat. That money can come locally because they'll use the perceived threat as a justifiable reason for raising more taxes or it will come from federal grants. The Feds are more than happy to pass around money to, quote, combat terrorism, and to show they've done all that's possible to protect against another Katrina."

"So, you think the government was responsible for the Katrina problems?"

"No way, man. Stuff happens, you know? But they've created this feeling they're taking care of everyone's needs, so, yeah, they figure it's easier to pass responsibility back and forth across the aisle than to be honest with people."

"OK, I think that makes sense, but how do grants and increased taxes benefit the politicians personally?"

"Are you serious? They're on the take. OK, not everyone but enough. They're awarded money to, say, buy heavy equipment to keep drainage ditches clean. They get to decide where they buy the equipment, what to buy, where they buy the diesel, insurance for it all ... and so on. Don't you think even a few thousand bucks might influence the awarding of a contract?"

"I'm new at this; guess I didn't realize how common it was."

"Man, what you and I've got going on is small potatoes," Franklin said. Wiley kept quiet, feeling his prey was about to spring the trap. "You've bought me a couple of meals and 'accidently' left several hundred dollars in my hands and I've been distracted while reviewing paperwork. Small potatoes compared to the big guys."

The two sat quietly for a minute. Once Wiley was certain nobody was within earshot, he tossed his new lure onto the water.

"Are you ready for big potatoes?"

Franklin just stared, but his interest was evident.

"Fred, we agree with you this storm is no big deal, but we want to get all we can out of the attention it's generating. I need you to certify the Cascades for use as an emergency shelter during the storm. Can you do that?"

"Sure, but why?"

"Are you asking why you would do it or why we want it?"

"Both, I guess."

"Our pre-opening sales are dragging well behind schedule and have stopped now with the storm. Remember our principle market is people living up north who have the money for a winter haven. They're all home now watching hurricane coverage. If we're taking in refugees, the TV cameras will flock to us. We'll make sure they get a look at the waterfalls and at one of our finished units and other amenities and they'll provide tons of free advertising."

"Brilliant ... and for me?"

Wiley scribbled a figure on a scrap of paper and pushed it across the table.

"How does that sound?"

Franklin returned the paper after adding a figure triple the original offer.

Wiley squirmed, putting on something of a show for the small town crook. Franklin had no way of suspecting the contractor had four times that much at his disposal and was looking at a tidy payday himself.

"OK, but this tops off what was made available to me. And I need the paperwork by 9 o'clock in the morning. I'll have the cash for you then."

"I can do that tonight. I don't mind collecting a little overtime from the city, either. You're picking up the tab, right?"

As Franklin walked away, Wiley signaled the waiter for the check and removed a voice recorder from his pocket. He made sure it was still running and then turned it off.

AUGUST 12, 1:00 A.M.

Doreen Strong started brewing another large batch of coffee as she rolled into the third hour of her night shift at the Coastal Cup Cafe.

Business was good for this time of the morning and tips were better than average. The journalists converging for the hurricane were good tippers and even the locals seemed more appreciative of Doreen's attention.

She fell back on 14 years of experience to keep things moving smoothly, neatly topping off one customer's cup while taking another's order. I'm a waitressing machine, she liked to think during such shifts. However, she and most of the customers paused and focused on the television as the latest hurricane report came in.

"Hurricane Clarice continues its single-minded advance toward the continent," said the anchor as she entered a new hour of broadcasting. Her voice was low and controlled, her countenance appropriately serious for the reporting of such a devastating story.

"Oh, man, she's loving this," sang out one of the grill's regulars.

"This is what they live for, dude," chimed in another, offering a high-five that was never seen by the first.

"The latest measurements from the National Hurricane Center show the storm is again at Category 5 with 165-mph sustained winds. Clarice's projected track is holding steady, as you see on the map here, but its speed has declined slightly, moving now at 8 mph. That slower pace helps the storm maintain its strength and I wouldn't be surprised if it grows even stronger.

"This is not what folks want to hear right now on the Gulf Coast. Let's check in with Frank Woffard in the town of Oldport for the latest there ... Frank?"

"Things get pretty quiet in Oldport this time of morning, Lisa, but locals tell me it's much busier than usual ..."

"Hey, I'm the one who told him that," Doreen yelled, drawing applause from customers beginning to return to their food. "I served him a chicken fried steak. He said it was the first he's ever had and I reckon he'll go home looking for one back there."

"They don't know how to do it there," someone called out.

"Where's he from?"

"Doesn't matter!"

By then, Doreen was again engrossed in juggling her numerous customers, more concerned about the present than worrying about possible storms.

AUGUST 12, 8:33 A.M.

The various department heads gathered in the main meeting room next to the publisher's office at the Odds and Ends.

"I don't have updated sales figures," the advertising manager started saying while people were settling in, but Martin Freer stopped him.

"We're dispensing with the ordinary this week," the publisher said, "to better focus on making sure we're prepared for this storm. Margaret, what's the latest?"

"I asked Ed to round that up," said Margaret Edmonds. She had been the paper's editor for several years but was more an administrator now, having recently hired Ed Roberts as managing editor. "Here he comes. Ed, you're up."

"Hope I didn't keep y'all waiting. OK, Hurricane Clarice is currently at a Cat 5 with 165-mph winds. Projections are for landfall in 48 hours or less. The forecasted path still has it zeroed in on our area."

"This is the 12th," said the circulation director, bouncing a pencil on the calendar opened before him, "so we're looking at trying to throw papers on the 14th during a hurricane."

"That is the first topic," the publisher said. "Ed, would you mind sitting in with us? I know we take pride in publishing through everything, but do we need to do so during a historic storm just to say we did?"

"We could have an extra early press run tomorrow and get the papers delivered by midnight or so," suggested the press foreman.

"There would already be severe weather here by then, given that the storm goes as predicted, worse if it speeds up," Ed said.

"And my carriers – the ones who haven't left town – would be out in that weather," said the circulation director. "Not only that, but people are already leaving town; how many readers will still be here? And how many of those are going out into tropical storm winds at midnight to pick up a paper before it blows away?"

"Are there any negatives to not publishing?" Freer asked.

"Lost revenue," said the advertising manager. "We cannot bill what we do not print."

"I don't see it being an issue with subscribers, unless Clarice totally turns away from us."

"I have a suggestion," Margaret pitched in. "I've actually given it a lot of thought.

"First, we announce our plans in tomorrow's edition, PI above the fold, so everyone knows what to expect. We do not print tomorrow night. In addition to what's been mentioned already, we will have little of news value that they won't already know.

"Whether the storm hits us or not, we'll tell our employees to get back here as soon as they can, realizing many of them will have issues to deal with at home or will be out of town. Our reporters and photographers will gather information on their way in.

"We'll put together whatever we can whenever we can and get it out to whomever we can. I'm moving well outside my territory here, but I suggest we don't even sell that edition. We'll put stacks on store counters, block open the doors to the paper boxes, hand out in the neighborhoods, whatever works. Definitely, put out plenty at shelters, the hospital, fire stations, etc.

"Then, we try to get back to normal for the day after the storm, if we're lucky."

"I like it," Freer said. "It's simple, gives incredible flexibility and we come out the good guys. Any problems with it? Any other thoughts?"

"All of this, any plan, assumes we have electricity," the ad manager said. "Indeed, it's assuming we have a building."

"We do have backup physical plant possibilities," said the press foreman. "I've already touched base with three other papers down the coast. Every one of us has volunteered resources to any who needs it. It's not easy, but it can be done."

"Again, that's why we say 'whenever,'" Margaret said. "We should add 'however.'"

"Does everyone grasp the concept?" Freer asked. "Put together plans for your department, integrate with one another where needed and understand you have considerable latitude to deal with this. One other thing ..."

Freer paused and looked around the table to make sure he had everyone's attention.

"As important as the Oldport Odds and Ends is to this county and to us, I do not want anyone to put the paper or a journalistic calling above his or her own safety. Promise me you will communicate to your people we will work with whatever they feel a need to do to protect their families and homes and then with whatever a recovery phase requires of them."

The publisher continued looking from one head to another until they all nodded.

"Finally, please understand this includes each of you. You and your families are more important than anything you're doing here."

As everyone started out, Ed motioned for Margaret to hang back.

"I like your plan. It gives us the ability to get something out quickly, if we can, instead of waiting for the TV guys to beat it to death. Did you read Lydia's piece this morning?"

"Did she really do that herself or did Weiscarver write it? It was a nice job."

"Stanley swears she did it and JP merely asked questions and edited. Both say there's a natural reporter inside her, that she merely needs confidence and guidance. He wants to use her as a full-time writer at least during the recovery stretch post-Clarice, give her a good look. It will mean bumping up her pay a bit, but we have room in the budget and we can structure it as a condition of continued reassignment, just in case she doesn't work out."

"By all means. We don't often find homegrown talent that wants to stay home. She showed insight to the community I've never seen on these pages."

AUGUST 12, 8:52 A.M.

Davis Wiley tapped twice on the office door as he walked in, knowing right where he would find Jeremiah Forge – staring at the television.

"Cheer up, Mr. Forge. Here's a little something to help you roll this nasty ol' hurricane into an economic boon." Wiley pulled from a legal size envelope a form entitled City of Oldport Special Use Permit.

"So, we're good to go. What did it end up costing us?"

"No worries; the money you gave me proved to be enough. Also in the envelope is a recorder. I played it and you can hear everything perfectly."

"I hope nobody has to hear it, but it's good to have in case Mr. Franklin develops a conscience along with a bad memory. When can I announce our big-hearted plan?"

"Any time, I guess. He did have some stipulations on there you'll want to look at," Wiley said, pointing to a paragraph on Page 2.

Forge read through it quickly.

The two ran through plans to get the condo ready for refugees.

"My men will remove or lock away equipment such as table saws and hand tools. In fact, they're at work doing that right now. As they run out of things to do, I'm cutting them loose; a lot of them are leaving town or want to work on their houses. Most will be gone today, the rest in the morning."

"What about you?" Forge asked.

"I'm headed home in the morning. It's about a seven-hour drive and I've not been home in a month, but I'll get back here as soon as everything blows over. Are you planning to sit here and watch over your 25-story baby?"

"Possibly, but I have some business in New York and may head on up there. You've got my cell numbers; we'll touch base after this thing passes." Forge was verbally pushing Wiley toward the door, anxious to put out the word about his plan and draw some prime media attention.

"One more thing," the project manager said. "Do you have a plan to manage all these people?"

"Certainly. You know a full security team has been in place for months. They're all required by contract to be available during emergency situations and will be the backbone of Operation Good Samaritan – I'm still trying to decide whether to go with that label. A good number of our housekeeping crew has been working prepping the units. Our maintenance people already on staff will assist them in setting up for the masses. I cannot force them to stay through the storm, but there's a bonus in it for them, plus they get to take advantage of our 'hurricane-proof' structure. So, yes, we're pretty well prepared."

"Please don't call it hurricane-proof, Mr. Forge. There's no such thing, really, but there is such a thing as karma."

AUGUST 12, 9:24 A.M.

It took Lydia Murray a little longer than usual to get settled in to work because a string of co-workers appeared to congratulate her for her front page story about those who are least prepared for a storm.

Just as she got into a flow keying a wedding story into the computer, the phone rang.

"Lifestyles; this is Lydia."

"Ms. Murray, my name is Jeremiah Forge and I'm general manager of Oldport Cascades Condominiums."

Forge paused slightly, possibly to allow Lydia to bask in the glow of his telephone presence. Her thoughts raced to her mother and unpleasant scenarios came to mind concerning what her mother said about winning a job so easily. However, Forge continued before she could formulate a question.

"I read your wonderful story this morning about the homeless and the poor who are put in greater jeopardy during a hurricane. As you probably know from the wonderful story JP Weiscarver did recently, we're planning to open the Cascades in a few months. That means the exterior of the building is complete, but most of the inside rooms remain in various stages of construction and finishing."

This time, when he paused, Lydia tossed in a comment about being familiar with the condos and JP's story.

"Well, Ms. Murray, we at the Cascades see ourselves in a rather unique position with the timing of Hurricane Clarice and the status of our construction. We approached city building inspector Fred Franklin, who's been monitoring our progress, about the prospect of providing shelter at the Cascades. Just this morning, I was handed a special use permit from the city and we are prepared to open part of Oldport's home of the future for those who need a safe place to stay during the hurricane."

By the time Forge finished his obviously scripted piece, Lydia had recovered and started asking questions.

"Pat," she said as she hung up, "I just got the strangest call about the hurricane. I think I need to talk to JP."

"Skip over JP, dear, and take it straight to Stanley. He came by while you were on the phone and said he wanted to talk to you."

"Oh, my, I bet he got complaints about my story."

"Get over there dear and quit worrying. I'm sure it's good news."

Before Lydia made up her mind whether to speak first to JP, she saw her mentor inside the glass-walled office of the city editor. As she approached Stanley's office, Andrea Munoz made eye contact and said, "I'm proud of you, Lydia. That was a great story this morning."

Wow, Lydia thought. Andrea, like her, was principally a typist, though she also doubled as an assistant to Stanley and helped others in the news room. Could it be she harbored a desire to be a reporter and found Lydia's actions heroic? Quickly, the modesty innate to Lydia took over and banished the thought as she acknowledged the compliment with a smile and a thank you. She quickly stepped into the office as Stanley waved her in.

Upon his invitation, she took a seat in a chair where she could see both Stanley behind the mountains of papers on his desk and JP, sprawled out on his favorite spot on the pea green sofa.

"Lydia," Stanley began, "as I told you yesterday, you did a great job on the homeless piece. JP insists I'm dumber than he already thinks I am if I don't give you a good look as a reporter. For once, I agree with him. I kicked it upstairs and both Ed and Margaret checked off on a trial period. If this storm lives up to half of its promise, we'll be able to use extra help."

"What about Mrs. Baird?"

"See, boss, I told you that would be her first concern," JP said, tacking on a big grin.

"Pat will be fine. Through her tenure and respect in this department, she's earned the privilege to recruit help whenever and wherever she needs it and she's not shy about asking."

"Hey, did I ever tell you I've done a couple of wedding write-ups?" JP asked.

"She may come to you or anyone else for help," Stanley continued.

"However, she'll probably have less to do except for a series of cancellation notices. Social life will grind to a temporary halt and then return with a fury, if I read those circles right."

"So, you said 'trial' period. Does that mean I can finish the period and be hired as a full-fledged reporter?"

"Yep," JP couldn't help but interject.

"That's not the way I'd put it," Stanley quickly corrected. "I'd say, unless you decline, you're a full-fledged reporter right now, just temporary. If you do what we both think you will, the worst-case scenario is you'll return to Pat after things settle down in a few weeks and will continue helping out news side until a regular position comes open. Best-case scenario is we convince the bean counters to let us keep you and hire Pat another assistant. The upside to this is we have a place for you either way."

"OK, when do I start?"

"Good. Pat tells me she can cut you loose as soon as you finish typing whatever you're doing right now. When you can, relocate to that empty desk next to Pam and let the receptionist know your new extension."

"I don't mind staying where I am, if that would be easier."

"No, you're part of my team now," Stanley said. "You need to be where you know what others are doing and where you can contribute to the process. Do not be bashful about making comments. You have a longer, closer relationship to this community than most of our staff. I suspect they'll quickly appreciate your input."

"So, what say we visit a few minutes about a story you might work on today?" JP suggested.

"Actually, I have one. Jeremiah Forge just called me to announce the Cascades will serve as a shelter during the storm."

"What?" JP blustered in an overly animated fashion. "My contact contacted you?"

"I suggested he talk to you and he gave me some line about being impressed with my story this morning and thinking it naturally dove-tailed into the Cascades' humanitarian gesture. Basically, he let me know in short order that he's full of it."

"Boss, this is purely a publicity move on his part," JP said. "How much do we cater to him?"

"I know what you mean, but we want to let people know their options. Is it ready for people to occupy?"

"Many of the rooms were complete, others in various stages when Cole and I were there."

"Oh, they won't be staying in the rooms," Lydia said. "He made that quite clear, probably to reassure any investors. They'll treat it like a shelter, allowing folks to put down sleeping bags or mats in the open, common areas."

"Can't say I blame 'em," Stanley said. "Remember what happened to the Dome in New Orleans."

"He did tell me he got a special permit from the city."

"You know, Lydia, that might be worth a phone call," JP said, rubbing his chin. "What was it you heard earlier?"

"I just heard grumbling on the street. You got an e-mail saying we should look into the city inspectors."

"What came of that?" Stanley asked.

"Nothing yet," JP said. "I replied to the e-mail in an effort to learn more and never heard back. Then this storm started brewing. Frankly, I left it on the back burner."

"Forge did drop the name of a Fred Franklin, I believe."

"I know Fred," Stanley said. "Good guy. The top inspector for the city, I believe. Make a call to him about the permit, find out what it's for, tell him we want to assure potential evacuees the building is safe. You're not looking for a boogeyman here, just doing good reporting."

"Looks like our baby girl is gonna kick off her new career with back-to-back PI stories," JP said.

"PI?"

"Oh, it's an archaic term for Page One the boss still uses."

"I'll go you one better," Stanley said. "Lydia, as soon as you confirm with the city, put together a short story for the Web site. Your lead may be the Cascades, but your story will be a roundup of all shelters here and those up north that you mentioned in this morning's story. We'll put it online now so people can start planning. Include a final graf about more information in tomorrow's edition. And, JP, why are you still here? Don't you have your own story to get out by this afternoon?"

AUGUST 12, 1:00 P.M.

Doreen Strong was worn out. Following an incredibly busy night waiting tables at Coastal Cup Cafe, she had worked hard to secure her apartment.

Being on the bottom floor was nice in that she didn't have to climb stairs, but she knew drainage wasn't good in the apartment complex and felt rising water could threaten her home.

She meticulously stacked important papers and electronics on the kitchen counter and anywhere she could get things off the floor. Closet shelves were stuffed with clothing, the most important items at the highest points. She had other items stacked up on the bedroom floor to pile onto the bed.

Doreen didn't have plywood, but she tacked and taped cardboard to the inside of her windows, hopeful for some protection.

As she crawled into bed with her television remote, she caught the latest information when the local station broke in on regular programming. Hurricane Clarice had strengthened, sporting 190-mph winds.

"Wow," she said out loud. "Is there such a thing as Category 6?"

AUGUST 12, 2:15 P.M.

"OK, people," Ed Roberts hollered to get everyone's attention. The entire news staff had gathered in one corner of the newsroom, some sitting and many standing.

"I don't know that we've ever had everyone together without there being food provided. None of us like big meetings, but I felt this was important. You have all heard we will not put together a regular newspaper tomorrow. Our challenge will be what we can get done after the hurricane passes. To that end, Stanley is taking charge of all personnel, including me. Sports, lifestyles, wire, feature ... all beats are out the window and we're all part of one team until things are back to normal. Stanley?"

"Did you want to address personal safety?" the city editor asked.

"Oh, yes. This comes from the top, from Mr. Freer through Margaret and with the whole-hearted endorsement of Stanley and me. Each of you carries the responsibility for your safety and for the safety of your family. We are requiring nobody to stay in town for the hurricane, especially not to get out in the storm or anything.

"We will fully respect your decisions, even if everyone packs up and leaves town, though we do want you back as soon as is safely possible. If you tell Stanley you'll be in town and then change your mind, that's fine. Let him know if you can, but then do what you need to do. Is that clear? Any questions?"

After a moment's silence, Stanley took over.

"OK, I'm going to run through our plans here. Even if you're leaving town, I want you to know what's going on; it will help you jump back in when you return. We do know our Web chiefs Bobby and Frieda are leaving town. Bobby's folks are putting them up at their home some 200 miles inland. They have great Internet access and that will be our command center of sorts.

"They set up what I guess you call a cloud where everyone can upload and download information. As soon as we finish here, Andrea's sending the information to each of your company e-mail accounts. They suggest you forward it to any personal accounts you have. There's also a concise information form telling us where you expect to be, how you can be contacted, etc. Include everything and note the information you do not mind sharing with the staff because it will be accessible to each of you. Keep in mind we have no idea just what communication we will have during the storm and possibly for quite a few days after. One little piece of advice, telephones require less bandwidth for text messages than for calls, so you might get them through when a voice message will not.

"OK, how will this work? We will explain in our paper edition in the morning that we will begin ongoing updates online as much as we can. Our editors will monitor this cloud thing from different locations and compile reports for Bobby and Frieda to upload to our Web site and to sites such as Facebook and Twitter as appropriate.

"Clarice is expected to make landfall sometime from tomorrow night to the next morning. We're not publishing a paper then because it's just impractical. We will throw together a paper with photos and hurricane news as soon as we can after the storm, even if we have to print elsewhere. The situation will dictate when we publish and how we'll distribute it. We realize our local residents may be unable to access the online information.

"Moving along, if you're able to access the cloud, you will see what's coming in. If you can contribute anything, even just a tidbit to illustrate someone else's point, upload it. This will be a monster collaborative effort, I suspect. Feel free to include any information, anything at all.

"Finally, whether you're staying or traveling, keep safe. Oh, one other thing. For those of you leaving, your packet includes a phone number you can call with information about our status, whether it's safe for you to start back, etc. The number is to my brother's house in Oregon. I'll get information to him, even if it's by ham radio. Calling him will be easier than trying to get through to someone here. If he doesn't answer, hang on for the message; he will keep it updated.

"We still need to tie up tomorrow morning's paper. I know Archie has the evacuation order; Jennifer has an interview with some Weather Channel superstar; Cole and Bob have pix of preparations at the animal shelter, county road and bridge, some surfside businesses and more; and JP has a survey of the plans of gas stations and grocery stores.

"I'm sure there are others, I hope there are others. See me individually after the meeting. We've tied up everyone else long enough. Y'all do be safe out there; we need you."

AUGUST 12, 8:28 P.M.

"Lydia, I am so proud of you," Maxine Murray said again. "I just can't get over them making you a real reporter."

"Mom, for the last time, it's temporary."

"Hush, child, I know good and well what all that means. You ain't got no formal education and they're just gonna make sure you know your stuff before they give you the really big bucks."

"Oh, so that's what it means," Lydia said, stifling a laugh. "Let me tell you this, no reporter in Oldport is making big bucks."

"Well, you sure ain't no cleaning lady at the new condo, either."

"Oh, Mom, but that's such a big step for you and who knows what will come next? Speaking of the Cascades, there's something I want to talk about now that we've got the house as Clarice-proofed as we can."

"'Clarice-proofed,' you sound just like a reporter," Maxine said as she set plates on the table.

Lydia waited until they were settled for their late dinner.

"Well, I told you about Mr. Forge calling and that they are opening the Cascades tomorrow as a shelter. I'd like to go there for the storm."

"But, child, after we did all the work on this place? This house has been here at least 60 years and never been blown away."

"The work we did was mainly to protect the house and the stuff as much as we can. No house in this town has ever seen a storm like Hurricane Clarice. Neither is a great argument. My main reason for going, however, is that I believe I can write a good story about the people who stay there."

Lydia watched her mother process the information for several seconds.

"Mom, you say you're excited for me and want me to do well. Don't you see? The big shot is opening his fancy new condo to the homeless and others who need a safe place to stay because of a story I wrote. People are getting help because of a story I wrote. I want to be there to see it through. I want to put names and faces on the people who benefit from this generosity, to let others know these are not animals but real people facing real problems."

When Maxine looked up, Lydia saw a huge grin on her face.

"Wow, I hadn't really thought of it like that. So, if I go with you, Miss Lois Lane, will I get to see how you work?"

AUGUST 12, 8:37 P.M.

"Staying here is the best thing for me, Momma. Not only would I hate myself for missing out on what might be the story of my life, but traveling the highways would be maddening. It's not just Oldport abandoning the coast, but people from all around are flooding the roadways."

As soon as he made the last statement to his mother, JP knew it was a mistake.

"OK, Momma, not everyone is leaving, it's not like I'm left alone to defend the city against Hurricane Clarice. And I'm being smart about it."

Another mistake, he thought. He mentioned being alone.

"Actually, I've decided while talking with you to call Jennifer and see if she'd like to weather the storm here. Her apartment doesn't seem all that safe and she has no family around either. Yeah, we'll see. She's a really nice girl, Momma, and I enjoy tremendously working with her and hanging out with her, but I haven't worked through all the demons yet from my last girlfriend.

"Yes, ma'am, I know. Besides, I don't really want to mess up a good work partner by dating her. Yes, I'm in church regularly. You should know there's a pair of widowed sisters there who, I've decided, are continually trying to deduce the person to whom I should be matched. Yes, I will indeed thank them for you the next time they get me cornered.

"OK, you have those phone numbers I e-mailed you, but promise me you won't start calling them for at least 24 hours after landfall. The likelihood is that I will weather the storm just fine but our power and communication infrastructure will not. Just as soon as the skies clear, I will try to get a message to you, even if it's just a text message saying I'm OK. Are you OK with everything? I mean, as OK as you can be?

"Yes, ma'am, I will. And I'll call Jennifer as soon as we hang up. I might give you a call again tomorrow, but don't worry if you don't hear from me until after the storm. I love you, too, Momma. Daddy, too."

JP released a heavy sigh as he slipped the phone into his shirt pocket and then reached down to scratch Bubba's back.

"She's worried, Bubba, but she's just being a mother. There's no way I can convince her we're taking adequate precautions. We'll be just fine. We will, won't we?"

The ferret gave JP one of its deep stares, its big, black eyes repeating the question.

"Yeah, yeah, we will. Oh, you're right, I promised to call Jennifer right away. She's not going to read anything strange into this, is she? No, I won't let things get uncomfortable. Why are you looking at me like that? I know you like her, especially compared to Sherry, but working with her makes things a little problematic along that line. Besides, it's highly possible any attraction I feel is more respect for the work she does than, uh ..."

As he paused, the ferret cocked his head.

"OK, Bubba, I'm calling her. Pushy, nosy ferret"

As JP dialed the phone, Bubba pushed his snout behind his owner's back.

"Hey, Jen, how's the preparation coming? Yeah, me too, I almost wish there was more to do. I feel like I'm sitting in a cave with all the windows boarded up. My front door is still open just so it feels like a cave rather than a tomb.

"You're right, bad timing for such a comment. I talked with my mother and kept sticking my foot in my mouth with comments like that. It seemed every time I tried to make an argument I was doing the right thing staying here and that I would be safe, she was able to turn it around on me.

"No, she wouldn't demand that I leave; she doesn't operate that way. You're right; I don't operate that way, either.

"Listen, I was telling her about what everyone was doing and, the more I thought about it, the less I liked that apartment of yours as a hurricane refuge. What do you think about staying over here during the storm, supposing Clarice stays the course? Well, think it over and you can decide tomorrow."

AUGUST 13, 1:00 A.M.

"Moose" MacDuff moved his large frame quietly around the house to not wake his family. A supervising lineman for the Oldport Regional Electric Cooperative, he had put in a long day making preparations.

Unlike most people, he was not getting ready for the storm to hit but for the days after it passes. While some held out hope they would not be affected by the storm, he knew his crew would be in the heart of the reconstruction effort wherever it hit, as they have done in many areas in the past. He could only pray it would lose strength before coming ashore.

With that thought in mind, he turned on the television for the regular update from the National Hurricane Center.

"For the first time in 48 hours, Hurricane Clarice has dropped to a Category 4, with wind speeds of 150 mph," chirped the overnight anchor, before giving out information on evacuation orders.

"Good," Moose mumbled as he clicked off the set. "Let's see if Mother Nature can turn it down a few more notches."

AUGUST 13, 7:08 A.M.

Jeremiah Forge stopped as he approached the Cascades and took in the magnificent view.

"You are my piece de resistance, my legacy, the signature to my life's work," he muttered. "Now, if we can milk some good publicity from this storm and then put it behind us, we should see a nice bump in sales to make for a profitable grand opening in November."

Any residual lift in spirits from admiring his work had wafted away in the early morning humidity before Forge reached the front door. He immediately spotted Davis Wiley, directing a couple of his men moving a large wet saw.

"You guys about through?" Forge growled.

"We've put the more cumbersome tools into a few of the sales offices since they've not been finished out. As for smaller tools, they're mostly in the exercise room on the second floor. We have various supplies – flooring tiles, trim, lumber, all kinds of things – in rooms here and there."

"All secured?"

"Everything's locked up; we shouldn't have your guests stumbling across anything valuable or dangerous."

"Once you're through, go ahead and lock down the resident and guest elevators. Double-check the employee elevator and make sure it's working by scan card only. Secure the stairway doors so my guests, as you call them, won't wander upstairs. I'll instruct the crew staying here to use just that one elevator."

"You're the boss. Tell them that if they have to use the stairs, they can come down, just won't be able to go up."

"What's he doing here?" Forge asked, eying the front door and the city building inspector.

"Oh, Franklin called last night and said he would drop off a few fire extinguishers and first-aid kits. I guess he figured it would look good on his paperwork."

While Wiley took care of Franklin, Forge walked around the ground floor of the Cascades, imagining a couple hundred storm refugees and, more importantly, film crews.

"Sandra!" he bellowed, getting the attention of his property manager, Sandra Lightley, who was hanging signs to direct refugees to rest rooms.

"Good morning, Mr. Forge. How are you?" she asked, knowing he would ignore the question. Her goal was to one day get a civil response from him.

"You got plenty of help lined up for this?"

"Yes, sir. Actually, a good percentage of the cleaning and grounds keeping crews responded to my request. I think most of them feel more secure here than in their homes. Are you sure you won't stay? I suspect we'll make it a fun experience."

"Part of me really wants to be here, to be honest, but I have commitments in New York. That's what I wanted to talk to you about. I'll be leaving by mid-morning, probably before many arrive. Once there is a good crowd here, if you've not been visited by a television crew, call those numbers I gave you and 'suggest' they drop by. When they do, invite the network cameras to ride with you to the ninth floor and offer them a bird's-eye view of the lobby. They won't be able to resist that image."

"Good idea. I'll go ahead and open up a unit to make it easier."

"No, let them see our security at work. That impresses people. Remember, the reason we're taking in these street people is to get some good public relations exposure."

"Of course, how could I forget?"

He stared through her a second and grunted something. She was young, he thought. She'll learn.

Holding her smile throughout his stare, Sandra decided she never would see anything pleasant from him. She again promised herself she would not become so greedy that she would be tempted to profit from those who needed help.

AUGUST 13, 9:09 A.M.

"It's all rather surreal, Bubba," JP said to the ferret as they headed to the beach in his little yellow pickup.

There were relatively few people on the streets. Like him, many people were off work either so they could evacuate or to be ready to respond after the storm hits. He did find long lines at a couple of gas stations, people topping off their tanks to either get out of town or to be prepared to wait out storm recovery.

Grocery stores appeared busy, too, though JP didn't know what they had left to sell. Seeing the crowds, he was glad he had taken care of his preparations early.

JP parked on a nearly empty lot on the edge of the beach and wandered toward the water. The tide was already higher than he had ever seen and waves broke more violently.

His eye then caught a gliding figure on the waves.

Of course, JP thought as he smiled at the image. "Look, Bubba, can you see the surfer? Yeah, there are some people enjoying the approaching storm."

Instead of the surfer slipping off the board as the waves eased and heading back out into the gulf, he rode almost all of the way to the shore, milking every last foot out of the ride. When he hopped off and headed toward the parking lot, JP recognized him as Manny Wellborn, a high school student who had already developed quite a name within the global surfing community.

The boy also noticed him and angled his way.

"Hey, Mr. Weiscarver, you about ready to take up my offer to go into the water?"

"I'm not sure these are learner waves today, Manny. I was surprised to see a surfer in a hurricane, but I wasn't surprised when it was you. Will nobody else go out on a day like today?"

"Oh, there are quite a few out there, you just can't see them for the waves. There's a bit of a lull now and they're just waiting for it to build up again. I decided it was a good time to get hydrated and eat a little something. Who's this?"

"This is Bubba. Bubba, meet Manny, a great surfer and a pretty dang good basketball player and student. Bubba's owner was killed last year and he adopted me. We've been best buds ever since. Maybe I'm letting my age show here, but I'm wondering, how do your parents feel about you surfing in a hurricane?"

"I'm not real sure, but if you stick around a while, you can ask my dad; I suspect he'll be coming in soon to get something to eat."

With a laugh, he said his goodbyes and headed toward his car.

"Hey, Manny, how much longer will you be surfing?" JP called after him.

"Dude, these are the best conditions here in my lifetime," the surfer yelled back. "I'm here until it washes me home. It's just gonna get better and better."

JP continued to meander down the beach until Bubba started wiggling. As if coming out of a daze, the reporter started back toward his pickup.

"I feel like I should be doing something," he said to the ferret, his voice serving to settle Bubba a bit. "It feels that, if I did the right thing, I could turn that hurricane around. I wonder if everyone else is as poor at waiting as I am. Tell you what, Bubba, let's stop by your old place on the way home and check in on George Saunders."

AUGUST 13, 10:48 A.M.

There was considerable activity at the Hodge Mansion on Alligator Way as JP parked in the large circle drive, enough to cause him to wonder what was going on, but he began to recognize faces and it all made sense.

Midge Moore was the first to notice JP and she stopped in her tracks and headed out to hug him.

"JP, my dear, I was just telling Bob earlier how delightful it would be to run into you while we were in Oldport. Oh! Irma's ferret! Bubba, right? Hello, Bubba. You look great; I think life with JP agrees with you."

JP eventually managed to squeeze in a proper greeting as the two made their way to the front door, where Michael Hodge was carrying in what he said was the last load. Inside, George Saunders was giving directions on where things should go. He, too, brightened at the sight of the young reporter.

"Dad gum, it, son, did it take a hurricane to bring you back around for a visit? Good to see you. You wanna shot?"

JP found himself awash in a mixture of memories.

The first time he visited the Hodge Mansion, it was doing research for a story about the recently deceased Irma Hodge, whose father built the mansion while developing the highly successful Yardarm Shipping Supply Company.

JP's first greeter then was Bubba, who was fleeing Juan Mendoza of the county's animal control department, which had responded to take possession of the dead woman's six dogs, twenty cats, fourteen birds, hundreds of fish and one ferret.

It was on a later visit when the reporter met the gardener, George Saunders. Police had privately admitted they were making little headway in finding Miss Hodge's killer and JP dropped in on George one Saturday morning unannounced.

The weathered old man asked him then if he wanted a shot of whiskey and JP took him up on the offer in hopes of keeping him talking, mainly because he considered Miss Hodge's 35-year employee a potential suspect in her poisoning death.

Michael Hodge was Irma's son, but he was raised in the mansion by Midge and Bob Moore because his single mother never took well to a maternal role. In recent years, they lived in neighboring mobile homes in nearby Queensland, the Moores with their own grown son, Charley, who was already eating a sandwich in the kitchen.

JP briefly marveled at the people he got to know in his line of work. To some, he was the equivalent of a service person best left in the shadows. He didn't really mind that because it left him in position to watch and listen to what went on around him, like a fly on the wall.

Some people, though, invited him into their lives. That was true of this extended family. He had been out of touch for some nine months, but they immediately put their figurative arms around him again.

"No, Mr. Saunders," JP said, "it's a bit early for me to start a hurricane watch party."

"Well, JP," Midge chimed in, "the first order of business here is for me to get some tea to steeping. Could I interest you in that?"

JP kept his visit brief, glad to know George Saunders wasn't riding out the storm alone in the big old mansion left him by the late heiress.

AUGUST 13, 1:00 P.M.

A reporter from a major East Coast television station brushed his microphone-free hand back and forth over his head, just to make sure his hair did indeed have a wind-blown look. With his back to the ocean, he leaned a bit unnecessarily into the wind and waited for his cue.

"That's right, Meagan, this town feels like it has a target on its back because Hurricane Clarice has been unrelentingly aiming at this spot on the

Gulf of Mexico for days now.

"Just-released figures from the National Hurricane Center say Clarice ended her brief respite from Category 5 status, returning with 160-mph sustained winds. Projections are for the storm to make landfall overnight in the Oldport area and they're expecting it to lose little, if any, of its punch.

"While you're looking at some footage shot around town late this morning, I'll tell you this will be our last live report from the hurricane zone. Yes, we're joining many other people from this area and taking the road north. Meagan, back to you in your dry, calm studio."

He and the camera operator both waited until they got an all clear and promptly started packing away the last of their gear.

"I've had quite enough of this place," the reporter said. "I'll be glad to haul it away from here and leave this storm to the big-moneyed cable guys."

AUGUST 13, 1:00 P.M.

Stanley Hopper and his new managing editor, Ed Roberts, had the "cable guys" muted on the television that hung on the wall overlooking the otherwise vacant news room.

"The Associated Press report is getting more specific about landfall," Roberts said while looking at Christine Finney's computer screen. "It says the eye is expected to come ashore just to the west of us. This may be my first hurricane, but I know that's not good news."

"Nope, that would put us receiving her right-hand punch, in the strongest quadrant of the storm."

"You don't seem too worried."

"It's coming ashore somewhere. In the immortal words of Bobby McFerrin, 'In every life we have some trouble; when you worry, you make it double.'"

"So, don't worry, be happy."

"Having a Cat 5 hurricane hitting you may not be happiness, but worrying won't make us better prepared. And, any true news hound will admit there's something special about having a front row seat to a major event."

"Are we prepared? I mean, it seems to me we are, but I don't really know my way around your team yet."

"We've got a cracker jack team, Ed, as strong as I've had in Oldport and probably as strong as any I've been a part of anywhere."

"It's obvious you bring the best out of them."

"Like to think so. But, the truth is, most of this crew could pick up and run just fine without me. But, if we're patting me on the back, I'll take some credit for getting them to that point."

Stanley gave his immediate superior a big, forced grin.

"Tell me something, if you don't mind me asking," Ed said after a pause, waiting for a nod. "I have to assume, when it was decided to insert a managing editor into the mix, that they offered you the job first."

The city editor gave what passed as an acknowledging shrug.

"Why, then, did you pass it up? I suppose they would have let you mold the position any way you wanted; why take the chance with them bringing in an ME from outside?"

"Bottom line, I know where I want to be. To add any level of administrative duties would take away from what I most enjoy. Right now, Pat's running lifestyle just fine, but she could up and leave any day and it would fall on your position to take care of it until she's competently replaced. Sports is always a potential headache. They are worthy challenges, just not what I want to deal with. Then, there's what nobody's actually said. Obviously, Margaret is eying retirement. You've already taken over quite a few of her duties. I'm certain Martin only agreed to add a new position so he'd have her replacement ready for a smooth transition. So, I'd then be at the top of the department, even further removed from what I most enjoy and, if I may say so, from my strength. And, as for taking a chance with an outsider, Martin and Margaret gave me considerable voice in your selection. For what it's worth, I gave you two thumbs up."

Ed sat quietly, occasionally nodding.

"Besides that," Stanley said dryly, "I didn't give it much thought."

"I appreciate that," Ed said after the laughter ended. "It's good to know the people you depend on are happy with what they're doing and are suited for it. I know what you mean. What I really wanted to do was be a sports writer, to eventually staff a Major League Baseball team and follow it around the country. It didn't take long to figure out I didn't really have the talent for that and, more importantly, didn't have the stomach for it. I tried to settle in as a beat reporter, but I wasn't really good at that either. Editing was better suited to my talents and, soon, I found a niche in administration. This, my contented friend, is what I do best."

Lifting his coffee mug in a toast, Stanley sealed the relationship, "Here's to a long partnership; may we happily stay out of each other's way."

As they soaked in the comfort of a deeper understanding of each other, both lifted their faces when something banged onto the roof.

"Tell me, Stanley, does it feel right to you for us to be sitting alone in a news room with what may be Oldport's story of the century pounding away outside?"

"Times have changed, Ed. Click onto our web page and I'll guarantee you the staff we bragged about earlier has been updating it throughout the day. This wouldn't work with just any collection of people, but my team cares about getting it done right. Doing it right doesn't mean throwing a paper into 150-mph winds. This is new territory and I'm looking forward to watching it develop."

"So, don't worry."

"Be happy."

AUGUST 13, 1:00 P.M.

As the cable weather reporter gave the news Hurricane Clarice had intensified to a Category 5 storm, again, Moose MacDuff stood silently in the background, filling the doorway to the living room.

"Virgil," his wife said when she spied him, "I was beginning to wonder if you intended to sleep through this amazing storm, but I wasn't sure when you came to bed."

"That's an idea," he mumbled. "Think my boys would miss me? It really wasn't all that late, but I made myself keep going back to sleep. Pretty soon, that'll be a rare commodity."

"Mommy, you know Daddy likes to be called Moose, not Virgil."

"Well, I call him Virgil because we're special to each other. Grandma calls him Virgil, too, because she's his mother."

"What about me? Am I special?"

"You?" Moose bellowed as he scooped the 5-year-old into the air. "You're extra special. You know why? You're the only person in the world who gets to call me Daddy."

When the tickling and giggling died down, Moose looked up from the floor and asked, with a begging look, "Kathy, honey, I'd do just about anything right now for a diet Dr Pepper. Would you fetch one while I see how many giggles are left in this little red-headed wonder?"

AUGUST 13, 1:00 P.M.

Joseph Lundgren led Suzette into the Oldport Middle School gym, which was serving as a shelter during the hurricane.

County leaders considered not opening an "official" shelter, fearful it would give people a false sense of security when they would actually be safer traveling inland. Finally, they decided to put the early emphasis on evacuation but open shelters for those who would not leave anyway.

The Lundgrens carefully prepared their home for the storm and felt confident in its safety, but their final decision was influenced more by their desire to not face their first hurricane alone.

As Joseph signed them in, Suzette looked around at their home for the duration of Hurricane Clarice.

It was more spacious than the gym at her home school in Outstate Minnesota, but the most noticeable sight was the array of exercise mats, many of which had already been claimed and rearranged into family groupings.

"We brought enough bedding that I don't think we'll need any mats," she said as Joseph caught up.

"Yeah, they said when they saw our quilts that it would be nice if we didn't need to use a mat. Apparently, they're expecting quite a few more people."

"Not so many, now, I suspect," interrupted one of their fellow evacuees. "Hi, I'm Sammy, two mats to the north."

As the men went through introductions, Suzette touched Joseph's elbow and nodded toward the television as almost everyone in the room fell silent to listen to the latest update.

"Wow, back to Cat 5 already and still aimed directly at us," she said. "Seems like our first hurricane experience might be a whopper."

"Your first, eh?" Sammy said. "Don't worry too much about the forecast; they always turn before making landfall. We might get a good blow but nothing like the media want you to believe."

"You're also not expecting a crowd here. Why?" Joseph asked.

"We've become second-class accommodations. I figure most people will be going to that new high-rise condo, the Cascades, just so they can say they were one of the first to spend the night there. Want me to give you a tour of the facilities?"

AUGUST 13, 1:00 P.M.

The updated hurricane forecast also came through two speakers piping a local radio station through the pens at Oldport County Animal Control Department.

The pets were beginning to get a little restless. The veterans were accustomed to seeing someone by this time of the day, even on weekends. It was a little warmer than usual, but not hot. The air-conditioner was blowing, but more fresh air than normal was also blowing through, raising the humidity. That was really no concern to any of the pets, but a few did seem to notice more noise from the wind.

Bottom line, though, it was comfortable enough and there was plenty of food and water.

AUGUST 13, 1:00 P.M.

As he had promised, Oscar Smith, one of the firefighters interviewed for Jennifer O'Hanlon's story, was some 135 miles away, the guest of a friendly fire department.

He had just shown off Oldport's newest engine to his hosts and moved back into the station's living area to catch the updated forecast. The other firefighters watched with him, finding the report of 160-mph winds more personal now.

"Any family back home, Smith?" one of them asked.

"Only my folks, except extended family, and they're on a month-long trip visiting my brother and sister in California. No wife, no kids, not even a steady girlfriend."

"Well, I guess that's good news," chimed in another, "excepting for the part that you're a sad, lonely case."

Amid a chorus of groans, Oscar shook his head. "Firefighters," he said. "You can teach them to save buildings, humans and cats, but you can't teach them manners."

AUGUST 13, 1:00 P.M.

Jennifer O'Hanlon slowly walked through her apartment, evaluating if there was anything else she should take or move to a safer location. Being on the second floor, she wasn't too concerned about rising water and she concentrated on putting things away from windows and inside closets and cabinets.

She cleaned the tub with bleach and filled it with water. She also filled various jugs and bottles with water, some of which she would carry to JP's place. As she packed up non-perishable food and several changes of clothing, she tuned an ear to the updated hurricane report, silently arching an eyebrow at the news of Clarice returning to Category 5.

The reporter finished the tour of her home at the front door, where sat her suitcase, a backpack of food and water and her laptop.

"That's sad," she said to nobody. "I'm running for my life and this is all I have worth taking?"

She smiled, though, as she gathered her belongings and headed to the car.

AUGUST 13, 1:00 P.M.

"It feels funny to be heading toward the beach," Maxine Murray said while trudging along beside her daughter. "It seems we should be going away from the storm we're running from."

"Do you need to take another break?" Lydia asked, though Maxine could tell the desired response was no.

"It's right in front of us. We'll rest when we get there."

"You seem to be holding up great, Mom. Had you not made this walk the other day, there's no way I would have asked you to do it, but it's smart to leave my car at home. While the Cascades will be safer for us, it won't be for the car."

"OK, run me through this again. Why is it safer here for us than it is for your car?"

"It's simply the quality of the structures, Mom. I probably wouldn't have thought about it before doing that story the other day, but our house isn't very sturdy. A storm as strong as Clarice might very well cause it to fall on top of us even though we're above the tidal surge."

Maxine shook her head while slowly plodding toward the giant structure that had been dominating the coastline the last year.

Sandra Lightley opened a door for the Murrays as they approached

"Welcome to the Oldport Cascades," she said cheerfully. "It's so nice to have real visitors before Hurricane Clarice comes calling."

AUGUST 13, 1:00 P.M.

After listening to the updated hurricane numbers, Rafael Ventura turned on the microphone to Oldport Supply Store's public address system and gathered his thoughts for just a second.

"Attention, friends and neighbors. May I have your attention, please? This is Rafael Ventura, manager of the store. I need to ask all our customers to quickly make their final selections and check out. We are glad to have been able to help everyone prepare for the hurricane, but right now I need to be able to let my hard-working employees go home and take care of their families.

"Please be aware that every hurricane-related supply we have left is on the floor. That is, we have nothing left in the storeroom. Fact is, all of our supplies are getting low and we are out of many things. Ask one of our employees wearing a yellow hardhat, most of whom are spread across the front of the store, if you need help finding something. They each have handheld computers that will help determine what is in supply and where it might be, since many items have been stacked away from their usual locations.

"Again, thank you for coming to us at this time and I hope we can help you, but please make your way to checkout as quickly as possible."

He clicked off the microphone and turned to an office worker.

"Well, that was too wordy and awkward, but I hope they get the idea. Delores, why don't you go home? There's no bookwork to do right now."

"I've been helping with the phones. We've been telling people the past 30 minutes to not bother coming down because we were closing. As soon as things slow, or you lock the doors, I'll head home. Robbie has everything under control there, so there's no rush."

"Thanks, Dee, but you do what you need to. Now, I'm going to make sure the entryways are locked and maybe round up a couple of guys to intercept people driving onto the parking lot and let them know we're closed."

Rubbing his eyes before pulling on his hardhat, he sighed.

"This part isn't any fun. Folks should have acted sooner, but I still wish we could help them out."

"You've got to take care of your OSS family, too, and we can do only so much for everyone else."

"You're right. Good luck, Dee. See you after the big blow."

AUGUST 13, 1:00 P.M.

Fred Franklin had a local radio station blaring out of his car's speakers as he loaded for a drive north.

"So, there you have it, friends. Hurricane Clarice is already back to a Category 5 storm, winds at 160-mph ..."

"Which is even faster than Zane drives."

"Thanks, Kristen. Anywho, this looks serious, folks, and it's still barreling straight for us. If you're not yet where you need to be, I suggest you put a little hurry into it. This storm could be making landfall in 12 hours and winds have already picked up considerably."

"I'm not where I need to be, yet."

"And where is that, pray tell?"

"I think I need to be in upstate New York right now. Can you arrange that?"

"Oh, Kristen, if only I could. Seriously, folks, it's time to ..."

Franklin turned off the radio to help him consider if he had everything packed.

It seemed like he was taking way too much and he knew his ex-wife would make fun of him. She had invited him to her parents' home because she knew he had nowhere else to go.

Going wasn't really supposed to be an option for someone in Franklin's position with the city. Critical city employees were expected to stay in town during a hurricane, but he knew he wouldn't be missed. After all, he had made a career out of keeping a low profile and cultivating even lower expectations.

With his house secured, the city building inspector crawled out of town on a northbound freeway.

AUGUST 13, 1:33 P.M.

JP Weiscarver was standing on his front lawn holding Bubba when Jennifer pulled her late model compact car behind his 11-year-old pickup on Oleander Drive.

"Is this the best place to park?" she yelled, but he couldn't understand her for the wind, which had picked up again, as it had been doing with greater frequency.

"Here, let me help you carry stuff in," JP said as he approached.

"Is this the best place to park?" Jennifer repeated.

"I don't know," he said and laughed. "I puzzled over that for quite a while. I finally decided it might be best if we parked in two different places so one tree couldn't take out both vehicles at the same time. After we get your stuff unloaded, you can pull around the corner and park there, if that's OK with you."

Unloading was not much of an issue and they were soon tucked away inside the house.

"I see why you were outside in the wind," she said. "It truly is a cave in here."

"Yeah, my landlords were set on sealing the house up. It's almost spooky, but I feel as secure as possible."

"What if the lights go out?"

"When they go out, we have a couple of kerosene lanterns that I'll introduce you to, if you're not familiar with them. Here's a small flashlight you can slip into your pocket now so you'll be able to get around. See on the kitchen table? There are a couple of larger flashlights and extra batteries for them all."

"Wow, I feel totally unprepared. I brought bottled water and potted meat to the hurricane party."

Soon, they were outside again so they could watch the racing clouds, seemingly oblivious to the increasing amount of rain that came with the storm's outer bands.

"You don't have to hear weather forecasters to know something's up," JP said.

"Nor do you have to be a coastal veteran," Jennifer added, clutching the stuffed animal that made the trip with her. "Those skies, the wind, just the feeling in the air, they all broadcast a feeling something's about to happen."

AUGUST 13, 5:28 P.M.

Doreen Strong struggled to maintain her balance while reaching for the door handle to the Coastal Cup Cafe with wind-whipped rain stinging her face. As she grabbed the handle, Jack Holliday unlocked the door and held it open for her.

"Hey, Doc," bellowed a regular customer, using Holliday's popular nickname, "it ain't time for Doreen to be here yet. You shoulda left her out there."

"What's with locking the door, Jack," asked Doreen, one of the few people who called him by his real name. She told him a real nickname would be something more original.

"I'm afraid someone will open it too casually and the wind will whip it off. There have been some crazy gusts come through. What are you doing here already? Your shift doesn't start for four hours yet."

"Are you crazy? I barely got in as it is. By 10 o'clock, it wouldn't happen. But the real question is why any of us are here?"

"Is that what they call a rhetorical question? 'Cause we both know the boss can't pass up a chance to make a buck."

"Truth is, Jack, I'd rather be here than home alone."

"Yeah, that's why Rita's here."

"Your wife Rita? Where is she?"

"In the kitchen. We decided to ride out the storm here. I mean, it was here or a shelter 'cause we couldn't stay in our trailer."

"You could have gone to the Cascades and sheltered in style."

"Heck, no, a place like that and they'd have me slinging hash in no time."

"Hey, Doc," came a familiar voice from the counter. "Would you like for me to refill my coffee myself or just wait for Doreen to clock in?"

AUGUST 13, 7:03 P.M.

Jeremiah Forge stood at the door of his 32nd floor Manhattan hotel room holding his carry-on bag, impatiently waiting for the bell hop to open the door.

Once inside, Forge headed to the television while the other man carried in his two large suitcases and garment bag.

"Does this thing get the Weather Channel?"

"Yes, sir, channel 105, I believe."

"... and we're seeing winds gusting near 100 mph already here in Oldport, but that's just a taste of what's to come."

"Thank you and we'll be checking back often. Take care. So, Clarice's latest figures obtained by the Hurricane Hunters include 170-mph sustained winds, putting the storm at one of the strongest to threaten the U.S. mainland. Needless to say, for those in the affected area, if you've not left yet, then you're likely riding out the storm. Nobody should be on the streets at this point."

"Maybe not on the streets, Margaret, but what about on the waves? Here's a story aired earlier by a local station about one young man who's in his element as the storm approaches shore."

As the interview with surfer Manny Wellborn began, Forge turned around to find the bell hop had left, leaving the key on the coffee table near the bags.

"Good," Forge grunted, "didn't have to listen to his happy talk or tip him for it."

AUGUST 13, 8:53 P.M.

Moose MacDuff reheated leftovers for a late snack as Hurricane Clarice pounded his sturdy home. His brother, Nick, twice declined a plate.

"I don't see where you put it all, Moose."

"It goes into my capacitor."

"Electrical humor, right?"

"Maybe. I'll need to leave soon and it may be quite a while before I'll enjoy home cooking again. Besides, eating keeps me from thinking about leaving y'all here."

"Don't worry, bro, we'll be just fine. You've made the house worthy of a bomb shelter."

"Well, I appreciate you and Carol riding out the storm with my girls."

Moose had finished the meat loaf and was digging into another slice of pecan pie, his favorite, when the lights went out, drawing a little squeal from his daughter. He scooped her into his right arm, down which ran his one tattoo – the MacDuff tartan, in honor of his Scottish heritage. He held her close while looking out the window.

"Don't worry, honey, we knew this would happen and we have plenty of flashlights. See, Mommy has your special flashlight," and he put her down to get it. Looking out the window again, he muttered, "I just hope the whole grid hasn't crashed this soon."

AUGUST 13, 8:53 P.M.

Jeremiah Forge ordered room service so he could continue to watch coverage of the hurricane.

He wasn't hearing a lot of what was said but was focusing on the background images, looking for his high-rise.

"The Cascades tower over everything in that burg," he said out loud. "Why is it the cameras can't find it?"

Suddenly, the street lights behind the reporter blinked out and an exclamation of surprise from a couple of people off-camera was audible.

"Not much chance now that you'll get a shot of my condo," Forge fumed and he started changing channels.

AUGUST 13, 8:53 P.M.

As the lights went out, a collective gasp rolled across the gymnasium where hundreds had gone for shelter. It was immediately followed by comments ranging from a soft "Oh, no" to a loud "There it goes!"

Joseph and Suzette Lundgren were already sitting cross-legged next to each other on a pad of quilts that had helped get them through Minnesota winters. When the room turned dark, they cuddled a little closer.

Joseph quietly stroked his wife's hair while she was caressing her belly and their unborn child.

"No way am I naming this baby Clarice," she said, squeezing out a smile.

AUGUST 13, 8:53 P.M.

Juan Mendoza put down the book he was reading when the lights went out and walked to the front door. For only a second he gazed out the small window on the door even though he knew he would see nothing.

Using the flashlight he already had in his pocket, he walked by the kitchen for a sip of water, topped off his last milk jug with fresh water and headed to the bed room.

He planned to get what sleep he could before the storm noise made it impossible. Once the danger passes, he'll start making his way to the animal shelter.

AUGUST 13, 8:53 P.M.

Lt. Angela Webb awoke when the station went quiet. She had developed the ability to grab shut-eye on short notice and to piece together short naps when needed.

When she walked into the living area of Station Four, she found a double crew of firefighters, eerily illuminated by emergency lights, itching to get into the fight.

One of the more experienced firefighters looked up and said, "It's time."

"Yes, sir," Angela agreed. "Let's get three trucks on the streets for patrol. Just as we discussed, keep in your assigned areas until we get a call. Cruise slowly with all eyes out for potential problems. You have wide latitude to address them as you see fit, to report them if you cannot. Check out any citizen waving you down, but try to not get tied down if it's not necessary. What am I saying? You know what you're doing; let's get Operation Clarice on the road! We'll trade crews in one hour and remember to top off your fuel tanks if you find an operating service station so we can hold our reserves for later."

AUGUST 13, 8:53 P.M.

The extinguishing lights were like a starter's pistol for Tim Grayson, JP's neighbor, and he walked first to the refrigerator to confirm the door was firmly shut. He then turned to the ice chest on the table and quickly reached in and blindly pulled out the first beer he found.

"Cool, a bock, one of my favorites," he said, pleased with the first round results of his beer lottery.

Popping the top, he settled into his recliner – Mission Control, he called it – where he was surrounded by an assortment of snacks.

"Happy is the man who has his priorities in order," he said just before a loud crack caused him to look around. "Dude, I hope that window holds up."

AUGUST 13, 8:53 P.M.

Sandra Lightley wasn't overly disappointed that Jeremiah Forge's publicity scheme failed so miserably. As he instructed, however, she placed phone calls suggesting camera crews visit the Cascades, but it seemed they were having no trouble finding good footage.

So, she thought the best thing she could do was make a good impression on the local newspaper by visiting with Lydia Murray. Well, she had decided that was how she would present it to Forge if she ever decided to answer one of his several phone calls. The truth was that she enjoyed the Murrays.

However, when the main lights went out and the backup lights clicked on, she excused herself in order to make the rounds and check on things.

"What a nice young lady," Maxine said. "It will be a pleasure working for her."

"You know there will be a couple of bosses between you and her," Lydia felt obligated to add, "but it will still be nice when you start work after the storm that the property manager knows you."

"She knows me because of my famous daughter."

"Quit it, Mom," Lydia chided, but a giggle gave her away. "And hand me a celery stick, please."

AUGUST 13, 8:53 P.M.

Sergeant Tad Ballew was working the social media angle to his public information job when his computer screen flickered. He had tweeted and posted numerous comments and answered questions on the department's blog, focusing on encouraging people to hunker down at home and stay off the streets.

He took the power outage, which inside the EOC meant a dimming of lights but no real interruption, as an excuse to take a break and get ready for the next phase.

AUGUST 13, 8:53 P.M.

Odds and Ends photographer Cole Thompson had just finished uploading five of his best photos for editors to post on the newspaper's Web site when he declined Doreen Strong's offer to freshen his coffee and darkness overwhelmed the Coastal Cup Cafe.

"On second thought, ma'am, I think I will have some more before it gets cold. Thanks. It might be good to sit here a spell and let the madness settle down some before I go back out."

AUGUST 13, 8:53 P.M.

Stanley Hopper was laboring away over his laptop computer at home, sluggishly trying to keep up with the information coming in.

He had just completed rewriting a cutline on one of Cole's photos in order to include more local background. It occurred to him in a slap-me-on-the-forehead type of moment that the online audience to the Odds and Ends hurricane coverage would be much broader than the usual readers who are familiar with the area.

When his overhead light went out, Stanley's computer switched to battery and he changed internet connections as he was instructed, though he still did not understand what that did. Like any good reporter, however, he went straight to the newspaper's blog and submitted his first personal entry of the night.

"Electricity went out in northern Oldport at 8:53 p.m. It is unknown at this time how widespread the outage is or its cause."

AUGUST 13, 8:53 P.M.

JP and Jennifer had been walking around outside his house, enduring the heavy rain and wind in an attempt to get a raw feel for the storm.

They were supporting each other near the curb when the street lights all went out. Jennifer added her flashlight to the one JP was already using and they made their way inside to find a sleeping ferret.

AUGUST 13, 10:00 P.M.

Few people in Oldport were able to receive the information, but the report on Hurricane Clarice showed winds still holding at a remarkable 170 mph.

Official landfall was forecast between 1 and 3 a.m.

At the Coastal Cup Cafe, everyone had abandoned the dining area and its plate glass window in favor of the kitchen.

In addition to three employees and Doc's wife, Rita, there were four regular customers who felt more secure there than at home alone. Doreen knew each of them by name and was familiar with their stories, at least the parts they made known, and the waitress even had a pretty good grasp of how much of their stories was true.

Each of these four men had no family at home and no children living in the area. She looked at them gathered around a preparation table, under the light of a battery-powered lantern, and recognized one thing each had in common with her. None of them wanted to face Hurricane Clarice alone.

AUGUST 13, 10:17 P.M.

Moose MacDuff's fear was realized, as he saw in his slow drive to the yard out of which he would work. Across Oldport, he saw no lights burning except for occasional spots powered by generators or batteries.

As soon as the winds become less dangerous, his crews would start surveying primary needs such as hospitals, emergency communications and major substations.

He also knew that within 12 hours of the storm's passing help would begin to arrive from other parts of the country, just as he and his crew had assisted them through the years. Within 24 to 36 hours, there would likely be hundreds of trucks and a thousand or more workers. They would work long days and grab sleep on cots or air mattresses in a tent city.

The scene had played out often enough around the country that key people knew what to do and it all served to getting hard-hit areas online more quickly.

AUGUST 14, 12:10 A.M.

After trying to sleep, Lydia Murray figured out few others were having any luck either, her mother being a notable exception.

Taking her slender reporter's notebook and a pen, she casually walked around the packed lobby of the Cascades. After several nods and hellos, she made eye contact with a mother trying to comfort a girl who had been startled awake by one of the loud bangs that occasionally rang through the huge building.

"Hello, my name is Lydia. What's yours?"

"Sarah."

"I'm guessing you're seven years old, Sarah; is that right?"

"No, I'm six."

"Six? Why, you're such a big girl for six. I bet you're pretty smart, too."

"Yes, ma'am. I can read a whole book. I brought it. Do you want to hear?"

"I would love it, if your mother doesn't mind."

"That would be wonderful, Lydia. My name's Becca. Sarah, while you read Miss Lydia your book, I'm going to walk around a little. I'll be back in just a minute."

"OK, Mommy."

Becca clasped her hands together at her chest and mouthed a silent thank you to Lydia and slipped away for a little alone time.

AUGUST 14, 12:31 A.M.

Firefighters Dominic Watson, Miguel Hernandez and Billy Green slowly drove through their section of Oldport, easing their way back to Station Four to wait out the worst part of the storm.

Dominic concentrated on driving while Miguel rode shotgun and scanned side streets and buildings to the right. Billy sat behind the driver and surveyed everything to the left. All three also spent a lot of time looking up, keeping a lookout for falling trees and power lines and even debris blowing in from elsewhere.

Fortunately, most of the utility lines had been buried in this section of town. They heard reports from other areas that streets were impassable due to downed lines.

"Wait," Billy said, patting Dominic on the shoulder.

They stopped often to get a better look at something that had caught an eye through the driving rain.

"Can you back up just a little? Yeah, there it is again, at 9 o'clock, do you see an arm waving back and forth?"

"No, but I've been staring into the glare of reflected headlights," Dominic said.

"It might be something blowing in the wind, but I'd almost swear it's an arm."

"Let's check it out, Billy Boy," said Miguel. "Dom, call the station and report our location and situation."

Billy opened his door and Miguel yelled at him to shut it.

"Slide to this side so we can buddy up as soon as we're off the truck," Miguel reminded him.

Once outside, they locked arms and moved deliberately around the front of the engine and picked up Dominic on the other side. With Miguel in the middle, they moved slowly and methodically with Billy guiding them.

"There," he said. "It is someone waving."

As they neared the victim, a building helped shield them from the heaviest winds and rain. Their flashlights revealed a middle-aged man pinned by a fallen awning.

He quickly assured them he was not injured – not seriously, at least – and that he was alone.

"I just had to get a closer look at the storm," he said, as his rescuers assessed the situation. Dominic radioed the station that no further need for help seemed likely.

"Think we need the Jaws of Life?" Billy asked as the squad leader examined the awning more closely. "Miguel?"

"Let's try it ourselves, first. Sir, what's your name?"

"Jim, Jim Madison. I just live around the corner above my pawn shop. I live alone, though, so there was nobody to check on me. I was carrying my cell phone, but it got knocked over there."

"OK, Jim, you say you're not in pain?"

"Only a little sore. There's hardly any weight on me, just not enough room to wiggle out. Speaking of wiggling, I can move my toes and I have feeling down my legs."

"Good, so here's what we're going to try first. We will try to lift the awning just enough for you to squirm out. We don't want to move it any more than we need to for fear it will cause things to shift. Make sense? Are you up to doing that?"

Madison gave a strong nod and positioned his arms to push against the ground. The firefighters chose their spots and made sure they had good grips before Miguel gave the signal to lift.

In a matter of three seconds, the man was out, hopping to his feet before Dominic was able to advise him to lie still.

"Sir, would you like to go to the hospital to get checked out?" Dominic asked. "Considering your mobility, we could transport you in the engine rather than call out an ambulance."

"No, no, I'm really fine and I promise to see a doctor if anything strange starts happening. I so appreciate you guys stopping, but I'll just get back inside and wait out the storm, but, uh, there is one thing."

"Yes, sir?"

"Would you fellows walk me to my door?"

AUGUST 14, 2:14 A.M.

Sandra Lightley felt she was losing control of the situation at Oldport Cascades Condominiums as winds beating on the front of the building sent screeching sounds through the mass of refugees.

The property manager had been moving all night, trying to calm people and assure them of the building's integrity. Most were willing to believe her. Indeed, they desperately wanted to believe her.

Lydia Murray, perhaps acting on natural instincts but maybe just trying to live up to her new role as a reporter, made her way to the front doors, now locked shut against the wind.

Alone, because nobody else cared to get that close to the storm, she peered through the glass, trying to catch a glimpse of the face of Clarice.

Lydia was surprised the lightning decreased dramatically as the eye approached, but an occasional flash helped illuminate the scene, reflecting off the wet ground. Gradually, her gaze focused on something and she finally figured out what she saw.

"Ms. Lightley," she yelled three times before spotting her. Sandra moved quickly toward Lydia, motioning her to quiet down and not startle the others.

"It may be difficult to see, but look toward the water," Lydia instructed. "It looks like a shrimp boat coming toward us."

"That's not unexpected, Lydia. Boats get pulled from their moorings all the time during a hurricane."

"That's not the point. Look where it is and, oh my, it's still getting closer. That means the Gulf is almost to our door."

In that moment, the threat became clear. The surge tide was indeed threatening the Cascades.

"We have to move upstairs," Lydia said. "Just the 10 feet to the second floor will make all the difference.

"I ... I don't know," Sandra replied, for the first time losing confidence. "Mr. Forge made it abundantly clear that everyone was to stay on the first floor. In fact, the stairwells are locked."

At that point, the first wave slammed against the building and the door strained to stay shut. Both women instinctively moved toward the center, from where several screams emanated.

"I don't have a key," she continued, "but there must be one." While talking, she opened the door to Forge's office and followed her flashlight beam inside. She and Lydia both started looking for keys and Sandra headed to the stairs with the first few they found.

"I'll continue looking while you try those," Lydia said.

While rummaging through drawers, she saw the special use permit and, after only a moment's hesitation, opened it. "It's OK; it's a public document," she said out loud.

AUGUST 14, 2:27 A.M.

The leading edge of Hurricane Clarice's eye officially waded ashore just west of making a direct hit on the town of Oldport.

Official readings recorded it as a minimal Category 5 storm with 160-mph winds.

AUGUST 14, 2:28 A.M.

As Lydia stepped back out into the commons area, she spotted Sandra eyeing the front door.

"It doesn't appear any worse," Sandra said. "The keys didn't work. I have some employees looking around for tools to break in, but I think the worst is over. I just keep falling back on the fact this building is supposed to be safe for a hurricane."

Two maintenance workers appeared from different directions, one carrying a crowbar, another with a fire ax.

"Thanks, fellows, but just hold on to them for a while. I think we're safe here."

"You might want to look at what I found while searching for keys, Ms. Lightley," and Lydia produced the special use permit.

"Yes, I'm aware of that; we had to have it before we could keep people here."

Lydia turned to the second page and pointed out a highlighted paragraph.

"This permit applies to areas more than 25 feet above sea level. Since the main floor of Oldport Cascades Condominium is only 20 feet above sea level and contains an independent knockout exterior, people should not be housed on that floor during a hurricane."

"What's an independent knockout exterior?"

"I've never heard of it," said the man holding the crowbar, "but it sounds like a tear-away jersey. It would make sense to make something where the bottom floor walls could give way without threatening the upper stories."

"Mr. Forge said it was safe," Sandra mumbled as she looked over her shoulder at hundreds of worried faces.

Just then, the front doors exploded under a pounding four-foot wave and water raced across the floor.

As Sandra yelled for the men to break down the stairway door, they were already en route to do so. She and Lydia began waving their arms to marshal people toward the stair.

Panic took over as children scrambled to get untangled from suddenly wet bedding, as mothers and fathers hoisted their offspring and tried to grab some private effects, as if there was anything important among them.

Children were crying, but the adults were mostly focused. Some were heeding signals to head toward the elevator area and many others followed, not knowing where they were going but hoping it was safer.

Others, still, scattered in different directions, looking for any place that might be safer. Some of them would choose well, some would simply choose the spot of their eventual demise.

Lydia made her way to Maxine, who had stayed glued to her spot, trusting her daughter would know where to find her.

"Mom, we've got to move that way toward the elevators and go up the stairs," Lydia yelled, noticing that the six inches of water had risen to just above her knees.

To her relief, the door to the stair had been ripped off by the men and was floating away. Anxious people were steadily streaming upstairs, most of the able-bodied ones carrying children or supporting elderly.

As they got nearer to the door, Lydia looked back and saw too many children struggling to walk through the rising tide, fighting to get through everything from seaweed to construction debris.

"Here, Mom," she said, thrusting the special permit into Maxine's purse. "This is very important. I want to make sure it gets to JP Weiscarver. Would you keep it for me? I've got to help some of these kids."

Maxine started to protest, but she saw the children and knew better.

"Be careful."

"I love you, Mom."

Maxine was pulled toward the stairwell. "I love you, too," she mumbled. "Please be careful."

AUGUST 14, 2:39 A.M.

The Weather Channel was on full alert, in spite of the early hour, as Clarice brought its fury to bear on the mainland.

The anchor was giving what information they had, including the rising death toll across the Caribbean, when she received the word she wanted.

"I understand we have just made satellite linkup with Frank Woffard in the eye of Clarice. What's it like down there, Frank?"

"Lisa, it's beautiful right now. We have maybe 5 mph winds and I believe our cameraman is right now showing you the bright stars above. It's a stark contrast to what we were hiding from just 10 minutes ago as the strongest winds of Hurricane Clarice ripped at Oldport from the east.

"We'll have maybe a couple of hours of calm before the winds will leap again to, we expect, at least 130 mph, this time from the west.

"We've not had a chance to look around, but we have not received any stories of damage. Then again, communication is very sketchy right now.

"Should anyone be listening to us as the eye passes over, we do want to warn you to not abandon your shelter; this storm is far from over."

AUGUST 14, 2:42 A.M.

JP and Jennifer made themselves wait a few minutes after the noise stopped and finally went out into the pitch dark.

"Well, it's official," JP said, "we caught the eye of the storm. That's the only way it would have subsided that quickly."

"Which means we're in for another bout with the backside," Jennifer confirmed.

Jennifer carried a lantern to light their path while JP had the strongest flashlight and they circled the house, inspecting for any damage. They had to take care for limbs and other debris that had blown into the yard, but there was no apparent damage.

"I think the old gal is holding up rather well," he said. "There are some shingles blown away, but not as many as I would have thought. Basica+lly, it looks pretty good."

"Hey, there, neighbor. Things are holding together in our area."

"Yeah, seems like these older houses were built to last," JP yelled at Tim Grayson. "You doing well?"

"Yep, the beer's still cold and plentiful."

AUGUST 14, 2:43 A.M.

Jeremiah Forge blinked his eyes a couple of times before he remembered he was in a New York hotel. It took another second to understand why he fell asleep with the television playing, something he just never did.

As the cobwebs cleared, he picked up on news reports that Hurricane Clarice had made landfall and Oldport was currently in the eye of the storm.

He dialed Sandra Lightley, but the call went straight to voice mail.

"Figured as much; the towers are probably out."

He turned over and went back to sleep, but not before turning off the television this time.

AUGUST 14, 2:44 A.M.

Cole Thompson was making the best of the break in the storm and was patting himself on the back in the process.

He figured it would be difficult driving around after the hurricane passed, so he had made plans.

He rented a motor scooter three days before Clarice hit and devised a way to carry his camera equipment. He then wrangled an invitation to stay with Chad Brooks during the storm, an easy task since Chad lived alone and nobody really wanted to ride out a hurricane in isolation.

Chad, a sports reporter, lived in an apartment complex, but he and Cole both thought it was sturdy enough to handle the weather. Actually, Cole was primarily interested in the fact that it was at a higher elevation than most of the town and had fewer overhead utility lines. Those two points seemed likely to provide better access to a larger area.

What Cole did not have the audacity to hope for was a break in the wind and rain while the eye passed over. When it happened, he spent a few minutes trying to read the wall clouds and then decided to go for it.

"OK," Chad said as he helped Cole get the scooter out of the apartment, "just don't wander too far. The backside will hit suddenly and with little warning."

"Yes, Mom. I'm thinking I'll do spokes on a wheel, head out for a ways, then come back to this area, then choose another way out. If I keep coming back the way I went out, it will lessen the chances of getting trapped."

He chose to head north first of all and within two blocks found the road blocked by fallen trees. He took some photos of local residents examining the tree and another group looking at a home damaged by another fallen tree. He used the audio recording feature on his camera to "attach" voice notes of names, locations and other information to the photos. He never really liked doing that, but it was better than keeping up with a notepad in this setting.

Instead of immediately backtracking as he had planned, he took a right turn and went three blocks, weaving in and out among debris, before he found another group of people using a couple of chainsaws to cut a fallen tree. Their objective was to clear the street before the storm resumed.

Cole headed back toward the apartment, taking time to closely study the clouds and visible stars. He figured the approaching eye wall would begin to obscure southern and eastern stars first, but he could still see quite a few twinkling lights in both directions and he chose a road headed west, carefully directing the beam of his headlight to find a safe course.

AUGUST 14, 2:45 A.M.

Moose MacDuff, anxious as he was to dart out and get to work, was the calm member of his team. Kevin "Kilowatt" Henderson, Stan Jowalski and Bud Richardson had all arrived at the yard before Moose and were engaged in swapping tall tales with other linemen.

Several dozen workers had gathered at the yard and were packed into the meeting room, which had been cleared of tables and chairs to make space. Moose knew it was a sturdy building, put together soundly just for this purpose; the company couldn't have a large segment of its work force wiped out just when they were needed most.

Located just north of Oldport, the yard had just become silent with the passing of the eye wall and the men inside became quiet as well. Robert Richardson, Bud's father and head of the department, stepped outside and quickly returned, slamming the door.

"We've landed in Oz!" he yelled and the room erupted in laughter.

"Settle down, now," he bellowed again, gesturing with his palms down to get the point across. "We've obviously entered the eye. That means we just weathered what is probably the worst part of the storm. It also means the second worst part is about to slam us again.

"I want y'all to fan out, check your trucks and make sure everything is still secure. If something's loose, tie it down or remove it to a safe spot. Then generally check everything around the yard, from the fences to the building, and see if there's anything that needs to be done. Do it if you can or get word to me or another appropriate person. Stay alert and do not wander off. We might have just a few minutes or we might have an hour, then it's back in here to hold these walls up."

AUGUST 14, 2:46 A.M.

All the fire trucks from Angela Webb's Station Four were on the street once the eye's calm settled in. The lieutenant was riding with her least experienced crew as they toured their assigned section.

Angela was using a handheld digital recorder to make notes of what they saw. Doing so, she neither tied up a dispatcher to take them down nor did she have to take her eyes off the road.

"We're encountering another blocked road in the 400 block of Wharf Street, approaching downtown. This looks like something we can safely clear ourselves."

Once they had done so, she was back on the recorder, breathing a little heavier.

"We did get that cleared without problems, clear enough to pass, at least, but it looks like some serious damage up ahead, hard to tell in such total darkness.

"We're entering the 200 block of Wharf now and, my gosh, there is debris everywhere. We're going to turn the engine to be prepared to leave quickly if the storm surprises us. Then we'll do a walk-through of the area."

Angela ordered her men to stay within sight and sound of each other and to all stay aware of the sky and the return of the eye wall.

Business after business had roofs missing, walls caved in and there were no unbroken panes of glass. Angela continued chronicling what she saw and added reports from her crew.

"Hey, Lieutenant," called her driver, "see that junk-covered slab? That's where the Coastal Cup Cafe used to be. There were people there yesterday as I was going to work. They said they intended to ride out the storm."

The four of them spent 20 minutes searching through debris without finding victims or survivors. Webb put the crew back onto the truck to continue its inspection.

AUGUST 14, 2:47 A.M.

Sergeant Tad Bellew was feeling a bit useless, isolated in the dimly lit emergency operations center, monitoring radio traffic and filling coffee mugs for those who actually had jobs to do.

When his phone beeped that it had received a text message, he was surprised that someone got through and realized there must be at least one cell tower still functioning.

"That girl is certainly following in JP's footsteps," he muttered to himself when he saw it was from Jennifer O'Hanlon, "can't even take off for a hurricane."

He read the message and was instantly engaged in action once again.

"We've got trouble at the Cascades," he said to the dispatcher. We need to get rescue and medical help over there ASAP."

As the dispatcher made contact with units in the field, Bellew reread the message: "FWD: Cascades damaged, ppl trapped and injured."

He replied, "Thx, on it."

"You got anyone in the area?" Bellew asked his dispatcher.

"No, sir, everyone says that area's all under water and too dangerous to enter. I've notified the nearest fire station, but they can't even get their trucks out right now. They have it on the top of their list, however."

AUGUST 14, 2:48 A.M.

"Sergeant Bellew says he's on it," Jennifer told JP while stroking the ferret in her lap.

"That was good thinking when you couldn't get the call out."

"The original good thinking was done by Lydia and she did so even though she's in the middle of it."

"Did you reply to her?"

"Yeah, I wanted her to know help was coming, but I've not heard back from her yet."

"I suspect she's busy. Don't worry about her, though. I've learned Lydia is a survivor. I sent a text to Stanley so he knows what's going on. He can decide whether to put anything online, if he can put anything online."

"I'm not looking forward to the backside of this storm, JP."

"And I'm not looking forward to what we find when it passes."

AUGUST 14, 3:04 A.M.

It had been relatively quiet outside the Cascades for several minutes – Maxine Murray really had no grasp of time – and the hysteria had settled down considerably.

Maxine's mind was caught in a tug-of-war between a mother's pride and her fear. Several times, she started to approach the frazzled Sandra Lightley to ask about Lydia.

Perhaps she was afraid of what she would hear. She calmed her fears, remembering Lydia was the most capable person she knew.

A male employee of the condo walked through the stairway door and approached Sandra, shaking his head. That's it, Maxine thought.

"Ms. Lightley, I know you're busy, but do you know anything about my daughter, Lydia, the Odds and Ends reporter?"

"Not really, ma'am, just that she was with me when the water broke in and she was helping get people to safety. We really have no idea where everybody scrambled. We suspect a lot of folks found safe places downstairs or maybe got through another stairway door. I'm sure she's OK."

AUGUST 14, 3:35 A.M.

Maxine now knew exactly how long had passed since talking to Sandra because she looked at her watch every few seconds. In between, she glared at the stairway door, begging it to open, but nobody was coming or going.

Suddenly, there was what sounded like an explosion, followed by shattering glass and screams.

"It's the eye wall," she heard Sandra yell to a couple of co-workers. "Make sure everyone is out of the condos and in the hall and shut the condo doors."

Maxine finally broke into tears as she heard a sound foreign to her. Indeed, few people on the floor would have known the incredible groaning and ripping noises were many of the knockout walls giving way.

Those on the second floor were relatively secure, but many on the ground floor who had found safety from rising water by climbing atop counters and desks discovered they were like golf balls on tees when the walls tore loose.

AUGUST 14, 3:39 A.M.

JP and Jennifer had both fallen asleep during the respite from wind and rain, he on the sofa and she in the recliner, Bubba nestled down next to her.

All three were on their feet when the backside of the storm rattled the house. It was all JP and Jennifer could do to resist the urge to crack open a door and take a peek outside, but the ferocity of the storm helped them curb the desire.

"Does it sound worse this time than it did the first time?" she asked.

"It does, but maybe it's because we built up to it before and this one was a rude awakening."

The sat quietly, trying to distinguish what the various sounds meant. Many times, they heard things bang against the side or roof of the house.

AUGUST 14, 3:43 A.M.

Cole Thompson completed his scooter tour as it seemed the eye wall was getting nearer.

He shot more photos than he normally would have because it was so dark and he often couldn't see what he was shooting. It wasn't uncommon to take a photo, look at it in the digital display and then try to reframe it using the initial shot as a guide.

Mostly what he encountered in the area was downed utility lines, snapped trees and blown out windows and signs. He had no trouble getting people into his photos. The thought had crossed his mind that there were more people out on foot than you saw in pretty weather.

He was in the process of copying photos from his camera to his computer when the backside of Hurricane Clarice slammed into Chad Brooks' apartment.

"Man, I hope you have a strong building here," he said.

AUGUST 14, 3:46 A.M.

In a way, the re-emergence of the storm was a blessing to a lot of people because they knew it had to come before things could get better.

Tad Bellew, who was often more distanced from events than other police officers, found himself pacing the floor because neither he nor anyone else could do anything about what was happening at the Cascades. Nobody even knew what was happening there, which enhanced the frustration.

Stanley Hopper was drumming his fingers on his desk at home, driving his wife crazy. The power went out so early and communication had been so sketchy, he was dying for more information. He spent a little while outside checking his house and his neighborhood while the eye passed, but mostly he sat by his computer and phone as if clear skies would enable him to reach someone.

Juan Mendoza found water leaking through the roof and into his dining room. He spread some towels and placed a waste basket to catch the water. His overriding concern, however, was the welfare of the animals at the shelter. I wish I had ignored policy and stayed there with them, he thought.

Moose MacDuff was glad to finally have the backside of the storm roll in. He and his crew, as well as the others in the building, were ready to get to work. They made good use of the period of calm to secure equipment. One crew went half a mile down the road to check a substation and came back with disheartening news; it was badly damaged.

The firefighters at Station Four had definitely been chomping at the bit.

A couple of them tried to convince their lieutenant that the huge fire engines could get through the water to reach the Cascades.

"There are too many low spots between here and there and you know it," Angela Webb said. "We all want to be there, but getting rescuers killed and losing needed equipment is not the way to help anyone."

She stood firm and she was correct, every firefighter in the building knew the best course, for the greater good, was to let the storm die down some. Each one of them was thankful, though, that there had been no reports of fires.

AUGUST 14, 5:15 A.M.

Jeremiah Forge was one of those people who could sleep well in a hotel. It probably helped that he only stayed in the nicest establishments.

So, it took several seconds before the twittering cell phone woke him and several more before he cleared his head well enough to answer.

"Yeah?"

"Are you watching the news about the Cascades?"

"Wiley? No, I was sleeping. It's about time they're giving us a little exposure."

"No, Mr. Forge, there's nothing good about it. You might be able to spin it if everything works out well, but..."

"Catch me up."

"There's not much of anything coming out of there yet, but the local newspaper put a blurb on their Web page that there were injuries."

"That sounds pretty generic."

"OK, the story gave a little background on the offer of using the Cascades as a shelter, quoting you as saying it was safe. It went on to say a reporter sheltered there and, during the height of the storm, texted a co-worker to say, let me read it, 'Cascades damaged, people trapped and injured.'"

"Good grief, that sounds like the paper is trying to sabotage us."

"Tell me, Mr. Forge, you did tell your staff to move the refugees off the first floor, didn't you?"

"Of course not. I don't want those people running amok where they could damage valuable property. Wiley, are you recording this?"

"You should know right now, Forge, I've recorded most of our conversations."

Forge cut off the connection and threw his phone into a pillow.

AUGUST 14, 7:09 A.M.

Water was still dangerously high in places, but rain was subsiding as Clarice moved farther ashore. Even more helpful, daylight was making its way through thick cloud cover well enough to allow rescuers to see where they were going.

Lt. Angela Webb got off the radio with command, operating out of Station One downtown, and looked around to see her men already in motion for the trucks. Everyone in the station heard the go-ahead. Over the past hour, they had put together a plan for action, at least until they started receiving more information.

This time, she would stay at the station to coordinate and to maintain contact with command. She and one truck and crew would remain free to respond where needed.

The first truck out of the station turned south toward the Oldport Cascades, the second toward downtown.

AUGUST 14, 7:31 A.M.

The first truck to reach its destination found a ravaged downtown district. The few people they saw on foot were OK, maybe lived in the area and maybe just got out early into heavy rain. Nobody reported finding anyone in trouble.

The driver noticed on a side street a man on a motor scooter, winding his way through obstacles, and he watched more closely when the rider quickly jumped off the bike.

"Hey, Matt," he said through his radio. "At my 2 o'clock a block over. Looks like somebody found something.

Cole Thompson, about that time, started waving both arms over his head to attract the firefighters' attention.

As a photojournalist, he had seen a lot of things that would have deeply disturbed others, but he had never been so struck by an image before. Seven bodies, best he could see, seemed to have washed up together in a ditch. Eventually, it would be determined they were Doreen Strong, Stan and Rita Holliday and four regular customers of the Coastal Cup Cafe. The other employee's body would not be found until evening.

AUGUST 14, 7:39 A.M.

"Engine 42 to Command."

"Command, 42."

"Command, we're pulling up on the Cascades area and already finding casualties on the north side of the building. We have numerous people signaling for help. Some seem mobile, others not. We're going to need help down here."

"Understood, 42, we'll send you what we can. Can ambulances negotiate the roads?"

"That should be an affirmative. We cleared major limbs in order to get by and if they take our route, water is not a major concern. Lt. Webb can give you the route."

"We will roll what we can and notify the hospital."

"Command, we have a clear line of sight to the structure now and it looks as if the bottom floor just washed away. There are people waving to us from second story windows. We will evaluate and report."

AUGUST 14, 7:40 A.M.

Sgt. Tad Bellew didn't wait to talk to the dispatcher, just put on his rain gear, grabbed his equipment bag and headed for the parking garage. If the ambulance could get through, so could he.

He had been in this business long enough to recognize a media lightning rod. A mega-million-dollar condo converted to a shelter that proved fatal to those it was supposed to protect ... he knew it would be all over the news today and he had to get ahead of the story.

As he pulled onto the street, he received another text from Jennifer O'Hanlon: "En route to Cascades."

AUGUST 14, 7:41 A.M.

Maxine was so numb she did not hear the chatter about an approaching fire truck.

It had been more than five hours since she saw her daughter and four hours since the resumption of the storm. During that time, it appeared they were locked in on the second floor.

Anyone who tried the stairway promptly returned. She overheard talk about all the stairways being impassable or dangerous. The best she could tell, it had been decided to wait for the storm to play out and for help to arrive.

That was OK with her because she had a bad feeling about what awaited her downstairs. She just couldn't imagine life without Lydia; she had absolutely nobody else.

That's not true, she thought, because she had imagined it before, over and over. And, she thought, she had always been wrong. She was a worry wart and Lydia was fine and trying to get to her.

But still Maxine had that nagging feeling.

AUGUST 14, 7:46 A.M.

Dominic Watson had dropped off Miguel Hernandez and Billy Green to evaluate the severity of injuries of those scattered behind the Cascades. He drove as closely as he safely could to the condo, all the while advising his commanding officer of the situation.

He moved underneath one of the broken out windows.

"Are there people hurt up there?" he asked. He got uncertain answers and then pressed to speak to an employee, maybe someone in charge. One of the refugees had already gone for Sandra Lightley and she appeared.

"We are safe right now," she said, "providing the building is sound. Can you tell if it's unsteady?"

"Ma'am, the load-bearing structure looks solid. It just seems like the walls blew out."

"We have only scrapes and bruises up here. We're anxious but can wait until it's a good time. Some water would be good if we're much longer. Can you tell us about the people who were downstairs?"

"All I know right now is we have a bunch of people back here. We'll get to you as soon as we can."

Dominic updated command on his situation. Miguel and Billy gave first estimates. They were aware of a dozen injured people, most of them rather serious but not imminently life-threatening. They had also confirmed nine dead and had been told of a few others.

"Best we can determine, they all came from the condo," Miguel said.

Before going back to help his partners, Dominic did his best to check out the bottom floor. Trash, furniture and building materials were packed into corners that stopped their flow. He could see why they were not able to get down the stairs; they were probably blocked by tons of debris. There was even a shrimp boat that apparently tried to sail into the building.

Convinced it would not be simple to use the stairs, he put in a request for ladder help while looking into some of the rooms and offices. In one, he found a young woman shielding two children. All were dead. In another, there was a sobbing elderly man. Dominic checked him out and slowly walked him over to wait by the truck.

AUGUST 14, 8:16 A.M.

JP and Jennifer had opted to walk to the Cascades, knowing roads would be questionable and deducing parking space might not be available.

Rainfall was decreasing, still throwing off intermittent cloudbursts but mixing in longer and longer breaks. One of those periods of pounding rain relaxed and as the pair could see better, a disturbing scene appeared before them.

The Cascades entry, through which JP had walked just nine days ago, was not recognizable. He wasn't sure, but he thought it was where a shrimp boat currently teetered. Not that an entryway was important because there were sections of wall missing everywhere. Not that one really wanted to enter, anyway, because it was a frightening mess inside.

The reporters picked up their pace, as well as they could in the mud thrown up by the storm, and started talking to each other about what they saw, as if each needed the other to confirm the sight.

On this side of the condo was the fire department's ladder truck, down which the storm refugees were slowly descending one at a time. Behind the condo were at least two ambulances and JP could see a large number of people moving about.

"They must be moving people from the condo to that area in back," he said.

"It looks like some of them are filing into that white bus. Is that the county's prisoner transport bus? I think it is," Jennifer said, her eyes darting from the scene to the debris she was stepping around.

"There's Sgt. Bellew," she added. "I'll start with him to see what he knows."

"That's good. I'm going to head back here toward the ambulances," JP replied, and they split up.

AUGUST 14, 8:19 A.M.

"Thank you, Jennifer, for your text," the public information officer said. "That was the only word we received about this until our fire unit rolled up. It's likely you saved lives today."

"The real hero is up there, I guess. Are there many injuries?"

"From what I understand, the people who made it upstairs are fine, but not those still downstairs."

"How bad is it?"

"We have several confirmed fatalities. Most of those who survived are pretty banged up. One ambulance has departed with one on a stretcher and four who were capable of sitting up. No idea of just how many there are."

Two school buses pulled up to help shelter and transport the victims.

"But we're organized for just such a thing," he continued. "It will take a little time to work our way through it."

"Any official statement for our online readers?"

"Just summarize what I've given you, Jen. I trust you."

Jennifer departed as a television crew rolled up and she worked her way through a group of survivors who had just climbed down the ladder. She was looking for familiar faces but saw none.

Heading toward the back of the complex, she ran into JP.

"Here's the notebook if you want to send your info to Stanley now," he said. "I just did. It actually has a fair signal here. I think he'd prefer a stream of stuff rather than long stories at this point."

"What did you find back there?"

"It's, uh, it's a mess, Jen. I'm practiced at disassociating myself from horror when I have a job to do, but this one is pretty difficult."

She squeezed his hand a bit while taking the notebook.

"Did you see Lydia?"

"Not yet. If she's upstairs, she'd probably be one of the last one's down. Wait, isn't that her mother?"

They arrived at the ladder truck just in time to take Maxine Murray's hand as she stepped off. When she recognized them, she gave both a joint hug and then backed away.

"Where's Lydia?" she asked JP.

He briefly looked at Jennifer, both realizing the possibilities. At that moment, Maxine broke down in tears.

"Mrs. Murray, don't go leaping to any conclusions," JP said. "We haven't seen her yet, but there are a lot of people around here. Some have gone to the hospital already."

"I've heard that a bunch of people have, that they're dead," she said between sobs.

"Yes, ma'am, but I haven't seen Lydia among them, either. When's the last time you saw her?"

"She practically pushed me up the stairs and then went back to help some kids. It was flooding fast. The last thing she said to me was, 'I love you.'"

"Mrs. Murray," said Jennifer, "why don't you get aboard this bus out of the weather. I understand water and sandwiches will be here soon."

The woman gave in, worn out from the overnight experience, but she stopped abruptly and reached into her purse.

"JP, Lydia said this was very important and that she wanted to get it to you. You might as well take it now."

Without waiting for a comment, she turned back toward the bus.

After JP read the highlighted section, he told Jen he was going to walk around and look at a few things, maybe snap a few photos.

"I'm going to hang out here a little while," Jennifer said. "I can help move people to the buses and might pick up a little information along the way."

AUGUST 14, 8:55 A.M.

After swinging by Chad's apartment to get more gas for the scooter, Cole Thompson worked his way by Oldport Middle School. The rain was fairly light by now and many people had moved outside, some to drag limbs and other obstacles from the parking lot and road.

Several were leaving, including the Lundgrens, whose photo he had taken for JP's story.

"Welcome to the Gulf Coast," he said.

Cole took just a couple of photos there and headed to Stanley's house three blocks over.

"How did you hold up here," he asked.

"I was more worried about you guys in that apartment. I've heard from quite a few people already, so I think we've weathered it pretty well. I haven't gotten any reports on the newspaper building yet."

"Well, I'm not going that way yet. I just wanted to download some photos on your computer just in case you have a chance to go through them. Then I'm headed to the Cascades. A constable's deputy told me they had some problems there."

"I was about to tell you that. JP and Jennifer have reported in from there. That's where Lydia and her mother were staying, but I've not heard from her yet."

AUGUST 14, 9:14 A.M.

After getting Stanley's report on the Cascades, Cole headed straight there. He still stopped to shoot photos on the way, including one of Moose MacDuff removing a power line from a road, but he did not tarry long at any place.

He was less than a mile from the condos when he noticed movement in the ditch and stopped his scooter.

"Hello, are you OK?" he called out, moving tentatively toward a mud-covered body. He was apprehensive after his experience behind the Coastal Cup earlier, but then he remembered, I did see movement.

He approached the person, talking all the while, and finally placed his hand on a shoulder, feeling a slight recoil. The head rotated toward him and then a child's head appeared from behind the woman.

"Lydia?" Cole asked, seeking not so much an affirmation as recognition from a blank face.

Gradually, he coaxed her to the roadside, where he sat her down and covered the two of them with his rain slicker. The young boy finally spoke to him, said his name was Buddy and he didn't know where his parents were.

"Who is this you're with?"

"I don't know, but she helped me out of the flood and helped keep me warm."

Finally, another vehicle approached and Cole flagged it down. It was an unmarked police car headed to the Cascades and they decided the best thing was for him to drive the pair in for triage and maybe link up with family.

With Buddy's help, they talked her into the back seat and Cole followed the captain to the condo. He took many photos there, but the most poignant proved to be of Maxine and Buddy's parents reuniting with their children.

AUGUST 14, 11:36 A.M.

Oldport County Animal Shelter was located about a mile outside the city limits on Queensland Road. The two-lane county road was not top priority after the storm, so it took Juan Mendoza a while to work his way there.

In fact, he was still half a mile short of the shelter when he gave up trying to drive, parked in an out-of-the-way spot and commenced to walking.

He wasn't surprised to find people already there tending to the animals. Alexa, for example, lived near enough to walk in. She and her husband had the backup generator running and were blowing fresh air into the pens.

"How do things look?"

"Solid. I haven't found any real problems. There's some loose metal flapping on the garage, but it seems like we've come through unscathed."

"Looks better than my place. What about yours?"

"We're really good, maybe lost a few shingles, but no major trees are down and no serious problems. I think this area got a reprieve. Was yours bad?"

"Apparently there's some roof damage because I had major leakage going on, but I didn't examine it closely."

With that, he went to work caring for his animals.

AUGUST 14, 12:29 P.M.

Jeremiah Forge had quit watching television. They were finally showing his condo, but none of the images were complimentary.

Why can't they focus on the fact that the bulk of the building was secure and that everybody on the second floor was safe? He tried hard to blame the media for sensational reporting, but his mind was too honest to let him do that without recalling his decision to ignore the city inspector's stipulation that they not stay on the first floor.

Room service had just left his lunch when his cell phone rang.

"Jeremiah Forge?"

"Who wants to know?"

"This is NBC News and Sandra Lightley said you would be the one to discuss the decisions made about boarding refugees at Oldport Cascades Condominiums and doing so only on the ground floor."

Forge disconnected the call and turned off his phone. Knowing that Goody Two-Shoes Lightley, she'd give them his hotel, too. He took that phone off the hook and turned to his meal.

AUGUST 14, 3:47 P.M.

By the time JP and Jennifer walked back to his house, they had written off the idea of checking on the newspaper building; those in charge would worry with that.

Their plan was to give JP's house a closer examination now that the rain had stopped, drive to Jen's apartment to check it out and determine if she could move back in.

As they completed the walk, they spotted Tim Grayson lounging in a lawn chair in his front yard.

"Any problems, Tim?"

"I only need electricity, man, and I'm good to go. And you know I had all the essentials taken care of. But seriously, man, did you see Jason's house?"

He led them through his back yard to where they could see a fairly large tree that crashed through the roof.

"Looks like he did the smart thing to evacuate," JP said.

"I sent him a text to let him know what to expect. I tried to get in to check things out, but the tree makes it impossible. Guess that will keep looters out, too."

While JP confirmed his house appeared to be in good shape, Jen loaded her bags in her car and they took both vehicles to her home.

They had to park a block away and walk in, carefully picking their way through trash, glass, limbs and various elements that had blown off buildings. When they turned a corner and could see Jennifer's building, she groaned.

The second-floor apartment looked like it held together, though the plate glass window was gone. However, a fallen tree had wiped out the stairs that provided access to two units. Most likely, the tree would have to be removed before they could get a ladder to get up to her place.

"Did your neighbors stay?" JP asked, realizing they could be trapped.

"No, they left two days ago, using this as an excuse to visit family in California. They offered to let me go, but, no, I had to be a big-time reporter."

"It's good to see your humor remains intact. Let's head back to my place; I hear some Vienna sausages calling my name."

AUGUST 15, 8:02 A.M.

"Let's go now to Oldport to get the latest about that hard-hit area from our own Frank Woffard. Frank?"

"Thank you, Lisa. Twenty-four hours ago, this town was getting its first glimpse at the devastation of Hurricane Clarice. Throughout the day and, for some people, through the night, they continued to search for victims and survivors, as well as lay a path back to normal operations, whatever that might be in a post-Clarice era.

"The latest figures we have are from last night, though we expect an update by mid-morning. That's at least 73 dead in Oldport County, and hundreds injured.

"On the good side, most of the injured are being cared for at Oldport's two hospitals, neither of which suffered debilitating damage and both of which have full electrical power restored as of last night.

"An often overlooked story in the aftermath of a huge storm is the cooperative help of power companies in getting hundreds of helpers from around the country. We encountered one of those this morning and asked him to take a breather and visit with us. Step over here, if you would. You're Moose MacDuff, right? And where did you come from, Moose?"

"I'm actually with the local power company, but you're right, there will be hundreds of trucks and thousands of workers here today, helping get power up not only in Oldport but in the entire region."

"What was yesterday like for you?"

"Well, we were actually at the yard when the storm came in so we could make sure our people were not separated from the equipment they would need. We started working by sunup yesterday, while still getting pretty good winds. One of our first objectives was getting the hospitals online. The system is designed to make it easier to do that, to be able to get them safely online even if the surrounding area is not yet ready. We were lucky and it went smoothly."

"I guess so. The hospitals were both off generators by early afternoon. Did you and your guys get any sleep?"

"Well, Frank, like most people in town, we didn't sleep when the storm came in, but most of us got a good four hours or so last night. We were back at it before sunrise this morning."

"There you have it, Lisa. There is no limit to the number of heroes this area has today. Back to the news room to find out more about massive rains being dumped inland by what's left of Clarice."

AUGUST 15, 9:09 A.M.

The city editor had put out word through the communication network set up for Odds and Ends staffers and had even placed flyers on the doors of the office building for all available news hands to meet at his house at 9 a.m. Once there, they found various chairs moved onto the driveway, along with a couple of tables.

"All the comforts, Stanley; you shouldn't have," piped up Archie Hanning as he arrived.

"Not only that, but we waited for you, Hanning," Stanley replied. "Now that Archie's here, we'll get started. I fully expect others to check in all day and I'll individually run them through what's going on. Everybody doing all right? Any problems you want to share?"

When nobody spoke up, he went to business.

"First, you probably all know the office is heavily damaged, quite possibly totaled. That stupid flat roof gave in. What we'll do for office space is way up in the air and is another reason I'm happy not to be higher up the ladder. This is a time when the publisher and department heads will earn those big bucks.

"I have no doubt we will operate out of temporary housing for a while, probably even separate places. It might even change a number of times.

"Printing will take place in Okley."

"What's Okley?" asked Christine Finney.

Pam Gipson, the regional reporter, fielded the question.

"It's a small town about two hours west of here, so it was on the dry side, but I didn't know it had a paper."

"No paper," Stanley said. "There's a small printing plant there that can handle our needs. How we're going to deal with the computer situation is still up in the air. For now, and maybe for some time, work on your own computers and place files on a flash drive to turn in. They tell me you should strip special characters, just use plain text ... oh, you know what they mean. If you don't, ask Dickey.

"Any questions? We'll consider my house news central until something else gets worked out."

"We always have, boss," JP said.

"Moving along with stories for this first thrown-together issue. First, we have plenty of photos, so filling pages will be no problem. I suppose we'll start with a damage roundup and casualty count. Jennifer?"

"Sure thing, Mr. Hopper. I've been rounding up information and beg anyone who's seen anything worth noting to share it with me. I saw Sgt. Bellew earlier and he said we're at 69 dead in the city, a few more in the county. Hardest hit might be the Sandpiper Subdivision, where it appears all of the homes were wiped out or at least severely damaged. That's where Lydia and her mom lived, by the way."

We're not the only area affected by Clarice," said Pam Gipson. "What about the adjacent counties and beyond?"

"Today, let's just focus on Oldport County. Ed has worked up something with the AP to get some wire stories to us for broader hurricane news. We'll probably toss in a column of briefs for the rest of the world. The eyes are on us today.

"OK, electricity? Big story," Stanley said, looking for a face. "Archie, that'll be yours."

"Already talking to them, boss. It's going to drag on for weeks, for sure."

"Relief info. JP, you're going to tell people where they can get help if they need it. Water, food, shelter."

"And ice," JP said. "Ice is like gold. Something else, I stopped by my church this morning. It weathered the storm pretty well, but several men in the church had brought out their grills and are planning on cooking up as much of the meat as they can before it goes bad. They'll make it available to those who need it and provide food for relief workers. I'm sure there are other such happenings; y'all let me know what you come across."

"Something Tad said this morning that might fit into your story," Jennifer said, "was how encouraging it was to see residents just show up to volunteer their help at distribution points and the shelter. I'll give you that quote later."

"Pam suggested a story about dealing with mounting issues," Stanley said. "She had researched it prior to the storm. One thing that stuck in my mind was being patient driving, turning all intersections into stop-and-go until lights are back."

"Pat!" he said, as Pat Baird walked up. "Glad you made it. Did you have any problems?"

"I'm a tough old bird, Stanley," she yelled, to group applause.

"Good, because I'd like you to put together a roundup of the medical services. Use anyone here you need to help run down information."

"That's a short list, folks, but we've got to get it together quickly. What else do you guys have?"

AUGUST 15, 9:21 A.M.

Once the meeting broke up, most of the staffers headed out promptly to take care of their assignments. JP held back until he could pull Stanley off to the side and explained to him about the special use permit, what it said, how Lydia came about it and the role she played in getting people off the deadly first floor.

"How do you know all this?"

"Lydia's mom gave me the permit; she didn't even know what it was, just that Lydia said she wanted me to have it. After I read it and things settled down, I was able to corner the property manager and she told me about Lydia pressing to get people off the floor. She painted her as quite a heroine."

"Can you get the story done today?" Stanley asked.

"I'd really rather wait a day just to tie things together a little better and so it doesn't get lost in the body count and all."

"Good enough. We'll still get it first, won't we?"

"I'm certain of it. Sandra Lightley is not going to take the fall for this, but I don't think she'll be telling these details to anyone else soon. At least, that's what she promised me."

"How is Lydia? Have you heard?"

"After meeting her mother, getting warm, getting water and nourishment, she started coming around and remembering the situation. I'd say she was simply in shock. Who wouldn't be? Just FYI, I intend to byline this story by Lydia and JP even if she's not able to contribute any more to it."

"I guess it really is her story."

"Yes, sir. When this plays out, I think people will say she saved a hundred lives."

"And, JP, when you see Lydia, tell her something for me."

"What's that?"

"When she's ready, we want her back here as a full-time reporter, even if I have to fire you to make room for her."

"With pleasure, boss."

ABOUT THE AUTHOR

Steve Martaindale likes to describe his specialization as generalist; saying his interest in many things, even though master of few, proved beneficial as a newspaper reporter and editor. His more than 20 years of working in small town newspapers has been punctuated with stints as diverse as running a courier service, volunteer firefighter, managing a condominium, delivering flowers and working in Antarctica. He also wrote a weekly self-syndicated column, A Texas Voice, for 18 years.

That breadth of experience has paid off again as Martaindale transitions from fact to fiction. He draws on associations with a wide range of people to apply reality to his characters and their stories.

He and his educator wife, Leah, have one daughter, a son-in-law, a grandson and absolutely no more pets.

"The Reporter, a Ferret and a Hurricane" is two standalone stories, "The Reporter and the Ferret" and "The Reporter and the Hurricane." The second story follows the first by about nine months. To keep up with the reporter, JP Weiscarver, like his page at facebook.com/JPWeiscarver.

Made in the USA
Lexington, KY
09 December 2012